IN TOO DEEP, OUT TOO FAR

He knew he was being watched. But when he turned around—nothing.

The front door opened to his touch, and he began to explore the barren, oven-hot interior, going down to the basement. He called for his friend.

"Cal? It's me. I'm alone."

"Where is he?" he wondered. Stepping carefully in the dark, his foot hit something soft. He jerked his leg away, then tentatively forward as he traced the contours of an arm, a shoulder, a head . . .

Suddenly, a powerful light sliced the scene.

"Against the wall!" the voice ordered. . . .

THE EPISODE

"FAST-PACED, OFFBEAT, WITH UNPREDICTABLE TWISTS."

—*ALA Booklist*

THE
EPISODE

Richard Pollak

A SIGNET BOOK

NEW AMERICAN LIBRARY

For Diane and Amanda

NAL BOOKS ARE AVAILABLE AT QUANTITY DISCOUNTS WHEN USED TO
PROMOTE PRODUCTS OR SERVICES. FOR INFORMATION PLEASE WRITE TO
PREMIUM MARKETING DIVISION, NEW AMERICAN LIBRARY,
1633 BROADWAY, NEW YORK, NEW YORK 10019

Permissions and Acknowledgments
Excerpt from *The Terminal Man*, by Michael Crichton. Copyright ©
1972 by Michael Crichton. Reprinted by permission of Alfred A. Knopf,
Inc. Lines from "They Couldn't Compare to You," by Cole Porter.
Copyright © 1951 by Cole Porter. Copyright renewed; assigned to
Robert H. Montgomery, Trustee of the Cole Porter Musical and Library
Property Trusts. Chappell & Co., Inc., owner of publication and allied
rights. International Copyright secured. ALL RIGHTS RESERVED. Used
by permission.

SIGNET TRADEMARK REG. U.S. PAT. OFF. AND FOREIGN COUNTRIES
REGISTERED TRADEMARK—MARCA REGISTRADA
HECHO EN CHICAGO, U.S.A.

SIGNET, SIGNET CLASSIC, MENTOR, ONYX, PLUME, MERIDIAN
and NAL BOOKS are published by NAL PENGUIN INC.,
1633 Broadway, New York, New York 10019

First Signet Printing, July, 1987

1 2 3 4 5 6 7 8 9

PRINTED IN THE UNITED STATES OF AMERICA

Chapter I

KATE called early, determined this time to keep Daniel out of the kitchen. On all but the first of their four dates he had insisted on cooking for her in his apartment. Like most of her woman friends, Kate found such gastronomic courtship immensely appealing, even when the lamb chops arrived a bit overdone and the *crème brûlèe* proved a transparent prelude to seduction—both the case a week ago. After each of these meals Kate had reflexively promised that next time was her turn. Her modest culinary skills, however, had lapsed after leaving home for Barnard; now she lacked both the confidence and enthusiasm for reviving them, even with the still-boxed Cuisinart her parents had given her for her thirty-second birthday last month. Tonight she would take Daniel to the restaurant of his choice, her treat.

Whoever picked up the phone said nothing.

"Daniel?" The name disappeared into the buzz of the open line. "Daniel Cooper? This is Kate. Are you there?"

"Are you there?" echoed Daniel.

"Of course I'm here. I've just slipped out of a

1

high-level meeting that may, even as we speak, be deciding the fate of the modern romance novel for all time. So, quick, tell me what splendid restaurant you'd like to go to tonight and I'll make a reservation. I'm buying.''

"I'm buying," Daniel said.

Kate had no time to argue over advance check-grabbing and started to say so, then stopped herself. Daniel's response had come after an odd pause, and he seemed to be simply repeating her words, not engaging them.

"Daniel? What's going on? Are you all right?"

"Are you all right." Again the reply came out of the hum after a few seconds delay. Daniel didn't really make the words a question; he just stated them—"Are you all right"—in a monotone, as if unable to shake himself from a task on which the call had intruded.

"Daniel, please, if this is some sort of—" The hum stopped. Kate hung up and redialed. After three or four rings she impatiently slammed the phone down and tried again. As she waited, she recalled Daniel's performance after their first lovemaking. When she had returned from the bathroom, he was no longer in bed, and no amount of pleading coaxed a sound from any corner of the dark bedroom. Kate had been about to switch on a light when, from the living room, Julie Andrews's voice swelled with "The Sound of Music." Kate found Daniel draped in his London Fog and standing on a chair, simultaneously conducting the record and practicing his flashing technique. "Wait till I get to 'My Favorite Things,' " he said. Laughing, she had thought, This is a nicely complicated man. Now she wondered if he was also a little goofy. Was his refusal to answer the phone designed to lure her up to his apartment early for some new prank? If so, she was not amused. She started to dial one more time when Maggie Burke appeared at her office door.

"A clamor for the pleasure of your company is rising in the inner sanctum," she said. Kate smiled out of her anxiety. She and Maggie had arrived at Glossary Books together two years ago. In their third week Maggie had proposed that a new Sylvia Smart romance be called *The Thighs of the Victor*. They had been friends ever since.

"I may not make it back to the meeting, Mag. I promised Sean Gallagher I'd go over corrections with him this afternoon, and his line is busy, busy, busy."

"His prose is busy, busy, busy too. Don't call him, just kill every other line. He'll never notice the difference, and the book will probably sell twice as many copies."

"If I can't reach him with a couple more tries, I may well do that. Meanwhile, please make my apologies to all assembled."

"There may be rioting," said Maggie, retreating down the corridor.

Kate dialed again. When Daniel still did not answer, she stuffed the Gallagher manuscript into her tote bag and headed for the elevators. She found a cab easily on Sixth Avenue and soon was moving steadily uptown in traffic not yet congealed into the Thursday rush hour. An urge to primp rose like lipstick out of a holder. Kate hated the impulse, and it seemed particularly stupid to fuss over her appearance to please a man staging an ill-timed stunt. "He thinks he's all three Marx Brothers," she thought, castigating herself again for leaving the office so precipitously.

Daniel lived in a typical upper-middle-class redoubt on Central Park West. A small, glass-enclosed vestibule formed the first checkpoint through which visitors could pass only if buzzed in from upstairs or admitted by a uniformed guard; toying with his nightstick, he usually made his appraisal from one of two cast-iron chairs chained to the lobby railing. The elevators were automatic; once an interloper made it that far, all manner of mayhem was possible. About a year ago Daniel had posted a notice on the laundry room bulletin board calling a meeting in his apartment to discuss the feasibility of digging a moat around the building. Three tenants came: the recently divorced social worker from down the hall, who wanted to meet such a funny man; and an elderly couple from the twelfth floor, prepared to contribute substantially to the project.

Kate was not surprised when Daniel buzzed her in without first identifying her over the intercom. He had gotten her this far; no need for further preliminaries—let the game begin. As she rode up in the elevator she prepared her preemptive strike: "Some of us, Daniel, have to go to an office every day and can't stay home playing sophomore. Besides, I like my job, and I don't appreciate having it jeopardized by your jokes in the middle of the afternoon when I still have a lot of work to do. Don't you think it's a little manipulative to trick someone into worrying about you like this?" Hoping she could keep from laughing at whatever awaited her, Kate arrived at 9A and pushed the bell hard.

It took Daniel more than a minute to open the door. He smiled at Kate but said nothing, neither inviting her in nor showing any sign that he wanted her to go away. He was dressed as usual: blue button-down shirt, khaki pants and running shoes. Daniel disdained coats and ties but was fastidious about the neatness of his chosen uniform. Kate thought he always looked as if he were about to take the field in a genteel softball game, no sliding permitted. She had never seen him, as now, with his shoelaces untied and his shirt untucked.

"Hi," Daniel said, finally, his voice distant, as on the phone. He remained in the doorway, his vague grin fixed noncommittally.

"May I come in?" Kate asked, no longer sure whether to be irritated, but her guard still up. After more of a pause Daniel withdrew from the threshold and Kate stepped inside. The apartment was dark, all shades pulled against the bright September sun. Kate knew that Daniel relished the light that streamed into his apartment. From the foyer she could see through the bedroom door that the bed was unmade.

"Daniel, did you just get up?" Kate asked, knowing that he rose almost every morning at six to run.

"Did I just get up," Daniel responded, again after a pause, again not a question. He stood with Kate in the foyer, as if awaiting instructions.

"Daniel, what's wrong with you? Why are you so distracted? Do you know who I am?" Kate watched anxiously as Daniel processed the question and reached for an answer.

"Faith," he said. The name banished any notion of a game. Faith was Daniel's ex-wife. Kate knew from Daniel's description that she looked nothing like Faith, who was tall and blond.

"No, Daniel, it's Kate. Kate Bernstein. We have a date for dinner tonight. Don't you remember, don't you recognize me?"

"Kate," he stated, not so much correcting himself as responding to her cue.

"That's better," she said, taking his hand and leading him into the living room. Daniel said nothing but offered no resistance. She guided him to the sofa, and after a moment's hesitation he sat down. She went around the room raising the shades.

"Nice day," said Daniel, as the westering sun warmed the room. Kate grasped at the phrase, tried to make it a piece of normal conversation. But Daniel had said it so absently, she knew nothing had changed. When she turned from the window, he had gotten up and was walking to the Steinway grand in the corner of the room. He sat down and began playing the opening bars of "Wait Till You See Her." His fingers stumbled immediately and although he made his entrance on time, he sang almost a tone off-key. He seemed not to notice these deficiencies as he forged ahead with the song. On their second date Daniel had played and sung two dozen show tunes for Kate, a performance that had astonished her with its bounce and wit. To hear him fumble at the keyboard now stunned her. She went to the piano bench and placed her hand on his forehead. She had decided to call a doctor; a fever would at least give her something more to report than his mesmerized behavior. She actually hoped Daniel would feel hot, but he did not.

When he finished the song, she asked, "Do you have a doctor?"

"Do I have a doctor," came the flat response.

"Daniel, please don't keep repeating what I say. I'm trying to help you." Kate sat down on the bench. Daniel put his head on her shoulder and began noodling "Send in the Clowns," missing at least half the notes.

"What is the name of your doctor?" Kate said, putting her arm around him.

Daniel kept chasing the song, humming the melody consistently flat. He seemed now not even to hear her questions. Kate contemplated calling Maggie at the office, or her sister, Martha, then realized that calling her own doctor made the most sense. She went over to the phone on Daniel's desk and started to dial when she noticed his address book on the blotter. No doctors were listed on the emergency page or under *D* or *P*. Kate looked over at Daniel, still preoccupied at the keyboard, then began with *A*. Her own name appeared in pencil among the *B*'s, and more women made their entrances on the pages that followed. Maybe one's a doctor, Kate mused, allowing that most of them had probably examined Daniel once or twice. She was about to give up and fall back on her own physician when, at the top of the first *S* page, under "Sawbones," three names appeared, including "M. Loring, neurologist."

Martin Loring was in the middle of rounds at the hospital when his secretary relayed Kate's call. He picked up the page phone, annoyed at yet another interruption.

"Doctor Loring." His voice barely hid his irritation.

"Doctor, my name is Kate Bernstein. You don't know me, but I'm a friend of Daniel Cooper. I'm calling you because your name is in his address book and I don't know who else to call. He's behaving very strangely. I think you should—"

"Now slow down, Miss Bernstein. You've done the right thing. Mr. Cooper *is* a patient of mine. Can you be more precise and tell me exactly what you mean by 'very strangely'?" He looked at his watch. Quarter to five. If this call meant trouble, he'd never finish rounds in time to make his six-thirty handball game, which he'd already missed twice this week. He listened impatiently as Kate recounted the events of the afternoon, beginning with her first phone call and ending with a description of Daniel's confused playing and singing at the piano, where he still sat.

"He's in some kind of trance, Doctor; I'm not sure he even knows where he is." When she finished, Kate expected Dr. Loring to take command, to say he was on his way or that he was sending an ambulance to bring Daniel to the hospital.

Instead he asked, "How long has Mr. Cooper been in this condition?"

"I don't know, Doctor. At least since three-thirty; that's when I called him from my office and first noticed his confusion. I came right up here."

"I'd like to talk to Mr. Cooper. Do you think you can get him to come to the phone?" The gears of his telephone manner meshed smoothly into place. Kate started to protest, then took the phone on its long cord and set it on the piano bench.

"Daniel, Dr. Loring wants to talk to you." Kate handed him the receiver, which he slowly put to his ear.

"Mr. Cooper? This is Dr. Loring. How are you?"

"How am I," said Daniel abstractly, after the pause that preceded all his responses.

"I'm your doctor. Do you remember me? Dr. Loring. Martin Loring. You've been to my office several times."

". . . Dr. Loring."

"Good. Now, can you tell me who you are?"

". . . Daniel Cooper."

"And where are you?"

". . . At my piano."

"At your piano where?"

". . . In my living room."

"Good. Can you tell me what day of the week it is?"

Daniel stared at the music rack, then at Kate; after a long pause he said, "Wednesday."

"Are you sure?"

". . . Yes."

Dr. Loring let the mistake pass and asked Daniel what year it was.

". . . Nineteen eighty-six."

"Right. And who is president of the United States?"

". . . Ronald Reagan."

"And what's his wife's name?"

"Faith," Daniel said, without a pause.

Dr. Loring did not know who Faith was, so he let this mistake pass too.

"Who is the mayor of New York?"

"Koch."

"Right. Now, can you tell me what you do for a living?"

". . . I'm a reporter."

"For whom?"

". . . *Tabula Rasa*."

"What are you working on right now?"

The question perplexed Daniel. When he failed to answer, Dr. Loring tried a different tack.

"Do you remember the last thing of yours that appeared in the paper?"

". . . The Bellemoor series."

"How long ago was that?"

". . . Last month."

"Now, can you tell me the name of the woman who's with you?"

Daniel looked at Kate as if caught in an introduction and unable to retrieve her name. Finally, he said, "Kate."

"Good. I'd like to speak with her again."

"Here," said Daniel, absently pushing the receiver in Kate's direction.

"You see what I mean, Doctor; his reactions are very slow and he's so confused. What's wrong with him?"

"Miss Bernstein, how long have you known Mr. Cooper?"

"About a month. Why?"

"Has he ever discussed his medical history with you?"

"No."

Dr. Loring sagged with the knowledge that he

might have an hysterical woman on his hands in a moment. He considered entangling himself in this case right now, skipping handball and getting home after eight yet again. Then he decided, no, this situation could be handled over the phone, at least until the morning. He prepared himself for Kate's reaction.

"Miss Bernstein, I don't want you to be alarmed, but Mr. Cooper has a history of epilepsy. It's not serious. I've been following him for several years now, and he's been seizure-free all that time. He does seem to be going through an episode of some kind at the moment, but I don't think we need be unduly concerned."

Kate wanted to explode. Epilepsy. Not serious. Don't be alarmed. "We" needn't be unduly concerned. What kind of bullshit doctor was this? Why wasn't he already on his way to help? Her head filled with the sight of Linda McCourt thrashing hideously in the center of the stage. No one in the cast knew she was an epileptic, but during a rehearsal of a Barnard production of *The Pirates of Penzance* she suddenly had gone into convulsions. Kate had only been able to look for an instant, but the sight remained indelible. How could epilepsy *not* be serious?

"Look, Doctor, I appreciate your calm," said Kate, attempting to conceal her hostility, "but I'm scared. Epilepsy scares me. The very idea of epilepsy scares me. Being here alone with Daniel scares me. Suppose his condition gets worse? I don't have the slightest idea what to do. I think Daniel should be brought to a hospital right away."

"If Mr. Cooper's condition doesn't improve in the next few hours, then we'll certainly consider hospitalization. But for now the important thing is to keep him comfortable. These things have to run their course. There's very little you, or I, can do once an episode begins." Kate found the word *episode* a maddening euphemism, as if Daniel were playing in some soap opera that would end promptly on the hour. "There *is* one thing I would like you to do," Dr. Loring continued. "Mr. Cooper takes medication daily. It's possible he forgot this morning. Regardless, I want him to have some now. I don't have his chart with me, but my recollection is that he takes phenobarbital and primidone, which is packaged as Mysoline. They should be in his medicine chest."

Kate reluctantly put down the phone and went into the bathroom. Both plastic containers of pills sat on top of the toilet tank next to the sink. She brought them back to the phone, and Dr. Loring instructed her to give Daniel two of the phenobarb tablets.

"And that's it? Suppose he refuses to take them. Suppose—"

"I'm sure he'll take them, Miss Bernstein. He's been taking them for years. He may want to sleep afterward. Let him. But make sure he's good and comfortable. Get him to lie down in bed. And try not to worry. I think the chances are very good that he'll come out of this soon. Remember, he's been seizure-free for many years. Whatever happens, I'm only a phone call away. And, in any case, I want to see Mr. Cooper in my office first thing tomorrow morning—at nine o'clock. Don't forget to give him the medication as soon as you hang up: two phenobarb. Any questions?" He sounded like a professor giving his class one last, quick shot before the bell freed him for lunch at the faculty club.

"No," said Kate coldly, and hung up. She had a hundred questions, not the least of which was why this doctor refused to get more involved with his patient. She had considered pleading, but fury quashed the words in her throat. She looked over at Daniel. He was no longer playing, but sitting on the bench gazing out the window. Seeing what? Kate wondered. Hearing what? Did he know she was now privy to his illness? Is that why he had fallen silent, staring out over the park.

"Mr. Softee," Daniel said with a grin.

"What? Mr. who?"

Daniel paused, then pointed to the window and said, "The Pied Piper of Ooze."

Only then did Kate hear the monotonous ding-dong summons rising from the street. She looked down at the white ice-cream truck parked on Central Park West and mobbed by children.

"You want some of that stuff?"

Daniel wrinkled up his nose and shook his head.

"I didn't think so, Mr. Gourmand. How about some orange juice instead?" She went into the kitchen and poured a glass and took it to Daniel with the pills.

"Dr. Loring wants you to take these," she said, hoping medical authority would overcome any recalcitrance.

Daniel looked at her, took the juice in one hand, the pills in the other, and, without protest, downed both. He handed her the glass and said, "I'm really hungry."

The statement jarred Kate, especially the *really*. It sounded in touch, aware, as if it had slipped out of the mists of Daniel's bewilderment. Maybe food would help shake him from his spin. Kate thought about calling Dr. Loring for advice, then went back into the kitchen, leaving Daniel on the bench. She wondered when he last had anything to eat, when his condition first set in. He had certainly not shopped that day; that was clear from the sparse contents of the refrigerator. In a cupboard Kate found a can of Progresso minestrone, one of the few commercial items Daniel deigned to stock. While the soup heated on the stove Kate sliced a wedge of Swiss cheese and arranged it on a plate with some matzos. When the soup began steaming, she poured it into a large cup, tasted it to make sure it would not burn his mouth, and then brought the meal into the living room on a tray. Daniel had moved from the bench to the sofa and was stretched out, fast asleep.

Chapter II

KATE turned the television set off at ten P.M. "How could I spend two hours watching such tripe?" she said out loud. She knew she was being too hard on herself, that under the circumstances she could hardly be expected to concentrate on the Gallagher manuscript she had so efficiently brought along. She looked down at Daniel on the sofa, where he had been sleeping for more than four hours, and felt her own exhaustion. She had not come prepared to spend the night, but it made no sense to think about going back to her own apartment. She went into the bedroom and rummaged through Daniel's dresser for a T-shirt. She rejected a yellow one with NO MORE MR. NICE GUY stenciled across the front in blue letters, promising herself she would ask Daniel its origins at the first opportunity. She chose as appropriate a plain gray model with no wise pronouncements, front or back. After undressing, she pulled it on, draped her clothes neatly over the director's chair near the bed, and went into the bedroom.

She was washing her face when Daniel screamed. Though loud, the throaty explosion lacked any sound of fear. For an instant she thought Daniel must have awakened, turned on the television set, and was now laughing uncontrollably at some sitcom joke. She ran into the living room half expecting to see him sitting up on the sofa grinning. Instead he lay facedown on the floor, wedged between the sofa and the marble coffee table. His body stretched stiff and he barely moved. His long sleep had convinced her that the crisis had passed, that he would wake up uneventfully. She wanted to bolt into the hall and bang on a door for help, to call Dr. Loring and make him materialize over the phone. Keep him comfortable! Kate wasn't sure she should even touch Daniel, or could touch him. Then, slowly, the ghastly howl subsided.

Kate knelt down, pushed away the table, and somehow summoned the strength to turn Daniel onto his back. She grabbed a cushion from a sofa and placed it under his head; he gave out a choking moan but showed no recognition. As she bent over his face Daniel started convulsing violently. Kate recoiled as a flailing arm struck her in the shoulder. Daniel's eyes bulged and rolled, and he seemed unable to breathe; his skin turned a pale blue, a pastel canvas streaked with bulging veins on his head and neck. Before watching television, Kate had tried to read; the book, a paperback of *Lucky Jim*, lay on the coffee table. She snatched it and jammed it into Daniel's mouth. Later Kate would estimate that the convulsions lasted a minute at the most. But now they seemed unending—vicious spasms that shook Daniel's frame with an invisible energy Kate found impossible to credit. She knew that a plausible physi-

ological explanation must exist, but she also re
reading that in the Dark Ages epileptics were thoug
to be possessed by demons. It did not surprise her.
Kate by now had branded Dr. Loring a monstrous
quack, but she kept operating on his instructions, as
if in a trance herself. She hurried into the bedroom,
pulled the quilt off Daniel's bed, and carried it back
into the living room.

The convulsions had stopped. Daniel now looked
incongruously beatific; his eyes were closed and his
breathing eased through his open mouth. He reminded
Kate of her three-year-old nephew, Mark, when she
and Martha tiptoed in on him at night. Her apprehension momentarily dissolved into an urge to comfort
Daniel, to tuck him in; but as she leaned over to
spread the quilt, she saw that he had soaked himself
through his khakis. Kate held the quilt, a good one of
some age, and wondered if Daniel would want it
soiled, would be angry with her for not finding something less valuable. She considered trying to undress
him so she could sponge him off with a wet towel.
Again aesthetics intruded. Kate was appalled by the
sense of bourgeois priorities that kept asserting itself.
Finally she leaned back down, draped the quilt over
Daniel, and moved quickly to the phone.

"Doctor's service," announced a starchy voice.

"I need to talk to Dr. Loring right away. It's an
emergency."

"What is the nature of the emergency?"

The nature of the emergency, thought Kate, is that
I'm in the apartment of a man I've known just five
weeks and he's frightened the hell out of me by

flipping out; the nature of the emergency is that I'm not altogether crazy about being here, especially alone.

"I'm with Daniel Cooper, one of Dr. Loring's patients. He's just had a very bad seizure. Please get—"

"Can you describe the episode?"

"Yes, of course. But please don't waste time. It's serious. He told me this afternoon that if anything like this happened to call him right away."

"Certainly. Your name, please?"

"Kate. Kate Bernstein. I'm at 555-4672. That's Mr. Cooper's number. Will Dr. Loring call right away?"

"Please stay off the phone," said the service, its tone unaltered. "Someone will call you as soon as possible."

Kate hung up vowing that if merely someone called, she would sue Dr. Loring for malpractice. She looked over at Daniel under the quilt; he seemed to have grown calmer in the brief time she was on the phone. Kate decided to let him rest on the floor; the pants could wait. To give him more space she pulled the coffee table farther from the sofa. As she did, she noticed blood and saliva seeping over Daniel's lips. She bent down and quickly removed the book from his mouth, staunching the flow with tissues from her shoulder bag and berating herself for not moving fast enough earlier to keep Daniel from biting his mouth. She held his face in her hands and began to tremble with the realization that, however sweet, this man had become a serious problem for her—and that he would probably wake up soon. Overcome by a need to talk to someone, she rose to call Maggie, then remembered that she could not tie up the line.

Dr. Loring called just before eleven o'clock, his phone-side manner diminishing rapidly as he questioned Kate about the attack. The new tone persuaded her that he or an ambulance would soon arrive and that Daniel at last would be in capable hands. But to her disbelief and renewed rage, Dr. Loring explained that now that Daniel had passed through the convulsions, the worst was over. This time Kate buried her anger and did plead, which revived the phone-side manner instantly.

"I realize this has been difficult for you, Miss Bernstein, but I really do think Mr. Cooper will be okay now. He should wake up quite soon. He'll be tired and doubtless upset—he hasn't had a seizure like this in a long time—but he'll be fine until I can see him in the morning. If he doesn't wake up in an hour or so, or if he's still confused when he does, then I want you to call me again. Never mind the hour. I'll get him to the hospital right away. Otherwise I would like you to bring him in at nine o'clock tomorrow. Can you stay with him tonight and do that?"

"No, Doctor, I'm due at the hairdresser in half an hour."

"I'm sure they won't miss you this one night," said Dr. Loring, flicking off Kate's sarcasm. "When Mr. Cooper comes out of it, he should get right to bed. And I want him to take another dose of medication, one phenobarb tablet this time. Were you able to give him the pills earlier?"

"Yes."

"Good. Now, do you have my office address? It's on East Sixty-eighth Street, six twenty. I'll see you at nine o'clock. After I examine Mr. Cooper, I'll try to answer any questions you have. I think I'll be able to reassure you that matters aren't really as bad as they seem. Now you try to get some rest tonight too. Is there somewhere there you can sleep?"

"Yes, on the sofa," said Kate, her anger deflating into resignation.

"Fine, then I'll see you in the morning. First thing."

Kate hung up but kept her hand on the receiver. She yearned for contact with someone: Maggie, Martha, her parents in Cleveland. She began dialing Maggie's number, then looked at her watch. Eleven-thirty. Maggie might be asleep; but, even if she weren't, what exactly was there to say? Since Daniel had not revealed his epilepsy to her voluntarily, could she now start blabbing it about? Kate thought of herself as an enlightened woman, but a stigma filled the room that inked out her education. She needed Maggie's comfort and advice, but she also didn't want her to know about Daniel, as if somehow that would make the last few hours go away for her too. "That son of a bitch, Loring," she said, fighting back tears of exhaustion.

Daniel squinted hard, trying to make sense of what he saw. He could not remember ever speculating about the meaning of a dream in progress. Yet Spencer Tracy had to be a symbol of some kind. Why else was he dressed so formally—white shirt, dark tie, black suit, even a fedora—as he walked into this

remote, ramshackle diner? Several men in dusty Western clothes menaced him, especially a beady-eyed
hulk who looked familiar to Daniel. He told Tracy to
get off "my stool" at the otherwise empty counter.
Tracy did. Daniel thought, How unlike him to be so
passive. The fat man offered to tie one hand behind
his back. Why? Daniel wondered. Was he a symbol
too? And why does everyone seem tilted to the right
in this dream? As Daniel struggled with his confusion, Tracy suddenly moved in on his looming foe.
With stunning and mysterious swiftness he sent the
bully crashing about the diner, flabbergasting his
cohorts. Their surprise—and Daniel's—was only compounded by the fact that it was Tracy who functioned
with one arm. Why? How was he able to dispatch his
murderous adversary so easily?

"Daniel?" The name sounded as a question; but
Daniel heard it as if the scene were about to acquire a
narrator who would explain everything. No narration
followed, however, only another "Daniel?"—to which
he could not respond no matter how hard he tried. He
felt as if someone had stabbed his hip with an ice
pick. "I must have been hurt in the fight at the
diner," he thought, trying to retrieve the scene. He
raised his head, hoping to find Spencer Tracy and not
the bully. He saw a piano and then a woman, dressed
only in a gray T-shirt, before falling back from the
intense pain in his hip. He looked up at the ceiling in
search of his socks. There were none, which was
odd; his father always said he knew the time had
come to change his socks when he threw the pair he
was wearing against the ceiling and they stuck. Daniel shut his eyes and tried to organize Spencer Tracy,

the woman, the piano, the hip, and the missing socks into some coherent explanation of his plight when he realized he was lying on the floor of his own living room. He again tried to sit up, but the pain pushed him back.

"Hi," said Kate, squatting down beside him. Daniel looked between her legs, seeking to program her bikini underpants into the muddle in his head. "It's Kate. Do you recognize me?" Daniel looked up into the round face and the big, brown eyes and did.

"What's happened to me?" As he spoke, he felt a sharp new pain in his mouth.

After a silence Kate said, "You've had some kind of attack. A seizure."

"Epilepsy?" The question drowned in disbelief.

"I'm not sure. I think so. Dr. Lor—"

"Oh, my God, my God. It can't be. I can't have had a seizure. I haven't had one since I was a kid." Daniel shut his eyes again, overwhelmed with embarrassment; he felt as if he had committed an obscene act in front of this gentle woman, whom he hardly knew. He tried to avoid looking at her, but tears began to flow, forcing his eyes open.

"Daniel, Daniel, it's going to be okay. I've talked to Dr. Loring twice. We have an appointment first thing in the morning." Kate bent over and hugged Daniel, who was now crying openly.

"Was it bad?"

"Pretty bad. But try not to worry about that right now. Do you think you can get up?"

"I'll try. My hip is killing me."

"You must have hit it on the coffee table when

you fell off the sofa. That's where you were when the convul—"

"Oh, Kate. You saw me. I'm sorry. I'm sorry."

"Please, Daniel, try to get up. Dr. Loring wants you to get into bed." Kate put an arm behind Daniel's back and sat him up. He probed his hip gingerly, coming away with the realization that he had wet his pants. Mortification now consumed him; he felt too ashamed to speak as Kate helped him to his feet. With an arm over her shoulder he hobbled against the pain into the bedroom and sat down on the bed. He ached with fatigue. Kate unbuckled his belt, unzipped his pants, and pulled them off; he looked at her sheepishly but did not protest. "Can you make it to the bathroom on your own?" she asked.

"Yes," said Daniel, not at all sure he could.

"Then try to wash up a little. I'll get some O.J. so you can take the medication Dr. Loring wants you to have."

Daniel fought off the temptation to fall back on the bed and go to sleep. Tasting the blood in his mouth, he struggled up and managed the few steps to the bathroom. He turned on the water and leaned against the sink, surveying his reddened lips in the mirror. As he reached for the washcloth he realized he could not recall waking up that morning.

Chapter III

DANIEL'S inner alarm forced him awake at six A.M. He felt drugged, then remembered that he was, with the extra dose of phenobarb Kate made him take before he collapsed in bed. He did not know about the pills she had fed him earlier in the evening. He burrowed back into the pillow, but the pain in his hip and mouth snapped at his torpor. He wondered when he'd be able to run again and if he could swallow any breakfast. He was famished. He was also neatly avoiding the main issue, Daniel thought with a weak laugh, as he conjured up the headline: "EPILEPSY STRIKES REPORTER AFTER TWENTY-FIVE-YEAR HIATUS; DIET TEMPORARILY RESTRICTED TO SOGGY RICE KRISPIES." Spurred by the smell of urine on his body, he leaned into his stupor, determined to get out of bed and into the shower.

As he pushed away the covers the freckled countenance of Arnie Royce thrust itself into his consciousness, as it had many times before. Arnie's worried face hovered over Daniel, who looked up bewildered at his counselor and the circle of bunkmates gathered around him. He was eight years old, spending his first summer away from Chicago at a YMCA camp

24

near Ludington, Michigan. That morning he had gotten up and splashed icy water from the pump on his face. "You must have fainted," Arnie said when he came to on the ground. For days this incomprehensible loss of control tormented Daniel, who already felt he lagged behind his fellow Bearcats on the playing fields of machismo the staff so noisily promoted. Only at Capture the Flag did he excel; he thought it a silly game but now threw himself into it with a vengeance, sprinting through the woods one step ahead of "sissy." The camp did not report the fainting spell to Daniel's parents, nor did he.

Three years later it happened again. This time he was alone, traveling to spend Christmas vacation with his cousin in Beverly Hills. Neither the excitement of his first trip west nor the angles of his coach seat made sleep easy, and he awoke exhausted as the El Capitan moved across the Nevada desert on the second morning. About two hours out of Los Angeles he went to the lavatory to wash up, and the next thing he knew, a nurse and two porters were bending over him. The back of his head throbbed from the bash it received when he fell against the steel armrest of a chair. His Aunt Dorothy was distraught when she saw Daniel assisted down the steps of the coach at Union Station, but she calmed down after the nurse explained that he had merely lost his balance on a sharp curve and knocked himself out on the chair. Daniel knew this interpretation fell short in some way but could not get a fix on what actually had happened. Nor, at eleven years old, was he inclined to pursue the matter, especially after the lump on his head receded and his fourteen-year-old cousin, David, began taking him on bicycle jaunts through this strange land of palm trees and elaborate crèches.

Daniel fought off the temptation to go back to sleep. "Don't forget to take your pill," his father's voice admonished. Recalcitrance and guilt roiled up, as they had not since the beginning in Chicago twenty-five years ago. Daniel purged his father only to sit before Dr. Hermann at Billings Hospital and hear again that he had something "vee call epilepzee." Daniel had often amused his parents at the dinner table with vaudeville turns mimicking their family doctor, a refugee from Nazi Germany; but when he made the diágnosis, he looked, with his high forehead and thick spectacles, like Dr. Sivanna, the evil genius in *Captain Marvel* comics. "You must take your medicashun effry day, wizzout fail, Daniel. Do you understandt? Wizzout fail. I haff alzo made ziss very clear to your parents."

No deal. Daniel flushed the pills down the toilet, watching anxiously as the red-and-white capsule of Dilantin swirled away in the morning, the white tablet of phenobarbital at night. Weeks went by without incident, convincing him that he was winning his gamble to prove that he didn't need these chemical crutches. Then he would find himself on the living room couch, or in his bed, or on the kitchen floor, looking up into frantic eyes. Still, he continued the hustle. When Ben and Elizabeth Cooper began standing watch in the bathroom, he faked swallowing and pushed the pills into his cheek with his tongue. Sometimes they dissolved before he could spit them out; but usually he managed to jettison them into some cranny of deception—a pajama pocket, a Keds, behind his radio—for later removal to the toilet.

Just after Daniel turned sixteen, his father, chairman of the English Department at the University of Chicago, asked him to tend bar at the Coopers' annual faculty cocktail party. Daniel jumped at the chance to earn the extra cash while demonstrating his newfound jigger mastery to a wider audience. He was making a whiskey sour for Professor Kenworthy, who had just told him a new knock-knock joke, when he lost the wager again, crashing into the bar table as he fell. He revived amid the spill of alcohol and a hush of conversation that sounded less concerned than knowing, as if these academics had long been privy to his secret. Only then did he strike a desperate bargain with the medicine, and it worked. The seizures stopped, and Daniel became a reluctant convert, a robust adolescent who had to remind himself each morning and night that he was ill. Ben Cooper also never ceased to remind him to "take your pills." Even now his every letter ended, "Don't forget to TYP."

These events had metamorphosed from trauma to anecdote over the years, but their original shock now welled up in force. Daniel swung his feet to the floor, rose against the spasm in his hip, walked into the bathroom, and ran a warm bath. He had expected to feel wobbly when he stood, but he didn't—only tired. He looked at the two bottles on the toilet tank, sentries that had inexplicably abandoned their posts for the first time in a quarter of a century. More medication would only zombify him further, and he wondered if he should take his usual morning dose.

More out of habit than conviction, he shook out a 250-milligram tablet of Mysoline. A bitter pill, Daniel thought, and washed it down, after which he put on his bathrobe and went into the living room.

Kate slept soundly beneath a blanket on the sofa, a blue bandanna tied over her eyes against the light. Daniel longed to kiss her awake, to apologize again, to thank her, to assure her he was now okay, to tell her he loved her, to explain his history so she would understand and love him back. He felt overwhelmed by a need for Kate's affection, for a commitment that she would remain in his life. He knew it was unrealistic, even absurd; once she awoke and found the emergency had passed, she might have little enthusiasm for entangling herself with him. Tears came again as he moved quietly back to the bathroom and slipped slowly into the tub.

He had gone to bed last night trying to summon up the day's events. When he couldn't, he drifted off, assuming that the shock of the seizure had momentarily disoriented him and that he would certainly remember everything in the morning. Now, enveloped in the amniotic reassurance of the warm water, he tried again. But his memory rolled like a projector threaded with undeveloped film. He shut his eyes and tried to focus on waking up yesterday. Nothing. He could not even recall getting up; the last thing he remembered was going to bed Wednesday night after watching Johnny Carson's monologue. Daniel couldn't be sure, but the stubble on his face seemed normal for a day's growth. Could he possibly have gone through so complex an act as shaving and not remember it? And if so, what else had he done? He had obviously dressed at some point, but when? After breakfast? Had he even eaten breakfast? His hunger suggested not. No matter how hard he tried to retrieve it, Thursday remained a blank.

Daniel looked over at his running clothes piled in the corner by the hamper. *Jesus*, he thought, *did I run*? He stared at the Yale sweatshirt, the shorts, the socks, and the Adidas, seeking some clue in their arrangement. He saw none, and now the questions began to cascade. Had he showered? Had he taken his medication? Had he gone anywhere, talked to anybody? For all he knew he had called Stephen Sondheim and asked him to collaborate on a new musical. Daniel slid lower in the water as a chill of panic invaded the steamy bathroom.

"Good morning." Kate stood in the doorway, looking half Florence Nightingale and half sex-kitten, Daniel's T-shirt falling just below her hips. "How do you feel?"

" 'High as the flag on the Fourth of July.' "

"Too easy. *South Pacific*. Mary Martin. 'I'm In Love with a Wonderful Guy.' "

"I promise to make the next one harder," said Daniel, looking away. Last night's embarrassment returned in force, along with a sexual urge that only compounded it. He felt utterly vulnerable, too, like a pubescent boy whose mother has just caught him masturbating in the bathtub. Still averting his eyes, he said, "Kate, what can I say except that I'm sorry you had to go through this?"

"You can say that you'll get out of that tub reasonably soon so I can use this bathroom, which I must with some urgency. After that we can have breakfast. How's your mouth?''

''Not so hot.''

''We'll figure out something; you must be starving.''

While Kate took over the bathroom Daniel dressed and went into the kitchen. He put water on to soft-boil some eggs and instantly fantasized about having a seizure and pitching onto the stove, charring his face. He stood outside the scene, horrified, but could not seem to cry for help. Daniel shrank from the burner and decided to wait until Kate joined him. For the first time since last night he was frightened, and a series of new accidents succeeded the image of his blackened face: a canoe overturned and he convulsed in the water; he fell off a platform and a subway train severed his legs; bus wheels crushed him; he had a seizure while driving and struck an oil truck head-on, exploding his life instantly. Daniel had contemplated such catastrophes before, but they were always abstract and remote. He and Kate had talked about renting a car soon and driving up to see the fall foliage in the Berkshires. Now he replayed the oil-truck conflagration with Kate screaming as she burned up beside him.

Kate emerged from the bedroom looking impossibly radiant. Her smooth skin seemed whiter than ever, and her obvious health made Daniel feel like hopelessly damaged goods. She raised the shades in the living room to let the sun stream in, then prepared breakfast and brought it to the table at the window. With some difficulty Daniel managed to down the eggs and a glass of milk, but when he tried to chew a bite of toast, he winced in agony and spit it into his egg glass. The realization that he would not be able to eat any solid food for—how long?—only deepened his gloom, and he stared angrily out the window.

"Question," Kate ventured. "Where'd you get the 'No More Mr. Nice Guy' T-shirt?"

" 'I don't want to talk small talk.' " Daniel sang the words sullenly; uttering anything hurt his mouth and he swung a foul look at Kate.

"I haven't the slightest idea what that's from and really don't care. I don't particularly like to make small talk, either, but I guess I'm not quite ready for a full-fledged seminar on epilepsy."

Chastened, Daniel looked down at his plate.

"Look, Daniel, I didn't mean to bark. I just don't think what's happened is musical comedy material."

"Janet Bartholomew gave me the shirt. She was one of the first women I went out with after my divorce. She didn't think I had enough moxie. She was always telling me I demeaned my talents working for a weekly rag like *Tabula Rasa*. She said that with my credentials I could be a really big deal at the *Times* if only I weren't so pure and had more ambition, more 'fire in my belly.' "

"Now *there's* a good song title."

Daniel laughed despite the pain and thought he had never loved anyone like this funny woman sitting across from him.

"Kate, I had the strangest dream last night. Spencer Tracy was in this diner out West—not the Old West, really, or at least he didn't seem part of the Old West. And he—"

"That wasn't a dream. That was a movie I was watching, *Bad Day at Black Rock*."

"You mean that was on television?"

"Yes. How much do you remember?"

"Only a fight. Tracy couldn't use one of his arms, but he was slaughtering this huge guy."

"Ernest Borgnine."

"Right. I remember thinking that I recognized him. Was I awake?"

"I didn't think so. You had your attack a few minutes after I turned the set off."

The word *attack* sent a wave of self-pity through Daniel. He felt as if he had a piece missing, like Tracy, but his confidence now drained away at the prospect of taking on anything. For most of his adult life Daniel had worn his epilepsy like a badge of courage. It had proved the perfect malady, full of scary mystery and myth yet, for him at least, free of apparent consequences once drugs put it under control. When Daniel told people he had epilepsy, as he almost always did eventually, they usually looked away in awkward silence. This cheerful man with the gangly good looks and the runner's glow did not square with their notion of an epileptic—a hard-edged, ominous word that most, if pressed, could not really define except by saying, well, it certainly does not describe Daniel. They seldom pushed beyond their initial incredulity, as if further probing might set Daniel off before their eyes. "If you ever write up your experiences for the *Times,* you can call it 'All the Fits That Are News to Print,' " one *Tabula Rasa* colleague had chanced a few years ago. His relief was palpable when Daniel laughed.

"Did you say last night that you talked to Dr. Loring?" Daniel asked.

"Yes, twice. We have an appointment at his office at nine o'clock." Kate's anger blew up again as she thought about Dr. Loring's offhand behavior. She wanted to spill it all to Daniel, but there would be time enough later. "We should leave pretty soon. It's eight-fifteen."

"You don't have to come. You've already gone way beyond the call of duty. I can get a cab right in front of the building. I'll be okay." Daniel looked away as Kate dismissed his fraudulence with a smile. He could not imagine getting through the rest of his life without her, much less the day. He leaned across the table and kissed her on the forehead, once more straining against tears. He wanted to guarantee it would never happen again, to say that it had merely been a fluke electric storm in his head that a small adjustment in medication would now prevent forever. He said nothing, silenced by the knowledge that, in fact, the storm could break again even as they waited for the elevator.

"No run today, Mr. Cooper?" said the doorman as they emerged into the lobby.

"Not today, Luis."

"Better be careful, you get fat."

"Probably," said Daniel, forcing a weak smile. He limped toward the vestibule, his hip rasping with each step.

"You have an accident, Mr. Cooper?" Luis hustled to open the heavy glass door.

"Nothing serious." Daniel watched Luis survey

Kate. He long ago decided that the staff rated the women who passed through his life and their lobby.

This thought and the rush of fall air cooled Daniel's depression as he and Kate walked to the corner to hail a cab. As they waited, Daniel glanced reflexively down Ninety-third Street toward the Bellemoor. Two patrol cars sat in front, and several cops milled about on the sidewalk; from the corner it looked as if the orange tape that indicates a crime scene was stretched around the entryway.

"Kate, something's happened at the Bellemoor. I'm going to take a quick look."

"Daniel, we're—"

"I'll only be a minute."

Kate started to protest again, but Daniel was already moving down the block. She trailed after him, a frustrated mother chasing a disobedient child. The doorway of the Bellemoor gaped like the mouth of a forbidding cave. A scarred dumpster at the curb brimmed with the detritus of the conversion under way inside. Plastic garbage bags lined the front of the building, shiny black pustules draining onto the sidewalk. The police appeared oblivious to the withered Hispanic man, his rheumy eyes streaming, who picked through the rancid overflow with his left hand and gripped a bottle in a brown paper bag with his right.

"What's happened here?" Daniel put the question to a patrolman slouched behind the wheel of a blue-and-white.

"A shooting," he said laconically.

"Who's been shot?"

"Who are you?"

"My name's Daniel Cooper. I wrote a series of

pieces about this building for *Tabula Rasa* recently. Who was shot?''

"You'll have to take that up with the lieutenant."

"Beaupre?"

"Yeah, he's inside."

"Thanks." Daniel showed his press credentials to another officer and was ducking under the tape when Kate grabbed him by the arm.

"Daniel, can't this wait? You'll be late."

"Someone's been shot. I've got to find out who. Just wait here, I'll be right out."

Daniel stepped into the peeling lobby, holding his breath against the stench as he had many times before. A pool of urine glistened on the grimy stone floor of an alcove where broken mailboxes flapped open. Daniel heard voices coming from the room at the rear of the ill-lit lobby. Lieutenant Ralph Beaupre stood with his back to the doorway as two other detectives dusted for fingerprints. Frames of cannibalized bicycles lined the walls, remnants of the distant days when this makeshift office had garaged recreation for the Bellemoor's once prosperous tenants. The room also once served as the building's shop, and rusted tools now lay strewn about among caked cans of paint. Years of dirt had left the single window nearly opaque. An air conditioner clattered on the sill, chilling the room without filtering out the odor of poverty. Beaupre leaned over a graffiti-carved desk, its top bare except for a telephone.

"Good morning, Lieutenant." Daniel looked at his watch as he entered the room.

"Cooper. What the hell are you doing here? I

heard you'd been benched." Beaupre looked genuinely surprised.

"Just some deserved time off for all my good works. Who's been shot?" Daniel had now guessed the answer, but asking the question seemed proper protocol.

Beaupre ushered Daniel back into the lobby and, when out of earshot of the other detectives, said, "I've got some good news and some bad news for you. The good news is that Billy Rourke has been murdered. That should make you happy."

"Murder doesn't make me happy, Lieutenant. I'm not particularly surprised, though. Billy boy had a certain enthusiasm for antagonizing people, as you know." Daniel had never disliked anyone more than Rourke. "Have you made a collar?"

"Not yet."

"Any suspects?"

"Well, your running buddy seems to have sprinted out of sight. That's the bad news."

"Cal?"

"Mr. Calhoun Bledsoe, right. He hasn't been seen around here since yesterday morning, and the people in his organization say he hasn't been in there, either. That's their story, at least. You didn't happen to run with him this morning?"

"No."

"I didn't think so. What about yesterday?"

Daniel realized again that he had no idea whether he had run yesterday morning—alone, with Cal Blesdoe, or with the 1984 Olympic team. Kate was right: He should be dealing with his own problems at Doctor Loring's, not nosing around the Bellemoor.

He looked at his watch again, then at Beaupre; in the dismal lobby the burly lieutenant seemed suddenly threatening, like Borgnine in *Bad Day at Black Rock*.

"Did you run yesterday?" Beaupre repeated.

Daniel tried to remain composed as he framed his answer. Finally he said, "No. I haven't been feeling well the last couple of days. As a matter of fact, I'm late for a doctor's appointment now."

"You do sound sort of funny. Hurt your mouth?"

"Burned it up with some pizza."

"That'll do it. Not the best diet when you're feeling poorly. What time did you and Bledsoe usually run?"

"Our agreement—for weekdays—is to meet at the corner at six-thirty. If either of us doesn't show by six-forty, the other takes off alone."

"How far do you usually run?" Beaupre had begun writing down Daniel's answers.

"Most mornings, three miles; twice around the reservoir."

"Impressive. How long does it take you?"

"Counting warm-ups, about forty-five minutes, door to door. Why?"

"So you'd get back around seven-ten?"

"About. Look, Lieutenant, I've really got to go." Daniel edged away, forcing himself to walk without a limp.

"Sure. Hope you feel better. What's the problem?"

"I've been pooped the last few days, so I thought I'd better go in for a tune-up. Just routine."

"If Bledsoe gets in touch with you, give me a call."

"I'm a reporter, I can't prom—"

"Save the First Amendment lecture. I don't need your promise, just call me, okay? I know you think Bledsoe is the Robin Hood of the Upper West Side, but Rourke is dead and Bledsoe's missing. So please get in touch if he calls up for a jog." Beaupre walked Daniel back through the fetid lobby to the doorway. "And one other small favor. When *Tabula Rasa* decides to let you loose again, how about writing a few nice things about our work up here in the Twenty-fourth. We do help a few schoolchildren across the street now and then."

"You can count on it," Daniel said, slipping back under the orange tape.

Kate almost yanked him to the corner and into the first available cab. He sagged into the seat and tried to purge the Bellemoor and Rourke from his mind and concentrate on his epilepsy. But as the cab turned east into the park's Eighty-first Street transverse, Kate chose the topic.

"Was it serious back there?"

"Fatal. A thug named Billy Rourke."

"Who's he?"

"Did you read my pieces on the Bellemoor?"

Kate had not. Daniel Cooper was just another byline to her when the series ran in August. She had meant to read it, as she always meant to read other muckraking pieces in *Tabula Rasa* or the sober investigations and the texts of presidential news conferences in the *Times*; she fully accepted the media's decision that these were important matters, even critical ones. But the seas of gray type overwhelmed her, and she went dashing for the trim lifeboats of the "Hers" column and the book reviews.

"No, I'm embarrassed to say I didn't."

The answer irritated Daniel, less because of his pride than because he was in no mood to summarize the twenty thousand words that had taken him weeks of legwork and writing to produce.

"Do you know what an SRO is?" He gave the question a patronizing edge.

"I think so. It stands for single-room occupancy, doesn't it? Like a welfare hotel?"

"The Bellemoor is one. Or was. It's owned by Bromley-Keller, the biggest real estate gonifs in the city. They've been forcing tenants out since last winter so they can convert it to luxury apartments, which is precisely what the good burghers in this neighborhood want."

"Just the news, please."

"That is the goddamn news, Kate. These poor bastards are being thrown out into the street while gentrification turns Columbus Avenue into Rue de Boutique. Even East Siders aren't afraid to come across the park for a promenade. The worst that can happen to them is that they'll drown in cream of broccoli soup." Daniel's passion made his mouth sting.

"Was Rourke a tenant?" she asked.

"He was Bromley-Keller's goon, a sadist first-class. One of his better tricks was to break tenants' windows in the dead of winter."

"Why didn't the police arrest him?"

"Because the tenants are too terrified to call them. Besides, the cops don't give a damn about these people. Gentrification works at all levels, Kate. When Bromley-Keller finishes converting the Bellemoor and nice, well-behaved white folk move in, it'll make the precinct that much easier to police.''

"Do they know who killed Rourke?"

"No." Daniel answered curtly, to close the discussion. He did not want to talk about Calhoun Bledsoe, who loathed Rourke even more than Daniel and with good cause. As the cab headed down Fifth Avenue Daniel shut his eyes tight against the possibility that his friend had finally lost control in Rourke's ratty command post.

Chapter IV

D ANIEL felt totally washed out by all the
extra medication in his bloodstream. As he
paid the cabbie he tried to remember when
he last saw Dr. Loring. At least a year, probably
more. Visits to neurologists long ago became few
and far between, happy confirmations that he had
outdistanced his epilepsy. His internist even pooh-
poohed the drugs. Edgar Grosbart, whom Daniel called
the Merry Medic, believed that suppressed anger was
at the root of every malady and usually prescribed
released steam three times a day. "That's the ticket,"
he had advised cheerfully at Daniel's last physical.
"You don't need those pills after all these years."
Daniel relayed this advice to Dr. Loring, who said
keep taking the medication, instructions Daniel welcomed. The pills had set him free as a teenager, free
of seizures but not of psychological dependency. Besides, the dosage he had taken up to now, as far as he
could tell, had not made him feel sedated. Or caused
any other side effects, for that matter, except for a
brief bout of gingival hyperplasia about ten years
ago. This excessive gum growth, a side effect of

Dilantin, disappeared soon after he switched to Mysoline.

Neither he nor Kate spoke as they walked to Dr. Loring's door. Miss Markham, the nurse-secretary, buzzed them in, waved them to a seat, and quickly resumed typing whatever information flowed through the earphones on her head. The waiting room was already full. Kate looked to Daniel as if she were about to scream "We're here!" at Miss Markham, even though they were now forty-five minutes late for his appointment.

"Quite a reception." Kate's loud sarcasm failed to penetrate the earphones and the typing clicked on.

"We may have to sit. I've been through this before." Daniel looked around the waiting room.

"Do you want me to go out and get a *Times*? Maybe there'll be something on the murder. I have to call the office, anyway."

"Sure. Get a *Daily News* too." Daniel started to add "and a toasted bialy," then remembered his mouth.

As Kate left, Daniel noticed that the girl on the couch by the door had contusions across the entire left side of her face. She looked about thirteen and wore blue pajamas, a white terry-cloth bathrobe, and sneakers. Daniel winced as he pictured the scenario: a grand mal seizure, a bad fall, the frantic cab ride. The child clung to her mother, who nervously stroked her hair. The girl's eyes unmistakably reflected heavy sedation, and Daniel recalled instantly the first time he had seen that vacant expression. An elderly man had collapsed while trying to operate a drinking fountain in a corridor of Billings Hospital in Chicago.

Saliva drooled from his mouth and he stared as if seeing nothing.

"Is he drunk, Dad?"

"No, Dan-Dan, he's not," said Bernie Cooper, as an orderly helped the man to the bench opposite.

"What's wrong with him?"

"He's sick, Daniel," said Betsy Cooper. "How do you feel?"

"Okay, Mom, I guess." Daniel drew a measure of security from sitting between his parents in the chilly hallway, but it did not banish the sense of dread that enveloped him. When he had regained consciousness two hours before on the second-floor landing at home, his anxious parents explained through his haze that he had fallen from the top of the stairs on his way down to breakfast. Daniel could not remember falling, as he could not remember falling at camp or on the train. As he lay on the landing trying to recover his bearings, he knew that this fall must somehow be related to the others, that something serious was wrong with him. He could not bring himself to reveal this fear to his parents as they drove to the Billings emergency room; instead he concentrated on his throbbing left shoulder, the more palpable legacy of this third mystery. But once seated in the corridor, Daniel sensed that the glazed eyes across from him signaled some awful truth he would soon be asked to face.

"Any sign of the good doctor?" Kate handed Daniel the *Times* and sat down beside him. He shook his head and turned quickly to the index, which guided him to B2, the next page. Bledsoe's familiar face, cherubic and crowned by an Afro, stared out of the paper's symmetry. The two-column headline over the picture read: BROMLEY-KELLER WATCHMAN DIES IN SHOOT-ING AT WEST SIDE SRO

"Watchman, my ass," Daniel muttered.

"Bledsoe's black," Kate said.

"Since birth." Daniel looked sharply at Kate, who retreated into the *Daily News* account of the shooting.

The *Times* article was by Marvin Hinkler, a dependable general assignment retainer with a deserved reputation for doggedness and getting his facts straight. Daniel did not share the *Times*' conviction that such journalistic vacuuming usually sucked up the truth; at the moment, though, he was grateful for any information at all, and Hinkler laid out what he had crisply.

The contractor for the Bellemoor renovation had come to Rourke's office shortly before nine o'clock Thursday morning, saw the body lying in front of the desk, and called the police. They estimated Rourke had been dead about four hours. Bruises and cuts on his face and body indicated he had fought hard before his attacker fired two bullets into his chest. Ballistics showed they were from a .45 caliber automatic believed, according to Lieutenant Ralph Breaupre, the detective in charge of the investigation, "to belong to the victim." Beaupre also speculated that Rourke knew his murderer and had had an argument with him during which he pulled the gun from his desk drawer; in the struggle that followed, the assailant managed to get hold of the gun and kill Rourke. Beaupre was looking for the weapon and for Calhoun Bledsoe.

"Very neat," said Daniel, looking at Bledsoe's

photograph and wondering if he really was on the run or just coincidentally in the mountains.

Bledsoe did disappear on occasion, bolting in his VW bug up the New York Thruway and into the Adirondacks. He rented a log cabin on Saranac Lake, a two-room hideaway with neither electricity nor phone. He had taken Daniel there in June, and for five days they almost managed to forget the cruel equation of the city, two men on a bender in the winy air. They rose early each morning and ran six miles through the embracing woods, three miles out and back along an old logging trail. On the first day Bledsoe immediately plunged off the wooden dock into the chill waters. Daniel waded in slowly, scooping up handfuls of water that he splashed on his chest, face, and neck. When a child, he had squealed derisively at his parents for such cautious submersions; now Bledsoe ragged him for his honky timidity. Over breakfast, around the warmth of the cabin's wood-burning stove, he told Bledsoe he avoided jumping into cold lakes in the morning because he had epilepsy and didn't want to shock his nervous system. Daniel watched for the usual response of embarrassed disbelief, but Bledsoe almost shrugged off the revelation, saying, with a grin, "Oh, I thought it was something serious, like maybe you couldn't swim." He asked Daniel no questions about his epilepsy and continued to cannonball off the dock whenever they swam.

Daniel had felt drawn to Calhoun Bledsoe from the moment they had met at a gathering of the West Side Tenants Council the previous January. Two representatives of Bromley-Keller's public relations department had come to field questions about the Bellemoor and other buildings the company planned to convert to co-ops. Bledsoe, who presided over the meeting as executive director of the council, sat at a table in the front of the hall wrapped in a gray woolen Army blanket, a somber Indian chief in a well-barbered Afro headdress. "I have ordered the heat turned off," he said. "to show our guests, and any reporters present, what it is like to live in certain Bromley-Keller properties these nights." The sullen tenants who filled the squeaking folding chairs stayed bundled up, but the two emissaries shed their topcoats and braved the near freezing temperature in their rep-tie livery. One was Puerto Rican, the other black; they sat like former major league baseball stars dispatched by the commissioner's office to prove that playing World Series games at night in the middle of October was a summery undertaking. Daniel actually felt sorry for them as they lamely tried to fend off the tattoo of hostile questions from the floor.

Daniel had been the only reporter present and wrote a long piece about the meeting and the Council for *Tabula Rasa*. Bledsoe provided remarkable copy, the kind Daniel found almost too heroic but knew readers loved. He had grown up in Brooklyn's Bedford-Stuyvesant ghetto. His father abandoned the family when Calhoun was eight years old, and his mother began working the steam table at the Schermerhorn, a vast cafeteria hard by Boro Hall. To augment her marginal salary Mary Bledsoe nightly toted home generous samplings of the day's menu to reheat for Calhoun and his two other sisters. Victor Kaplan, the corpulent owner, blinked at these transgressions, especially as Mary became the star attraction at "The Horn." Every weekday scores of courthouse denizens and all-wise politicians lined up to banter with this animated woman while she loaded up their trays. Only once did she ask them a favor: to help get her son into New York's elite public school, Hunter Elementary.

Calhoun thrived there and performed even better after matriculating to Hunter High. By his senior year he needed no political clout to get into Williams College on a full scholarship. After four more years, during which he starred as a guard on the basketball team, he graduated *magna cum laude*, Phi Beta Kappa, and moved smoothly on to Harvard Law School, again with full financial support. When he finished with top honors in 1974, he had metamorphosed into that peculiarly American phenomenon, the golden black. Major corporations and three-floor law firms put on the full rush, long-exclusive fraternities now panting at the prospect of such a fashionable prize. Government agencies weighed in enthusiastically, too, dangling an assistant this or a deputy that at up to $50,000 a year. The elders at the cafeteria eagerly sought to advise their protégé, whose basktball exploits and other achievements were now enshrined on the wall behind Victor Kaplan's cash register. As Mary pushed the meat loaf over the counter she received surefire counsel in exchange: "If he goes with the Jenkins firm, he'll be on the Federal bench in ten years. Then he can throw us all in the slammer for overeating. Tell him, Mary."

Mary told him, but her son went back to the old neighborhood to work for $17,500 at the Bedford-

Stuyvesant Restoration Corporation, a quasi-public housing agency seeded with Kennedy money in the sixties. In 1979, when the corporation's head, Franklin A. Thomas, was tapped to succeed McGeorge Bundy as president of the Ford Foundation, Bledsoe could have named his position there. And he seriously considered making the jump until he visited the foundation's hushed glass box, with its airless atrium of embalmed vegetation. The staff seemed mummified, too, philanthropoids somnambulating through reams of reports that often seemed less important than the coffee that arrived in silver thermoses. Bledsoe stayed in Bed-Stuy for a few months after Thomas left, then accepted an offer to lead the newly formed West Side Tenants Council. He had to take a pay cut, but he welcomed the chance to challenge Bromley-Keller and the city's other real estate barons on their own turf.

More than anything, Daniel envied Bledsoe's involvement. He had always regarded journalism as something of a dodge, even the so-called advocacy brand practiced at *Tabula Rasa*. After fifteen years he felt unfulfilled, as if he had typed millions of words into a memoryless word processor. He knew this wasn't true, that some of his work had helped make a difference. He conceded, too, that the cumulative efforts of the media sometimes made a big difference, as in Vietnam or Watergate. Yet, now more than ever, he felt relegated to the sidelines, running up and down in an irrelevant profession.

Calhoun Bledsoe laughed when Daniel unburdened his discontent as they canoed along the shoreline on their last afternoon in the mountains. ''Cooper, half the city knows who you are because of all the hell-raising you and that paper do; if I vanished in these woods tomorrow, nobody'd even notice.'' Bledsoe's false modesty echoed on the lake, faintly derisive. ''But if you're looking for involvement, how about this: I've decided to move into the Bellemoor when I get back, and I'm gonna squat there with as many tenants as I can persuade to stay. Bromley-Keller will have to dynamite us out. We'll need all the publicity we can get. You could put the spotlight on us and keep it there. And if you do, the TV crews will eventually pick it up. Maybe the *Times* won't give it a big ride, but the television boys love the kind of visuals we can give them. You've gotta admit, it's your kind of story; and all you have to do is walk around the corner to cover it.''

The idea seemed as natural to Daniel as the silent glide of the canoe, and he grabbed at it instantly. Chopping wood at sunset, sitting by the fire that night, driving down the next day, the two men plotted their strategy. Once or twice this cozy conspiracy gave Daniel pause for its violation of standard journalistic ethics; but he easily vanquished his misgivings with the sword of justice. By the time they crossed the Harlem River into Manhattan, he no longer remembered, or cared, whose idea the Bellemoor series was.

''Does the *Times* say there's a reward?'' Kate's voice pricked Daniel back to the present.

''A reward?''

''Yes. The *News* says Bromley-Keller is offering twenty-five thousand dollars.''

Daniel skimmed down to the bottom of Hinkler's

story. It was there, a statement from Steven C. Bromley, Jr. himself: "William Rourke was one of Bromley-Keller's most loyal and devoted employees. As president of the company, I join all members of the Bromley-Keller family in deeply mourning his death and offering sincerest condolences to his grieving family. We are cooperating fully with the police in their efforts to apprehend the person or persons who committed this crime. Toward that end, Bromley-keller will pay a twenty-five-thousand-dollar reward for information leading to the arrest and conviction of William Rourke's murderer. We ask anyone with such information to call 693-8210, the special number the police department has established for this case."

"Bullshit." Daniel put down the paper.

"The reward? Why?"

"Bromley-Keller doesn't give a damn about thugs like Rourke. They're a dime a dozen."

"Then why bother with the reward?"

"Window dressing. Twenty-five thousand buys a lot of PR, especially when the odds are that they'll never have to pay it. They—"

"Mr. Cooper?" Dr. Loring stood in his office doorway, chart in hand.

Daniel rose as if jolted by an electric shock in the carpet. He handed the *Times* to Kate, who eyed her adversary across the waiting room. From her phone encounters she had conjured up a model of imperiousness: slim, graying, smug. What she saw was yet another collapsing American male of about fifty-five: bulging midriff beneath stooped shoulders, eyes rimmed from too little sleep, and the smile of a man with less time than he needs. He looked at Kate and said something to Daniel, who signaled that she should wait and disappeared with the doctor behind the closing door.

"Sit down." Dr. Loring motioned Daniel toward a leather arm chair in front of his desk, behind which on the wall a half dozen diplomas and certificates attested to the neurologist's curative powers. In the midst of these hung a sign in calligraphy that read, IF I WISHED TO SHOW A STUDENT THE DIFFICULTIES OF GETTING A TRUTH FROM MEDICAL EXPERIENCE, I WOULD GIVE HIM THE HISTORY OF EPILEPSY TO READ—DR. OLIVER WENDELL HOLMES. Daniel did not remember seeing the quotation on his last visit.

"Abandon hope all ye who enter here?" Daniel nodded at the wall.

"What? Oh, that. Not at all. My daughter made it for me recently, and I decided to put it up. Epilepsy is sometimes a tough nut."

"It certainly was for me last night."

"Suppose you tell me about it."

Dr. Loring's cue triggered the rush of well-being Daniel always felt when a doctor took over and actually began to care for him. The very process of answering questions made him feel secure, as if each probe were an acupuncture needle that each answer brought in right on the mark. This time, however, Daniel could furnish virtually no answers beyond what Kate had already reported over the phone. As he turned back one question after another Daniel prayed for a flicker of memory that would help his case, would shine even the weakest beam into the nearly twenty-three hours he had lost. It did not come. "Why can't I remember anything?" he finally asked, convinced that the questions were pointless.

"I'll get to that, but first I'd like to put you through a few paces. You've done all this before. Would you stand up and walk over to the door?" Daniel rose, again suffused with the sense that some sort of progress was being made. "Now walk back toward my desk putting one foot in front of the other." As Dr. Loring watched, Daniel negotiated the invisible tightrope, losing his balance twice. Was it normal to falter that way; had he done so last time he faced this test? Daniel could not recall.

Dr. Loring next pointed him onto an examining table where new challenges followed. Could he hold his right hand in front of him and then bring his index finger to his nose? Could he stretch both his arms to the sides and then bring his index fingers together in front of him? Could he see Dr. Loring's finger as it moved across his field of vision? Could he hear the vibrations of a tuning fork at his left ear? Right ear? When Dr. Loring tickled the soles of each foot with a large, blunt needle, Daniel saw his big toes turn down. This tested the Babinski reflex, he knew, but he could not remembr which response was normal, up or down. Dr. Loring's expression revealed nothing, and Daniel could not bring himself to ask.

"That's all for the moment; put on your shoes and socks and—" The intercom on the desk intruded. "Yes." Dr. Loring looked at his watch and frowned. "Just now? That's her third seizure this week. This time I think we should get her to the hospital again. Will you arrange it with admitting—and order an ambulance if she can't get there on her own. Is someone with her? Good. Tell them I'll see them at the hospital at around eleven-thirty.''

"Three seizures in one week, isn't that rare these days?" asked Daniel as Dr. Loring hung up the phone.

"Anticonvulsant drugs have a high rate of success in many cases, Mr. Cooper. You are one. But for some people they don't do the job." He waved toward Oliver Wendell Holmes. "We don't know why. The patient I was just talking about is in her late twenties; she's been married about four years and has a two-year-old daughter. She had no history of epilepsy until about six months ago when it just hit her, bam." He socked his fist into his palm. "She's been in and out of the hospital ever since."

Daniel had been genuinely curious about the phone conversation. Now he found Dr. Loring's explanation excessive, as if aimed at softening him up. What's one bam after twenty-five years in the face of this woman's grim story? Daniel quickly pushed aside this starving-children-in-India equation.

"Why has my epilepsy returned after all this time?" he asked.

"First of all, Mr. Cooper, it hasn't returned. It never left. As you know, your electroencephalograph readings have been abnormal ever since you were first diagnosed"—he looked into Daniel's chart—"by Dr. Hermann at Billings in 1960." He unfurled a shiny scroll of graph paper. "You had your last EEG with me five years ago. This is it." He spread the evidence out on the front desk, and Daniel leaned over it, trying, as he had at other times, to comprehend the march of peaks and valleys. They had been explained to him by various doctors over the years, but Daniel seemed determined to block any sustained understanding of this black-and-white proof that something didn't work right inside his brain.

"Okay. It never went away. But why a seizure now? And why was I out of it for so long beforehand?"

"I wish I had some solid answers for you, Mr. Cooper, but I'm afraid I don't." Dr. Loring sighed inaudibly as he began his recitation, by now almost a recorded message.

"Unfortunately we don't know much more about what epilepsy is, what *causes* it, than we did at the turn of the century. We know that a seizure takes place because of excessive electrical discharges in the brain, but we still don't understand what triggers the discharges. What we have discovered, over the past fifty years or so, is that a variety of drugs can reduce and, in some cases, totally eliminate seizures. They don't cure epilepsy, Mr. Cooper, they just control it—sometimes. Actually, you've been very lucky to go so long on so little medication without a major episode."

"Until now."

"Yes, until now."

"Frankly I don't feel particularly lucky at the moment. Besides, you've explained all this to me before. I know that you don't even really understand how the drugs work, mine included—only that they do. Sometimes. I've discussed this with other neurologists and I don't expect miracles, but surely you must have some ideas about why I had a seizure last night. What about the tests you just did?"

"All normal. But they're just the beginning. When you leave here this morning, I want you to go to a lab on Third Avenue for some blood tests. One thing that will show us is whether or not your drug level is too low after all these years. As soon as it can be arranged, I also want you to have a brain scan and a new EEG. Miss Markham will set them up when we're finished. Do you have insurance?"

"Yes."

"Good. The scan and EEG are expensive."

"What if I had no insurance and were broke?" Daniel knew this was not the moment for politics, but he couldn't reign in his hostility. "Why are they necessary? What do you expect them to show?"

Dr. Loring looked at his watch. "I don't necessarily expect anything. The scan takes a sophisticated computerized cross section of your head. It helps us rule out the possibility that something other than epilepsy might have caused the seizure—a tumor, a small stroke. The EEG—"

"A tumor or stroke? You mean my attack might have had nothing to do with epilepsy?"

"As I said, it's only a possibility; I'd be derelict if I didn't explore it. The scan isn't painful. You'll have to have a dye injection, which may make you a little nauseous, but that's about the worst of it."

"The worst of it, Doctor, is that I came here looking for answers about epilepsy and now you're telling me that I could have a tumor in my head. Or that maybe I had a stroke yesterday. Jesus, I'm thirty-nine years old."

"And you'll probably live at least another thirty-nine," said Dr. Loring, again consulting his watch.

"All those hours I was out of touch yesterday, could that have been caused by a stroke or tumor?"

"It's a possibility that should be explored." The trace of impatience in Dr. Loring's tone clearly indicated that the session was ending. "One more thing," he said, walking around the desk. "I'm going to adjust the dosage of your medication. Beginning today I want you to start taking a grain and a half of phenobarbital and 750 milligrams of Mysoline daily—a tablet of each when you get up, the same after lunch, and again when you go to bed." Dr. Loring bent over his desk and began filling out new prescriptions.

"Christ, Doctor, I'll be catatonic. That's three times what I've been taking all my life. I already *am* catatonic after only a day—from all those extra pills I took yesterday."

"No. You're feeling the way you do because of the seizure itself. They take a lot out of you, especially one that lasted as long as yours. It's like running forty miles in a minute, or having electroshock. But every day you'll feel a little stronger."

"Not if I really ran twenty-four hundred miles per hour. I'd be dead."

Dr. Loring smiled peremptorily and held out the two prescription slips.

"Do we have to go this route?"

"Yes. Maybe we can cut back later, but right now it's important to get more medication into your bloodstream until we see what the levels are."

Daniel accepted the slips like sentencing decrees. Dr. Loring told him to rinse his mouth out with warm salt water several times a day until it felt better and ushered him toward the waiting room and Miss Markham.

"He certainly was anxious to talk to me," said Kate when they left the office.

"I'm sorry. It's my fault. He would have, I'm sure, but I completely forgot to ask, and then I got all involved in making test appointments."

"What kind of tests?"

"Blood tests, for openers. I'm going to a lab now. It's only a couple of blocks. Walk with me and I'll give you all the gory details. Then you can abandon this mercy mission and get back to Glossary."

Daniel didn't really want to discuss anything. His chewed-up tongue made it literally a pain to communicate even if he didn't want to stew alone in silence. But he could not treat Kate like an anonymous night nurse about to go off duty. As he described his session with Dr. Loring he wondered if she sensed the perfunctoriness of the account.

"Well, I guess he sounds as if he knows what he's doing," she said when Daniel finished. Her commitment to raising hell about the doctor's behavior last night waned. "When are the brain scan and EEG?"

"Next week. Monday and Wednesday." They walked awhile in silence, then Daniel continued. "It looks as if I have more than a nickel's worth of epilepsy, after all."

"I didn't know they put a cash value on these things."

"The Army did."

"The Army? You were in the army?"

"Two years. From 'sixty-nine to 'seventy-one. You are walking with a trained killer."

"Very funny. I'm amazed that they took you."

"So was I. I had just graduated from Yale and was taking the summer off at home in Chicago before taking a reporting job at *The Washington Post*. When the call to arms came that June, I simply assumed, as I had for years, that the Army would never take me. When I went to the physical, I had a whole sheaf of letters from doctors about my epilepsy. This Army neurologist, a captain named Farson, read them and was not impressed. I had been taking a capsule of Dilantin and a half grain of phenobarb daily since I was fourteen. He seemed to find this astonishing. His exact words were, 'You know, son, that's about as close as you can get to taking no medication at all. It seems to me you have about a nickel's worth of epilepsy.' Then, before I could utter a bleat, he pointed at the letters and said, 'These doctors say you can't serve in the military. What do *you* think?' " Daniel had dined out on this story for years and warmed again to the telling, despite the realization that his wounded mouth gave his diction a distinct Brando quality. "Do you get the picture, Kate? I'm sitting there in my skivvies feeling like a fifth-grader and this kindly, white-haired principal is, in effect, asking *me* if I want to join the Army."

"What did you say?"

"I said yes, because I realized as I sat there that I did."

"But what about Vietnam?"

"I know. It seems crazy now. This was only a year after the Tet offensive. Fortunately I spent the whole time doing information duty at the Pentagon— except for basic training."

"Where did you go for that?"

"Fort Leonard Wood. Missouri in July and August. The guys in my platoon bitched about everything—the fuckin' heat, the fuckin' food, the chickenshit Army—but I absolutely loved it. I was so gung-ho that by the fourth week I could do more push-ups than anyone in the platoon but the drill sergeant. I marched twenty-five miles in the sun with an M16 and a full field pack, and finished at the head of the column, feeling great."

"But why? You didn't know at that point that you'd wind up at the Pentagon."

"I just didn't think about Vietnam when I was in basic. I was having too much fun. My medical records said that because I had epilepsy I should 'avoid common industrial hazards.' I suppose that meant that they didn't want me smashing up one of their jeeps. But it didn't stop them from ordering me to crawl under live machinegun fire in the dark."

They turned down Third Avenue as Daniel's enthusiasm mounted. "You know what the sergeant called me? 'General Brown Nose.' My platoon mates were somewhat less imaginative. 'That Yalie asshole' was one of their favorites. But I didn't care. From the day they shaved my hair off I converted basic into my private war, into a personal test of my fragility. I know this sounds preposterous—it sounds preposterous to me *now*—but when I shouted 'Kill! Die!' during bayonet drills, the target was not the Viet Cong but my epilepsy. I literally stabbed it to death again and again. By the end of the two months I had never felt so physically confident, and I was convinced I had skewered epilepsy forever. The Army *had* made a man of me. Now I'm back at square one—or worse.''

Kate laughed.

''What's so funny?''

''I'm sorry. I know you're upset. But the idea of you yelling 'Kill! Die!' at anything is pretty bizarre, you must admit. I can't quite picture you with a bayonet.''

''Listen, I was the best,'' said Daniel, lunging at Kate's rib cage with his finger. ''I got straight A's in death.''

When they arrived at the entrance to the lab, Kate made a halfhearted offer to come upstairs with Daniel and then accompany him home. To her obvious relief he shooed her off to work. He promised to call her as soon as he got back and agreed to let her cook dinner for him. The blood tests took about half an hour, and Daniel arrived at Ninety-third Street by noon. He started toward the Bellemoor to find out if the police had developed any leads, but the lone cop posted in front suggested that they had returned to the Twenty-fourth Precinct.

''Did you hear about the shooting, Mr. Cooper?'' Luis said when Daniel entered 329. ''You knew the guy, didn't you, and the guy they're looking for too? Do you think he did it?''

''No, Luis, I don't.''

As he rode up the elevator Daniel wondered if Ramirez actually had read the Bellemoor series or just seen him on the subsequent television coverage. The pieces had made him and Bledsoe popular talk-

ing heads, recounting for earnest, well-tailored an-
chormen in their antiseptic studios how rats and roaches
scuttled with proprietary tameness in every corner of
the Bellemoor, how bathrooms were never cleaned
and toilet paper was unknown, how the elevator had
not worked since March when, according to Bledsoe,
Rourke unbolted the cables from the roof of the car.
Tenants climbed the stairs to their apartments, arriving to discover their locks changed or their posses-
sions stolen. Such harassment was commonplace at
the SROs across the West Side, but the army of
storefront lawyers that eagerly marched for the poor
in the sixties was now a faded pang of conscience.
The reduced pro-bono cadre of the eighties, ragged
and overworked, was no match for the landlords'
high-paid gunslingers and the inertia of the courts.
What few cases made it onto the docket dragged on
for months, delayed by legal stalling or stalemated by
the refusal of frightened tenants to testify. Occasionally a judge would lecture a landlord for accumulated
violations and levy a fine. Bromley-Keller routinely
appealed these convictions and had managed, Daniel's tally of court records showed, to pay only twelve
thousand dollars for its overzealous relocation proce-
dures at the buildings it was converting. A studio
apartment in the Bellemoor would soon bring in more
than that in a year.

Daniel liked delivering these TV lectures, especially when they were accomanied by footage of
evictions that tugged at the conscience of the viewer.
"Look at those poor bastards, where will they go?"
But by the next commercial for cheap flights to the

Sun Country, who cared? When the "poor bastards" silently disappeared into the outback of Queens and Brooklyn, the cameras never followed. Nor did they pay much attention to the power players, like Bromley-Keller, who so far had proved untouchable. With the cooperation of the mob-controlled construction trades they were converting Manhattan into one large co-op city for the rich, smoothing the way with cash that flowed as regularly as sewage but proved not nearly as traceable. The cliff dwellers thrilled to the metamorphosis. Fifteen years ago Columbus Avenue had been nightmare alley, block after block of slums oozing their threat onto the avenues and side streets. The ladies of Central Park West often made the three-block shopping trip to Broadway in taxis, stagecoaches rattling through Indian territory. Now the Upper Left Side was going up in flambé, Daniel thought as he reached his door.

The midday sun buoyed him as he entered the apartment, and he decided to see if a workout at the piano would boost his morale further. Let's see what kind of healing power the Gershwins have in a crisis, he said to himself as he sat down and began playing "Someone to Watch Over Me." He laughed at the dollar-Freud quality of his choice and imagined Dr. Loring perched on the Steinway in a sequined red dress, torching out the number in some smoky boite. But when he sang the refrain, the words became: "Dooooon't you forget the new dose."

He supposed it could wait, but he had taken only the old amount that morning. He might as well get started on the new regimen and find out how dragged out it would make him. He went into the bathroom and shook out a tablet of phenobarb and one of Mysoline and drank them down, eyeing his running clothes on the floor. Again he tried to get them to yield some indication that he had or hadn't run yesterday morning. They looked like dirty laundry, nothing more. Daniel gave the pile an annoyed kick as he started back to his song. The muzzle of a gun poked out from beneath his sweatshirt.

Chapter V

"**W**ELCOME to the black hole," Billy Rourke said as Daniel entered his grimy lair at the Bellemoor. "Shut the door. Mustn't let any of the coolth escape. This July heat is a bitch." Rourke wore faded Army fatigues, a white T-shirt that accentuated his muscular relief, and sat with feet propped on the desk next to a set of earphones and a Walkman.

"I didn't know you were a music lover," Daniel said.

"Absolutely. Good for my image with the tenants." Rourke did not stand up or reach out to shake hands; he waved Daniel to an overstuffed armchair in front of the desk.

"Antimacassars?" Daniel fingered the white doilies on the headrest.

"Is that what they're called? It came with the chair. Mrs. Rubenstein left it when her son finally carted her off last week. Gives the room a certain charm, don't you think?" Nothing in Rourke's neutral blue eyes suggested irony.

"Didn't she want it?"

"She left it. Nobody wants what's in these dumps.

The son didn't want Mrs. R. He told her she could stay with them for a few weeks, but that's it. 'I don't want the children doubling up forever; they need their own space.' He didn't give a shit about her tears.''

"Where'd they go?"

"Who knows? Westchester, I think. In a station wagon with plates that said HERCAR. The wife probably has a steel cunt to go with it."

"Could be." Daniel tried to sound congenial. He began all interviews in this conciliatory tone, the soothing voice of a benign judge merely doing his job by seeking the facts. The approach generally worked with politicians and bureaucrats. That Daniel often proved to be a hanging judge seldom seemed to bother them when he came around again, testimony less to the power of the press than to its lack of it.

"I have a few things to do, Cooper. You're here. Why?" Rourke stared at him icily.

Daniel was used to setting the pace in interviews; Rourke's abrupt challenge caught him off-balance. He considered stalling by lobbing a few innocuous questions, then took the plunge.

"I thought maybe you could help me explain Councilman Wilder's recent behavior." Daniel looked for some recoil, but Rourke displayed none.

"Why? Is he baying at the moon?"

"No, but he's acting rather odd for a politician who's been the darling of West Side liberals for the past nine years. One week he's the champion of the tenants living in those three buildings Bromley-Keller needs demolished for the Dickinson high-rise; the next week he's leaning on the health department to close them down as uninhabitable.''

''Maybe he took a look inside.''

''Maybe. And maybe someone got to him with some cash. Fifteen thousand, to be exact.'' Daniel thought he saw Rourke flinch at the figure.

''Mr. Incorruptible? Are you telling me that *Tabula Rasa*'s all-purpose good guy is on the take?''

''From your employer.''

''Who says? Bledsoe? He's full of shit.''

''Among others. Everything leaks in this city, including Bromley-Keller. Three sources have told me you passed the money to Wilder at the Three Brothers coffee shop.'' Daniel exaggerated the number of sources by two. ''I've enough information to go with the story now.''

''Then why come to me? Write whatever you want. You may have Bledsoe in your pocket, but I'm not getting into the other one.''

''You don't have to. But why take the fall for Bromley?''

''Mr. Bromley pays me to help relocate tenants, not to bribe city councilmen or anyone else. I have nothing to do with the Dickinson project. I've got my hands full with this fleabag.''

''All I'm asking—''

''Look, Cooper, I spent four years in Vietnam trying to make soldiers out of the kind of dumb animals that used to live in this building. Did a pretty good job too. And what do I get? A dishonorable discharge. Just because of some penny-ante dope-dealing between chopper trips into the countryside to get my ass shot off. You know how long it took me to find anyone who would give me a permanent job? Two fucking years. That was Bromley-Keller. So find yourself another pigeon."

Daniel did not know any of this history and was scrambling to play off it when a tentative knock sounded on the door.

"Come in," Rourke shouted into the din of the air conditioner.

Daniel turned to see a child of about seven standing in the doorway. She wore no shoes, and her tattered, unwashed clothes hung loosely on her malnourished frame. She looked at Daniel like the young Third World supplicants who gaze out of the creamy pages of *The New Yorker*; only, instead of the standard ad agency smile of hope, fear masked the child's dark face.

"M-my daddy said to come down and tell you that the toilet still don't work," she said, stammering. Her eyes darted to Daniel, probing to see if this stranger was an ally.

"Bernice, I told your Daddy that the toilet wasn't gonna be fixed. He's got to move out of this building and soon. He knows that." Rourke stood as he said this.

"He made me come down." Bernice fought hard to stem her tears.

"Don't cry, honey. Tell your dad to come down and I'm sure Mr. Rourke will work something out." Daniel moved to comfort her, but she backed away.

"He can't come down, he's too drunk," said Rourke, looking furiously at Daniel. "And I already have worked something out. They can use a crapper in any of the empty apartments on the floor."

"They *all* broke," the child said.

"Then go to another goddamn floor. But don't bother me about it. Better yet, go live with your mother." Rourke moved from behind the desk.

"We don't know where she gone." Bernice began to weep openly.

Daniel again tried to approach her; again she retreated. He held out his handkerchief and said, "Here, dry those tears. Maybe I can help you. My name's Daniel and I'm a reporter. Go upstairs and tell your father I'd like to talk to him. Tell him I'll be up in a few minutes."

Bernice looked at Rourke for permission. When he shrugged, she backed into the lobby and disappeared toward the stairway.

"Stop worrying, Cooper, that kid'll survive. They all do. Maybe the boozer won't—who cares. But poor kids learn the ropes early. I saw it on the streets of Saigon, and I saw it where I grew up in Kentucky. I didn't have any shoes most of the time, either."

"Was your father a drunk?" Daniel challenged.

"Sometimes. And he beat me too. You manage."

"For God's sake, the child doesn't even know where her mother is."

"Probably hooking somewhere. The kid's better off." Rourke dropped back into his chair and returned his feet to the desktop. "If you're so concerned about Bernice and her drunk daddy, why don't you take them in? You have a nice, comfy apartment at 329, and I'm sure the toilet works. They'd like it there, and I'm sure your neighbors would love to have a cute little pickaninny running around the lobby. Daddy could hire out as a butler, if you can sober him up first. Make them an offer when you go upstairs. Then we'd both be happy. They'd be out of here and you wouldn't have a guilty conscience. Or are you only interested in getting a good story?''

''I've already got a good story, and maybe I *will* make the offer.''

''The sooner the better,'' said Rourke. Daniel knew his alliance with Calhoun Bledsoe in pursuit of Bromley-Keller drew its considerable energy as much from an embarrassment of privilege as from a commitment to liberal principles. He could afford the luxury of muckraking for *Tabula Rasa* because his moderate salary was substantially augmented by a bountiful trust fund left by his grandfather, a Chicago grain merchant. This largesse also made possible the purchase four years ago of his apartment, whose five spacious rooms could easily provide a temporary shelter for Bernice and her father. Rourke, of course, was right. Should they move in for even a few days, 329 would begin to rumble like Mt. St. Helens. No blacks or Hispanics lived in the building, and even so Ivy-stamped a lawyer as Calhoun Bledsoe would not be able to buy an apartment, even if he could afford it. The co-op board, like most on the liberal West Side, kept watch on the apartments like bankers overseeing their portfolios.

Daniel had moved in eagerly nonetheless, relieved at last to be out of the cramped, two-room sublet he had occupied since separating from Faith. He had never challenged the status quo at 329 by running for the board or even bothering to seek out and push a black or Hispanic purchaser. Nor did his concern for

Bernice and her father extend across his threshold. Rourke's grasp of this truth moved Daniel onto the offensive.

Pulling out a notebook for the first time, he said, "Bledsoe has given me a sworn affidavit saying that he's seen you in the corridors at night firing off a gun, and a half dozen other tenants tell me the same thing."

"The cops have been here three times on that one. If I did what Bledsoe says, the walls and ceilings would look like Swiss cheese. The cops didn't find a single—"

"I assume you use blanks. I don't think even you want to kill these people."

"I don't give a shit what you think." Rourke swung his feet to the floor and leaned forward across the desk.

"Do you own a gun?" Daniel asked.

"Damned right I do, and it's not filled with blanks." Rourke reached into the bottom right-hand drawer and lifted out a 45-caliber automatic. He placed it deliberately in front of him and then pulled a folded form from his wallet. Pushing it toward Daniel, he said, "My permit."

Daniel had not expected a direct answer to his question. The sudden presence of the shiny weapon itself made him feel as if someone had switched off the air conditioner. He looked nervously into his notebook, scratching for a follow-up question in the tightening atmosphere.

Seizing the pause, Rourke patted the gun and said, "Do you really think I'd work in this hellhole without protection? For all your snooping, Cooper, I don't think you really have any idea what kind of people live in a place like this.''

"Bernice and Mrs. Rubenstein?" Daniel's reflexive sarcasm sucked up more air.

"No, smartass. How about the pimps who come here to shack up with their whores in the middle of the night? Or the coke heads who are so strung out they'd stick you in the back just to get a subway token to make their next connection? Or Robinson on the sixth floor? Bledsoe probably says I broke those mailboxes out there in the lobby, but take my word for it: Robinson trashed them looking for welfare checks. When I caught him, he threatened to kill me with a machete he says he keeps under his mattress. And the loonies. The state says let 'em out of the bins, they're no threat to society. Bullshit. Two weeks ago one of 'em—a woman—just walked in that fuckin' door behind you and tried to dump a bucket of scalding water on me, screaming that I was her husband. She was black as the ace of spaces." Rourke picked up his gun and put it back in the bottom drawer. "So, yes, I do have a gun. This place is no different from Vietnam. You never know where the next ambush will come from, or when, especially since your pal Bledsoe moved in and started looking for publicity."

Daniel recalled this July confrontation with Rourke with perfect clarity, but the clear pool of his recollection filled instantly with the silt of incredulity as he stared at the gun on the bathroom floor. He bent down and reached for the weapon; perhaps the feel would explain how it got there. His hand hovered, then withdrew, whether because he didn't want to leave fingerprints or was afraid to jog his memory he wasn't sure. Probably the latter. His fingerprints must be all over the gun already. Unless somebody planted the thing, slipped in during his epileptic blur yesterday, and stashed it under his running clothes. When the phone rang, he had to wrest himself from the apparition at his feet.

As he walked into the living room Daniel prayed that the caller was Bledsoe. At the very least he could say whether they had run together Thursday morning, and maybe even supply some absurdly simple explanation for how Rourke's gun had materialized in his bathroom. It was Kate, her voice concerned and affectionate. How did the tests go? How did he feel? She was coming up after work. Sixish. Did he think his mouth could handle some soup and French bread? If so, she'd pick it up at the Silver Palate on her way.

"That's fine," said Daniel, trying not to sound eager to get off the line.

"Anything else I can bring? How about some sexy underwear?"

"Sure," said Daniel, feigning enthusiasm. "See you later."

"You're okay?"

"Absolutely. See you at six." Daniel hung up.

As he returned to the bathroom the Torsney case burst in his head. On Thanksgiving Day, 1976, six cops had investigated a family quarrel at the Cypress Hills housing project in the East New York section of Brooklyn. The dispute was settled peacefully, but as the officers left the building they encountered several teenagers loitering near the entrance.

"Did you just come from apartment 7-D?" asked fifteen-year-old Randolph Evans.

"Damned right," replied one of the cops, Robert Torsney, who drew his revolver and, at point-blank range, shot the boy in the head. Evans fell and Torsney shined a flashlight in his face, then headed back to his patrol car, ignoring the calls of his fellow officers.

"What did you do?" Matthew Williams, Torsney's partner, asked when he got to the car.

"I don't know, Matty; what did I do?"

Randolph Evans died that night in Brookdale Hospital. Three days later two thousand mourners gathered in the First Baptist Church in Crown Heights, their hymns and eulogies moaning helplessly over yet another loss to a white cop.

"We are going to be the instruments of a judgmental Christ," cried the Reverend Timothy Mitchell. "We cannot sit idly by while our little ones are killed."

And for a few days they didn't. Bitter denunciations and formal protests rained on the police department. To the surprise of even the most skeptical, Torsney did not escape with the usual suspension "pending an investigation." Instead he was arrested on the spot and, on the day of his victim's funeral, indicted for second-degree murder. That seemed to satisfy the multitude, which meekly returned to the quiet simmer of the ghetto.

To Daniel, Torsney was just another headline, another trigger-happy racist cop, until the papers reported that he was claiming epilepsy as his defense. Torsney's lawyer maintained that the officer fired while in the throes of a rare form of psychomotor seizure. Daniel thought the whole thing reeked. Torsney had no history of epilepsy, psychomotor or any other kind. Evans was unarmed, but Torsney said he had hallucinated a weapon of some sort in the boy's waistband. Almost a year to the day after the shooting a jury acquitted Torsney by reason of insanity, a plea that rested heavily on the epilepsy claim.

Furious, Daniel wrote a memo to *TR*'s editor, Malcolm Fosdick, offering to do several articles on the case. When a day passed with no response, he invaded Fosdick's office. The memo lay in his in box, unread, so Daniel delivered its contents in a bristling diatribe. Torsney had shot the kid in cold blood. Now he had literally gotten away with murder by taking refuge behind the myth that epilepsy produces violent behavior.

"*You* sound fairly violent at the moment," said Fosdick, tugging at his broad red suspenders and leaning back in his swivel chair.

"Come on, Mac, you know the verdict stinks. It leaves the impression that an epileptic can be normal one minute and then suddenly turn into a homicidal maniac."

"Aren't you overstating things a bit, Dan? I haven't read your memo, and I certainly haven't followed the case as closely as you have, but from what little I've read in the *Times*—and what you tell me—I get the impression that Torsney got out of a tight spot with a slick lawyer. It's happened before. Besides, only Neanderthals think epileptics are potential killers."

"There are a lot of Neanderthals out there, Mac."

"Look, Dan, I know you had a few seizures when you were a kid. But that was years ago. Ancient history. Forget it. You're the best reporter in this shop, in the city for that matter. I'd never have cajoled you away from *The Washington Post* if I thought you'd be anything else. But your judgment's skewed on this one. Sure, it's our kind of story, and we'll do it. But not as a series and not by you. You've got bigger fish to fry. I'll give it to Victoria. She'll do it justice."

Daniel sulked for a week, during which he considered the treason of doing the pieces for another publication. He also toyed with the idea of writing a book about the case. But fresh injustices soon pushed the Torsney verdict out of the papers, leaving Daniel with no daily information to fuel his outrage. He thought about pursuing the facts on his own: reading the trial transcript; interviewing the psychiatrists who testified so confidently for each side; exploring the legal tangle of the insanity defense; even bearding Torsney if he could get at him. He had never written a book; maybe this was the one. Daniel made several starts on a magazine piece, but in the face of his *TR* assignments and Fosdick's wet blanket, the project quickly began to seem like too much trouble. With each passing day his interest flagged, especially after Vicky Antonelli's tidy summation appeared in *TR* and co-opted his fury. Now, almost ten years later, he hadn't the vaguest notion of what had become of Robert Torsney.

Daniel tried to summon up the angry skepticism he had felt about the case as he reentered the bathroom.

But all he could think was: Did I kill Rourke? His intellect pronounced the question ludicrous, but could he trust the inside of his head anymore? Something had gone terribly wrong, and a lifetime of logical thinking seemed to be falling away, as if the running path around the reservoir had suddenly been swallowed up by jungle. At the time Daniel had attributed his failure to pursue the Torsney case on his own to simple laziness. Now he wondered if a subconscious fear hadn't made him drop it. Maybe Torsney *had* suffered a psychomotor seizure; maybe there *was* a connection between violence and epilepsy and he had been afraid to find out any more than he knew.

Daniel gazed down at the gun again and tried to remember—or at least imagine—grappling with Rourke. He had encountered hand-to-hand combat only in the make-believe world of Fort Leonard Wood. He still stayed in shape by running, but that hardly provided the nerve or training to wrestle a gun from Rourke, who considerably outweighed him in both pounds and malevolence. Yet epileptics in seizures, he had read, could unleash physical energy far beyond their normal capacities, sometimes breaking their bones by the violence of their convulsions. Daniel pictured himself going to the Bellemoor in the middle of the night, cocked like a robot with this superhuman strength. It was sci-fi madness.

He erased this nightmare momentarily by concentrating on where to hide the gun until he could think more clearly. Almost shutting his eyes, he picked it up with a sweat sock, placed it in the wicker hamper, and threw the rest of his running clothes on top. The smell of his sweats made him yearn to run. A jog around the reservoir always jacked him up, aerated his mind. Maybe that would nudge his memory or at least help him deal with this incredible incubus. Just contemplating the exertion, however, made him sag with fatigue. Determined to face down the extra phenobarb, anyway, he began unbuttoning his shirt; then he said the hell with it: Even if he ran three four-minute miles, he'd still come back to the gun.

Daniel dropped the hamper lid and looked at his watch. Only two-thirty. He wished he could put the digits on fast forward so Kate would appear in minutes; yet he wasn't at all sure he could handle her when she did arrive. She had been saintly yesterday and this morning, but he had no idea how she really felt about his epilepsy. If he showed her the gun, she would be terrified, would insist he tell the police. If he refused, she might go herself. If *he* now feared that he might have killed Rourke, why shouldn't she? Her independent spirit had drawn him from the start; she was not likely to roll over because he wanted to keep this problem to himself while he . . . while he what? Put on a deerstalker and solved the case himself? Kate was no Watson, and Beaupre certainly no Inspector Lestrade. Doubtless he was progressing quite nicely on his own.

Daniel went into the kitchen and brewed some tea. He put two spoonfuls of honey, an oatmeal cookie, and a dollop of milk into a large mug and poured in the steaming liquid. The sight of this pablum made him feel infantile, but he knew his mouth could deal with it and hoped the shot of glucose would boost his energy and morale. He was walking with the mug to the living room window when the sheet music on the

piano rack arrested him. The notes seemed to be
staring at him, a gallery of accusing eyes fixing him
from every corner of the page.

Robert Torsney had seen eyes, too, Daniel recalled. A few weeks before he shot Randolph Evans
he was on routine election-day duty at a polling place
and called a superior to say that the voters in line
were staring at him "with death in their eyes." The
superior laughed. So had Daniel when he read about
it in the *Times* report of the trial. Someone in Torsney's
corner had apparently read *The Idiot*, knew that Prince
Myshkin, Dostoyevsky's epileptic hero, saw fright-
ening, disembodied eyes at several dramatic points in
the narrative. No need to introduce Dostoyevsky to
the jury, just the eyes. At the time Daniel regarded
them as just one more invention in Torsney's deft
defense.

Daniel yanked himself from the gaze of the notes
and went to the bookshelf. He took down his battered
Penguin paperback of *The Idiot* and began searching
for the passages about the burning eyes. Instead he
fastened on the scene where the prince encounters his
rival, Rogozhin, on the stairs of his Petersburg hotel.

Rogozhin's eyes glittered and a frenzied smile
contorted his face. He raised his right hand and
something flashed in it. The prince did not try to
stop him. All he remembered was that he seemed
to have shouted:

"Parfyon, I don't believe it!"

Then suddenly some gulf seemed to open up
before him: a blinding *inner* light flooded his
soul. The moment lasted perhaps half a second,

yet he clearly and consciously remembered the beginning, the first sound of the dreadful scream, which burst from his chest of its own accord and which he could have done nothing to suppress. Then his consciousness was instantly extinguished and complete darkness set in.

"He had an epileptic fit, the first for a long time. . ."

Daniel had read this passage many times. He knew what came next and tried to close the book and shut out Dostoyevsky's vivid description. But his eyes would not relinquish the page.

. . . the sight of a man in an epileptic fit fills many others with absolute and unbearable horror, which has something mystical about it. It must be assumed that it was this impression of sudden horror, accompanied by all the other terrible impressions of the moment, that paralyzed Rogozhin, and so saved the prince from the inevitable blow of the knife with which he had been attacked.

Daniel took the book over to the sofa and sat down to wait for Kate.

Chapter VI

THE sun glistened on the reservoir against Daniel's black mood. Joggers streamed steadily around the track, spurred by the absence of job deadlines on this crisp Saturday morning. Their command infuriated Daniel. Two days ago he could run this 1.6-mile lap two times in under twenty-five minutes and hum with energy for hours afterward. Now he wondered if he could summon up the thrust to get around even once.

"Do you honestly think you should do this?" Kate put the question gingerly, but it didn't work.

"Yes, damn it, I do. And, as I said back at the apartment, I don't need you to ride shotgun."

"I'm not riding shotgun, Daniel. I just want to be with you. Is that so terrible?"

"Then stop hovering."

Kate watched in silence as Daniel sat at the edge of the track and began his stretching exercises. She sympathized with his instinct to remount the horse that had thrown him, but why so soon? She saw him wince as the warm-ups pained his hip. She had tried to keep him in bed, urging him to take it easy over the weekend, to let her pamper him, to hold off running at least until he had gone through the CAT scan and EEG tests next week. Daniel had exploded, shouting that he had coped with epilepsy all his life and wasn't about to let it nail him now. Kate finally had to settle for a sullen promise that he would not start running until she could go home, change, and meet him in the park.

Gulls swooped and turned over the water. Daniel stood up and watched as one plunged for food and then soared off, bouncing off its own reflection. He touched his tocs a few last times and moved onto the track.

"Go slow for my sake if not for yours." Kate fell in with his trot. "I believe in exercise but not excess. I've never done this, and it looks like a long way around. Besides, neither of us should be in a hurry on such a beautiful day."

"Why don't you just wait here?"

"Not a chance. I've threatened to try this for years. Now that I'm here, I have no intention of missing this opportunity to record the world's first two-hour mile."

"Suit yourself."

Daniel cursed his prickliness. Kate deserved better, much better, but the events of the last forty-eight hours drenched him like acid rain, poisoning his affection. While waiting for her yesterday afternoon he had immersed himself in *The Idiot*, obsessively searching for links between his plight and that of Dostoyevsky's prince. This was chutzpah, he knew. Leo Nikolayvich Myshkin was a Christ-like vessel, the creation of a genius. All they had in common was epilepsy. But for the moment that was enough; that and the sense of foreboding that chilled almost every page of the novel. By the time Kate had arrived at the apartment, depression had locked Daniel in. She had brought with her freshly baked challah, vichyssoise, and chocolate ice cream, a meal to go down easy. Daniel had consumed it eagerly and gratefully but throughout deflected Kate's questions with petulant, monosyllabic replies.

After dinner he retreated into the Yankees game on television. Kate treaded water by trying to work on the Gallagher manuscript, a bodice-ripper whose sex passages, though absurdly purple, slowly made her want Daniel in bed. When the game ended, he found her in the bedroom propped up against three pillows, penciling at the manuscript. She wore only transparent, white bikini panties, her softness aglow in the yellow light of the bed lamp. The sight touched Daniel and he undressed quickly; but he could not create the emotional alchemy that merged love and lust. He lay in Kate's arms, his head swarming with the fear that he had killed Rourke, that his arrest was only hours away. He replayed the Torsney case again and again, wondering where *he* would find a slick lawyer when the time came. He imagined a courtroom scene unfolding: a butch woman prosecutor held up the gun and shouted the details of Rourke's death. They made no sense, but the members of the jury nodded knowingly each time she pointed at Daniel.

Kate took command in bed, but her loving efforts only triggered a new anxiety. He began to fear that the exertion of sex would set off another seizure, that the consonant pleasure of orgasm and the terrible dissonance of epilepsy were somehow connected. He knew of no medical evidence that supported this, but as Kate's warm hands played over his body, he recoiled at the vision of fucking himself into another convulsion. He wanted to confess the dread, to have Kate's boldness sweep it away. He wanted to tell her about the gun, too, and Torsney, and how afraid he was that seizures would plague him the rest of his life. He needed an ally badly, but the revelations remained sealed as he lay staring up at the shadows on the ceiling. After half an hour Kate kissed Daniel gently and turned out the light. He had hoped the dam against his words would break in the dark, but it did not.

"Hey, pull your elbows in," Daniel snapped at a sprinting runner who jostled him in passing.

"Sorry, sir." The boy could not have been more than sixteen; he had the rail-thin look of a fledging marathoner and made his apology without turning his head or breaking stride.

"Is it always so crowded out here?" Kate had so far managed to keep abreast of Daniel.

"Yes, especially on Saturdays."

More runners weaved by them, sending Daniel deeper into his funk. Normally he did most of the passing. To relieve the monotony he and Bledsoe often kept count of the runners they overtook, congratulating themselves like gold medalists each time they set a new record. They excluded women from these homemade Olympics, and Kate's presence at Daniel's side only confirmed his hobbled gait now.

At the quarter-mile mark he harnessed his anger and began to pull away.

Kate watched as he disappeared around the south end of the reservoir and headed for the East Side. Her concern for his condition melded with a desire to cheer him on, and then she ran out of breath. Her chest felt as if it had just filled up with three-alarm chili. She considered stopping and waiting by the track until Daniel came around, or reversing directions to meet him. She shifted down to a walk and, once her lungs revived, opted to continue at that sedate pace until Daniel lapped her. She moved to the outer edge of the track to make way for the procession of pounding feet.

In a few minutes Kate arrived at the long straightaway that parallels Fifth Avenue. About a hundred yards ahead, a knot of people had gathered in the middle of the track. She began running again instantly, trying to spot Daniel in the crowd now spilling over onto the grass embankment. After only half the distance her chest heaved again and her legs throbbed perilously. By the time she reached the scene, she had to grip the reservoir fence for a moment to keep her balance; then, still gasping, she pushed through to the center of the crush. Daniel lay on his back, his face a mask of blood and dirt; blood oozed, too, from the rips in his knees and upper legs. A runner bent over him, taking his pulse.

"Oh, shit. Daniel!" Still sucking her breath, Kate knelt beside him; she took off the bandanna with which she had tied up her hair and started to clean up his face. His eyes seemed to recognize her, but he did not speak.

"You know him?" The runner released Daniel's wrist and looked at Kate.

"Yes. We started running together about ten minutes ago. Are you a doctor?"

"An intern. At Mount Sinai. I was only a few yards behind him when he fell."

"Have you called for help?"

"It only just happened, miss."

Kate bridled at the "miss." This man, in his sweatshirt and satiny Bill Rodgers running shorts, looked about twenty-five, seven years her junior. He struck her as curt, a budding Dr. Loring.

"Look, he had a very bad seizure the night before last. Now he's had another one. Look at him. We've got to get him to an emergency room. He's an epileptic."

The word sent a murmur washing to the edge of the crowd, which moved in for a closer look.

"I don't think he's had a seizure, I think—"

"I don't care what you think, I want you to get him some help." Kate turned imploring eyes up at the bystanders, who looked away: a doctor was present; they would wait their cue.

"Right now the best thing we can do is help him right here. Does anyone have any tissues or a handkerchief? Or a clean T-shirt?"

"I have some diapers, Doctor." A nanny in her starched white uniform pointed to a pram at the foot of the embankment.

"Yes. Good. Can someone take them and get them wet? There's a drinking fountain at the Nintieth Street exit."

Several runners made for the pram. The nanny,

who introduced herself as Miss Ruppert, gave the diapers to a muscular redhead who quickly doused them in the fountain and returned. Meanwhile the clot on the track dilated with morbid curiosity.

"What happened?"

"I don't know. Someone said the guy flipped out."

"Yeah. He had a fit."

"Whadaya mean, a fit?"

By way of explanation a bearded runner rolled his eyes and said, "Epilepsy."

"Epilepsy? And they let him run? That's crazy."

"He could really hurt himself."

"Could? Look at his face, it's shredded."

"An epileptic? I've never seen one before, have you?"

"Never. He actually had a *fit*. Right here? On the track?"

"My aunt's an epileptic. She takes some sort of pills. It's really not that big a deal."

"Tell that to him."

"He really looks in shape. Do you think he runs, like, every day?"

"Come on, folks, could you all move back a little." The policeman's laconic request had only a modest effect on the growing crowd, which, after spotting the patrol car just pulled up on the bridle path near the pram, rearranged itself for a better view of the proceedings.

"Officer, my name is Philip Cohen. I'm an intern at Sinai. This guy is pretty banged up. Do you have a medical kit in your car?"

"Sergeant Delvecchio. No, we don't carry them."

"We don't need a first-aid kit, we need to get him to an emergency room. Can't you just take him in your backseat?" Kate pointed down the embankment at the cruiser.

"Who are you, miss?" the sergeant asked.

"A friend. I told the doctor—or whatever he is—that Daniel is an epileptic. He's just had a seizure. Please take him to the hospital." The dark slab of Mount Sinai rose over Fifth Avenue only a few blocks to the north.

Blood-smeared diapers littered the track, and dark stains blotched Miss Ruppert's whites, making her look like a field nurse. She and the intern had managed to wipe away most of the dirt and blood from Daniel's torn face, and his head now rested on Dr. Cohen's sweatshirt. Miss Ruppert held a wad of tissue against Daniel's nose as the doctor worked over the still bleeding lesions on his legs. The crowd wound tighter as Kate and Delvecchio pressed back through.

"He took a pretty bad spill, but I think he looks worse than he is. He may have broken his nose, though. We ought—"

"Oh, Daniel." Kate knelt down on the track and began to cry.

"—to get some pictures taken and clean him up properly. I don't think we need an ambulance if you can back your patrol car up the hill."

"I'll be okay," Daniel said, as the vise that gripped his chest loosened, letting in the first full breath since he hit the ground.

The words startled Miss Ruppert, who jerked her hand away from Daniel's nose, releasing a gout of blood. She grabbed a clean corner of a diaper and again stanched the flow.

"Sure you will," the intern said. "How's the nose?"

"I'll be okay," Daniel insisted. Out of the corner of his eye he saw the crowd parting as Delvecchio's partner backed the patrol car up the embankment.

"I'd like to get you into the backseat of the police car. With some help do you think you could walk a few steps?"

"I'll be okay, Doctor. Just let me lie here for a few more minutes."

Kate bent over Daniel, her eyes still teary. "Honey, please don't try to be a martyr. You've had another seizure. They want to take you to the emergency room."

Daniel looked up at Kate, then into the amphitheater of eyes staring down at him. They seemed to reflect back the vision of a freak. Why had Kate blurted out so much? He wanted words like *seizure* stashed back in the closet, not broadcast to a parkful of strangers and police. Besides, he wasn't at all convinced he had suffered another attack; like the clear autumn sky, his memory was free of a single cloud. He did hurt all over, though, and the prospect of a hospital's antiseptic ministrations tempted him, but that would mean forms to fill out, questions about epilepsy, information for the police.

"I don't need an emergency room, Kate. Just get me back to the apartment by cab and I'll be fine."

"No!" said Kate, frustration blotting her tears.

When Dr. Cohen strongly seconded this motion, Daniel gave in. The intern and Delvecchio helped him off the track and gingerly negotiated him toward the cruiser. Miss Ruppert walked beside them, awkwardly holding the diaper to his nose. Rivulets of blood began to trickle from his other wounds, now prey to gravity. Daniel stared down at his leaking body in dismay, then into the crowd flanking his path to the car. He wanted to tell off this collective gawk, but he let it go and slowly edged himself into the backseat. Dr. Cohen sat beside him, and Kate squeezed in front between Delvecchio and his partner, a rotund officer named Bennett, who seemed primarily preoccupied with the balance of his Styrofoam coffee cup on the dashboard.

"Did anyone thank that nurse?" asked Daniel, now pressing the diaper to his nose himself. As the car rolled down the slope he managed to twist around for a glance out the rear window. With the help of two women runners Miss Ruppert was gathering up her unlikely bundle.

"I have her name and the number of the people she works for," Delvecchio said.

Daniel caught a glimpse of the nanny's sleeping charge as they pulled past the pram and back onto the bridle path. He speculated silently on the kind of reception she would get from her employers when she appeared with her blood-soaked laundry. He wondered, too, if the city would bill him for the stains now spreading where he sat. In front, Kate squirmed anxiously between the two policemen as the car headed out of the park.

"Metropolitan's only at Ninety-seventh and First. We'll be there in a minute," said Delvecchio.

"Metropolitan? Why Metropolitan? Why not Mount Sinai? It's even closer." Kate's voice rose in dismay.

"Those are the rules, miss. Street accidents go to city hospitals. They'll take good care of him."

"If I take responsibility, officer, I'm sure they'll take us at Mount Sinai," Dr. Cohen said.

Delvecchio looked across Kate at his partner, then nodded and said into the windshield, "You're the doctor."

Bennett turned the cruiser up Madison Avenue, bleating the siren only two or three times in the thin Saturday morning traffic. At One Hundredth Street they rolled down the emergency ramp, and Daniel limped through the sliding glass doors on the arms of the two cops. Dr. Cohen led them up to the registration desk, in front of which the morning's wounded had begun to collect on pastel chairs. They sat stiffly, anesthetized by the soothing presence of *Mister Rogers* on a television set suspended from the ceiling. Daniel felt as if he had just run through a field of concertina wire, but he feared he ranked low in the triage and steeled himself for a long wait.

"Another jogger? You'd think with those expensive shoes more of you would manage to stay on your feet." The registration nurse, a squat black woman with a nameplate that read BAKER rose to take charge. "Why, it's young Dr. Cohen; I didn't recognize you in your underwear." She feigned serious scrutiny. "Nice legs. What's going on here?"

They took Daniel right away, Dr. Cohen leading him down a corridor toward a warren of treatment rooms. Kate tried to follow, but Baker politely detained her with registration questions. Bennett, a new coffee cup restored to his hand from a nearby vending machine, hovered idly by the desk as Delvecchio moved off to a pay phone on the orange wall of the entryway. He dropped a quarter in the slot, dialed the Twenty-Fourth Precinct, and asked for Beaupre.

"Hello. Frenchie? Sam. Your man Cooper has just fallen in our laps." Delvecchio retraced the morning's events, starting with the plainclothesman who followed Daniel into the park and then radioed him over to the cruiser, which trailed him from the bridle path that circles the reservoir just below the track. After describing Daniel's accident he said, "Did you know that Cooper is an epileptic?"

"I know he went to a neurologist yesterday. A doctor named Loring. I haven't been able to get through to him yet. Go on."

"That's all I know, really. His girlfriend was nearly hysterical on the subject. She said he fell because he had an epileptic fit. He had one the night before last too."

"Thursday night? How do you know?"

"The girl. I think that's what she said."

"Well, make sure, Sam. It's important. Stay there. Pump the woman while you're waiting. Is Cooper being treated now?"

"Yeah."

"Good. Find out everything you can from the woman. And if the hospital doesn't admit Cooper, drive them back to the West Side. They were out running; chances are they don't have any dough for a cab. Insist on taking them, Sam. If he protests, tell him you have to do it, it's regulations or something.

See if you can get him to open up on the ride, especially about Thursday—all day. Then get back here. Andy will keep an eye on the apartment.''

"How goes the struggle?"

"I could use a lead or two, Sam. Better yet, find me the gun."

"Any word on Bledsoe?"

"Not a peep. See if you can get the girlfriend to drop a hint. But don't come down too hard on either of them. We don't want to upset those screamers down at *Tabula Rasa*."

"I'll be as gentle as a lamb, Lieutenant."

Delvecchio hung up and walked back to the registration desk. He sent Bennett out to baby-sit the cruiser and sat down next to Kate in the first row of the waiting area. Between craned glances at the television set, now offering *Sesame Street*, she told him the whole story, beginning with her phone call to Daniel Thursday afternoon. What was the harm? Daniel's epilepsy was hardly a secret now. She had already provided some of the details for Mrs. Baker, and Daniel was probably revealing even more himself as they bandaged him up. Delvecchio's questions were warm and solicitous, not the probes of a nosy cop. Kate liked him. He had rescued Daniel, taken him to this hospital, something she had wanted desperately since Thursday evening's collision with Dr. Loring. She ached to unburden herself, too, to release all the oppressive information she had reluctantly accumulated. Delvecchio listened sympathetically, a decent, caring man. His kids were probably watching *Sesame Street* also, he told her.

Daniel finally reappeared looking like a battle casualty, his legs painted with dark seas of Betadine solution on which adhesive tape anchored islands of gauze. The same rouge brightened his face, highlighting the rents in his flesh; wads of cotton plugged his nostrils. Dr. Cohen steadied him as he walked.

" 'A wandering minstrel, I, a thing of shreds and patches,' " Daniel mumbled as they approached.

"*The Mikado*?" said Kate, rising to embrace him.

"*The Mikado*," he replied wanly. He pushed her gently away. "Careful, I'm broken."

"Your nose?"

"No. That's still half Jewish. Just the rest of me."

"The nose came out okay in the X ray," said Dr. Cohen, "but Dr. Martinson would like Mr. Cooper to see a neurologist before he leaves."

"Who's Dr. Martinson?" asked Kate.

"The resident who glued me back together. An eager beaver, very thorough. But I think I'll skip it."

"Why, Daniel?" pleaded Kate.

"Because I have my own neurologist, and I'd like to get back home."

"It's a chance to get another opinion, Daniel. Take it."

"No!" Daniel turned to Dr. Cohen. "I'm glad you were running behind me, and I appreciate everything you've done. But I'd like to go home. Is that against the rules?"

"No. We can't keep you here against your will. I think you should stay until a neurologist can check you out, but if you sign an AMA form, you're a free man."

"What's that?"

"Against Medical Advice. It lets the hospital off the hook."

"Daniel, this is really stupid."

"Who has the forms?"

Dr. Cohen pointed to the registration desk where Mrs. Baker was now talking to Delvecchio. The sight only made Daniel want to escape sooner. He pushed his way into their conversation and asked for the form; looking skeptical, the nurse produced it, and he scrawled his name as Delvecchio watched silently and Kate stood by, resigned.

"At least we have a ride back. The sergeant says he'll take us."

"I think we can manage." Daniel eyed her angrily.

"Come on, pal, it's no trouble. We're going that way, anyhow. The station house is on West One Hundredth Street." Delvecchio measured Daniel's reaction.

"Thanks, but I think we'll go it alone."

"Daniel, what's wrong with you? Half the world is trying to help you today and all you do is buck. I know you're hurt, but you're behaving like an infant. You can get back any way you want, but I'm going in the police car." Kate looked at Delvecchio. "Whenever you're ready."

The pitch of this dialogue had risen sufficiently to pierce the narcotic of the television set. Their drama now played to a growing audience in the rows of plastic chairs. Suddenly Daniel felt that any exit would do. He looked at Kate, then at Delvecchio; warily he headed for the sliding doors and the cruiser beyond.

Chapter VII

THE ride back to Central Park West took less than ten minutes. Delvecchio probed around the edges of epilepsy, never mentioning the word as he tried to get Daniel to talk about what had happened to him Thursday. Each question drew opaque responses that increasingly irritated Kate. Daniel ignored her, concentrating instead on repeated examinations of his palms. He sat scrutinizing them even after the patrol car pulled up to the canopy at 329.

"We're home, Daniel," said Kate.

Her tone reminded him of a college girlfriend's observation that an evening with him was sometimes almost as much fun as being alone.

"Sorry." Daniel twisted out of the backseat and onto the sidewalk, grimacing as his lesions stung.

Like a grateful fare tipping a considerate cabbie, Kate leaned forward and thanked Delvecchio. She wanted to apologize for Daniel's rudeness, too, but checked the impulse out of a sense of loyalty she was not sure she could maintain much longer.

"Glad to help, miss," said the sergeant, turning to look out the driver's window at Daniel. "Take it easy, Cooper."

The admonition struck Daniel as a bit too polite. "I don't think I'll be running for a while, if that's what you mean." He had meant to sound civil but knew from Kate's stare as she joined him on the sidewalk that he had failed.

They stood at the curb in silence as Delvecchio and Bennett pulled away and turned down Ninety-third Street. Daniel considered walking to the corner to see if they stopped at the Bellemoor. The notion faded as the warm autumn sun bathed his wounded body, a welcome fix of salubrity that lasted only until Kate spoke.

"Why did you treat those men like the enemy?" she said.

"What happened to me Thursday is none of their business. Or anyone else's."

"They already know what happened to you, Daniel. I told the sergeant while you were in the treatment room. He couldn't have been more solicitous."

The last word opened a sluice in Daniel through which forty-eight hours of suppressed anger now began to rush. It would have washed over Kate like a tsunami had they not been standing in the counterflow of people walking along Central Park West.

Kate sensed his fury and pleaded, "Daniel, Delvecchio knows you had a seizure on the track. I saw no reason not to tell him about—"

"I didn't have a seizure. I tripped. Look." Daniel held out his palms.

"They seem fine. I don't understand."

"What's the first thing a person does when he starts to fall forward?"

"I don't know. Let's not play twenty questions out here on the street."

"You shoot your arms out to break the fall, and your hands hit the ground first. Always. But mine didn't. There's not a scratch on them."

"Which means?"

"Which means that Loring now has me so doped up that my normal reflexes are shot. When I tripped, the message didn't make it from my brain to my arms in time, so I pancaked flat on my chest and face."

"Daniel, you were unconscious, just like the other night."

"No, I wasn't. I simply had the wind knocked out of me. I remember everything. Tripping. You telling that intern about my attack Thursday night. The comments of all the assholes who gathered around to watch the freak show. One guy said, 'He's an epileptic and they let him run?' Or something like that. Am I right?"

"I don't know. I wasn't paying any attention to the crowd. Look, I'm not crazy about Dr. Loring myself. I haven't even told you about how difficult he was to deal with on Thursday. But it doesn't sound reasonable that he would prescribe so much sedation that you'd endanger yourself simply by running."

"Well, he has. His goddamn treatment is worse than the malady. I'm wiped out all the time, including now."

Kate didn't know whether that was meant as a cue, but she decided to make it one. Daniel's interpretation of his running accident sounded like a classic case of denial to her, not a subject to raise here under the canopy, if at all. He had said his epilepsy was nobody's business. Maybe that included her. Suddenly Kate yearned for some time apart.

"You must be exhausted," she said. "Why don't you go up and get some rest? I'm going home and get out of these running clothes. And I've got to plow through some pulp this afternoon. I'll call you later; put your machine on if you go to sleep. Is there enough left from last night for lunch?"

Daniel nodded, both relieved and perplexed by Kate's abrupt decision to depart. "We'll talk?"

"Of course." Kate gently took his face in her hands, bent his head down, and kissed him above the dressing on his nose.

"That's about the only part of me that isn't damaged."

"And your hands. Maybe I'll come over later and you can play me some Cole Porter."

"How about 'Down in the Depths on the Ninth Floor'?"

"How about 'You'll Get A Kick Out of Me' if you start feeling sorry for yourself?" Kate kissed him again and left.

In the lobby Mindy Frey rolled a tennis ball for Linguini, who skittered in hot pursuit across the freshly waxed stone floor; she splayed into the wall like a beginning ice skater as her eight-year-old mistress squealed merrily. When the terrier saw Daniel push through the glass door, she scrambled toward him, leaping against his scraped legs and thrusting the ball at his hand.

"Down, 'guini. Bad dog. Down." Mindy gave her a stern spank on the rear. "Oh, Mr. Cooper, she pulled a bandage off. I'm sorry. Bad dog." She slapped the dog on the snout.

"Don't hit her, honey, she's only playing." Daniel pressed the adhesive back against his skin.

"What happened, Mr. Cooper? You look terrible."

Daniel smiled at her honesty. "I tripped and fell while I was running."

"My mom used to be a nurse. Do you want me to get her? She's upstairs."

"That's sweet, Mindy, but I'll be okay. Just keep Fang away from me until the elevator comes."

She dragged her pet to one of the lobby chairs as Ramirez emerged from the package room. Before the doorman could react to Daniel's appearance, Mindy announced, "He tripped on the running track."

"Pretty bad." Raimrez responded with uncharacteristic coolness. He and Daniel always engaged in the artificial badinage of doorman and tenant, and Ramirez often trapped him in the lobby with conspiratorial discourses on the latest laundry room gossip or the drinking habits of the new handyman. Now he seemed to be eyeing Daniel suspiciously, and by the time the elevator door slid open and Daniel entered, he had turned his back.

Daniel was still contemplating this strange behavior as he rewound his answering machine tape. He eased into his desk chair, turned up the volume, and played back the single message.

"Phyllis here. It's eleven A.M. Saturday. Please call Mac as soon as possible. He'll be in the office all day."

Daniel clicked off the machine. He was surprised the call had not come yesterday, as soon as Fosdick learned of Rourke's murder. Doubtless all was forgiven and they wanted him to get on the story.

Tabula Rasa came out on Wednesdays, so he still had two days until the Monday afternoon deadline. To report what? That he had the murder weapon in his laundry hamper and had no memory of how he acquired it? That he might have killed Rourke himself in some kind of epileptic trance? That his partner-in-justice, Calhoun Bledsoe, who might provide an answer or two to these questions, was incommunicado? His eyes tightened against his fatigue as he realized it was time for another dose of Dr. Loring's opiate. He ached to retreat into bed and burrow his troubles in the pillows for a few hours of sleep. Then he would somehow deal with *Tabula Rasa*. Fosdick had ordered him to take a leave of absence—benched him, as Beaupre had so succinctly put it. Fosdick could wait.

Daniel appraised his grated body in the bathroom door mirror. Mindy was right. He did look terrible. He shook out a tablet of Mysoline and one of phenobarb and washed them down with the enthusiasm he usually reserved for liver. He then checked the hamper, where the gun still rested like a fox in a coop. Until this moment it had not occurred to Daniel to wonder if the weapon was still loaded. Two bullets had been found in Rourke's body, but Daniel could not recall if the papers or Beaupre had said how many had been fired altogether. Nor did he know how many cartridges a 45 caliber automatic held. As he eased down the lid the gun triggered a phantom bullet, splintering the hamper and ricocheting around the cramped bathroom. The phone rang through the ghostly reverberations.

Daniel moved to the night table and sat down on

the bed, berating himself for not resetting the answering machine before leaving his desk in the living room. He wanted desperately to let the phone ring, to fall back on the bed and give in to his fatigue. But he had never been any good at ignoring phones, at reining in his reporter's curiosity. It might be Kate, who would worry and probably rush over if he didn't pick up. Or Bledsoe. At that prospect Daniel grabbed the receiver. His hello was greeted by the familiar basso profundo of Malcolm Fosdick.

"At last. How's the man of leisure?"

"Fine, Mac."

"You've heard about Rourke, I assume?"

"Yes." Instinctively Daniel began rummaging around for a pencil and paper in the night-table drawer.

"Do you think Bledsoe did it?"

"Christ, you too? Yes, and he's stalking Steven Bromley right now. With a howitzer."

"Calm down. A simple yes or no will suffice."

"Then no. Just because he's not around at the moment doesn't mean he's a murderer. It's only been two days. Less. Maybe he's up at his cabin. Maybe he doesn't even know about Rourke."

"The State Police checked the place. He hasn't been there."

Daniel didn't really think he had, but this confirmation, plus the realization that Calhoun was now the object of a serious manhunt, unnerved him. He pushed off his running shoes, swung his legs onto the bed, and leaned back against the wall.

"Have you heard from him?" Fosdick asked.

"No," Daniel said wearily.

"You'd level with me?"

"Mac, I haven't heard from him. Don't you think I'm sort of curious myself?"

"I should think you would be."

"What the hell's that supposed to mean?"

"Come on, Daniel, let's not waste time going over old ground. You know I was never comfortable with Bledsoe's role in the Bellemoor pieces."

"You ran them."

"Because *most* of the material was first-rate, as usual. Except when you were carrying Bledsoe's spear in his vendetta against Bromley-Keller."

"Okay, forget it." Daniel was in no mood to review this history, either. "Do you want me to do the Rourke story for Wednesday or am I still in the doghouse?"

"Some doghouse. A few extra vacation weeks with full pay. Relax, we'll handle the story down here. But if Bledsoe contacts you, call me."

"And you'll call the cops."

"Not necessarily. We'll discuss it. How's the singing?"

"I'm booked into the Music Hall next week."

"With the Rockettes?"

"No, just the Mighty Wurlitzer."

"I'll be there. Meanwhile, call me if you hear anything."

So all was not quite forgiven, Daniel thought as he hung up. He knew he was in no shape to pursue the Rourke story for *TR*, even if he worked it by phone from the apartment; he had no idea what he would have said had Fosdick told him to get on it right away. But he wanted to be asked, to hear that his cooling-off period was over.

Daniel now deeply regretted blowing up at Fosdick last month. He slid down between the sheets and shut his eyes against the embarrassing replay of the explosion and the events leading up to it. Despite his inconclusive collision with Rourke in July, Daniel had remained convinced of the man's guilt. Too much pointed to his involvement in the Frank Wilder bribe, especially Bromley-Keller's eagerness to demolish the three squalid tenements and erect the Dickinson. The thirty-story high-rise was Steven Bromley's pet project, a pool and solarium at the first setback and closed-circuit TV security in every cranny. At the press conference announcing the structure Bromley called it "the beacon for a new neighborhood stability on the West Side above Ninety-sixth Street." He even implied he might move his family into one of the triplex penthouses. But after six months the residents of the three buildings, organized by Bledsoe and the West Side Tenants Council, not only refused to budge but were on a rent strike.

Calhoun had told Daniel he had overheard Rourke discussing the bribe on the phone at the Bellemoor, presumably with Bromley. When Rourke went to the Three Brothers coffee shop a few days later, Hilda Purvis, a WSTC secretary, followed him and sat two booths away when he and Wilder met. Bledsoe told Daniel that she saw Rourke hand Wilder an envelope. Within a week Wilder's office announced that the buildings were a health menace and should be torn down as soon as the tenants could be relocated. Wilder usually courted *Tabula Rasa*, which over the years had cast him as the city council's liberal mensch. After reversing his long-standing opposition to high-rise construction on the West Side, however, he proved remarkably difficult to reach. When Daniel finally did get him on the phone at home, his normally bluff politician's tone had modulated to a whine.

"I made a thorough tour of those traps," he said. "They're worse than I ever imagined. Not just the usual stuff, like rats and broken pipes. They're structurally unsound too. It's criminal to let human beings live in such conditions."

"So why not force Bromley-Keller to fix them up? Why wasn't that a condition when the city sold the buildings to B-K two years ago? At fire-sale prices."

"We tried. They've done nothing but stall. Besides, off the record, what's the difference? The only fixing up they'd even consider is total renovation. The tenants would have to move out, anyway, and they'd never be able to afford the remodeled apartments."

Two assistants in the councilman's Broadway office confirmed independently that Wilder had never visited the tenements, as far as they knew. Daniel then called his single source inside the Bromley-Keller hierarchy. When he summarized all he knew, the panicked executive said, "How the hell did you find out so much?" and hung up. Daniel now had the makings of a story that would give his final article real clout. He was not ashamed of the first four, but he had no illusions about them. Their muckrake of Bromley-Keller's tactics and vivid description of conditions inside the Bellemoor would rend a few hearts, but most readers of *Tabula Rasa* would sigh "how true" and move quickly on to the cultural coverage and personals. The bribe story, however, was a scoop that would be picked up all over town and might even slow down the Bromley-Keller bulldozer—if he could link the payoff directly to Steven Bromley. Rourke could provide that connection, and Calhoun Bledsoe had persuaded Daniel to lean on him that hot July day at the Bellemoor.

That proved a mistake. Daniel was no district attorney with a bagful of immunity and other legal lures. All he could offer Rourke was a vague promise that his role in the bribe scheme would be put into context in the pages of *TR*. Rourke did more than sneer at him. By the time Daniel went to the office the next afternoon, two of Bromley-Keller's lawyers had been to see Fosdick with a catalog of Daniel's offenses: slandering Steven Bromley; harassing one of his employees; trespassing at the Bellemoor, and invading the privacy of the tenants. They said they certainly did not want to leave the impression that they believed in prior restraint; they would simply read the series carefully when it came out.

Their visit made Daniel determined to go with what he had about the Wilder bribe. When Fosdick killed the material, Daniel threw a tantrum that culminated in his smashing his video display terminal, a feat accomplished with an aluminum softball bat grabbed from the desk of the *TR* team captain. En route to this Luddite frenzy, which the staff witnessed with varying degrees of dismay and hilarity, Daniel accused Fosdick of being "a pussyfooting eunuch." As calmly as he could under the circumstances, Fosdick reminded Daniel who edited *Tabula Rasa* and pointed out that he simply hadn't brought home the goods. He had only Bledsoe's word about

Rourke's phone conversation, which may or may not have been with Bromley. Again, it was Bledsoe who told him that the Purvis woman saw the envelope passed. And even if she had, how did Daniel know it contained money? Wilder could have visited the three buildings without his aides' knowledge; as a result he simply could have changed his mind about them.

As for the petrified Deep Throat at Bromley-Keller, his bleat was worthless, even were Daniel willing to name the man, which he wasn't. Fosdick blamed Daniel for the lawyers' visit too. He had let Bledsoe manipulate him into seeking a shortcut to the story, overplaying his hand with Rourke instead of slogging after the facts until he had more than his sand castle of circumstantial evidence.

Daniel sagged as he recalled socking the VDT out of the park. He wondered if it had been repaired and whether Mac would eventually ask him to pay for it. He would write the check today if that would help heal their rift. Daniel no longer blamed Fosdick for putting him on leave; his behavior had been outrageous. Mac was the best editor in the city and had been fighting New York's rapacious officials and business leaders since he had joined *TR* as a reporter in the fifties. He would like nothing better than to swing a wrecking ball at the whole Bromley-Keller empire. But he recognized weak reporting when he saw it, and Daniel knew that's what he had provided. Some time ago he had accepted all blame for trying to force the bribe story, rejecting Fosdick's accusation that he had been set up by Bledsoe. Now he began to wonder if he had misjudged his absent friend. Where the hell was he? Daniel struggled to focus on this question as doubt merged with sleep.

Four hours later the door bell sounded as if spliced into his cortex. The shimmering dancers on the poster of *A Chorus Line* across the room seemed to prance toward him as he drifted back into the pillow. The bell electrified him again, awakening him to the realization that someone had made it upstairs without first buzzing from the lobby. It must be Kate, he concluded: Luis tended to be gallant with recognizable girlfriends and pass them up unchallenged. Daniel wished the door was unlocked so he could simply shout, "Come in." Yet he felt so tired, he was not sure he could muster the necessary decibels, anyway. As he dragged himself from bed the recollection that Kate had said she would call before coming over pierced his coma. The bell rang again.

"Coming," Daniel yelled hoarsely. He opened the door on Lieutenant Beaupre.

"Bad time, I know. You were asleep."

"Fast."

"I really am sorry. You're bleeding." He pointed at Daniel's leg as he crossed the threshold.

"Come in," Daniel said sarcastically. The bandage Linguini had loosened had rubbed off in bed; blood trickled from his knee. The sheets must be a mess, Daniel thought.

"I'm in no hurry. Go patch that thing up." Beaupre looked into the living room. "Nice place."

"Make yourself at home."

Back in the bathroom, Daniel washed off his knee and attached clean gauze with fresh adhesive tape. As he looked at the hamper he reflected on what a fortunate life he had led; what had passed for tight spots up to now no longer qualified. Even the trauma of Thursday's seizure seemed tame. Kate, for all her anxiety, had been there when he needed her, made him comfortable, seen him through the worst, just as others had done at camp, on the train, in Chicago. He was very lucky. Maybe he'd stay lucky if he simply told Beaupre the truth: "You see, Lieutenant, Thursday I had this epileptic attack that lasted, well, I'm not sure precisely how long, and afterwards I found Rourke's gun under my jockstrap." That was as much of the truth as Daniel knew. By now Beaupre might know much more himself, might even be there to make an arrest.

"Quite a view," Beaupre said as Daniel returned to the living room.

"I like the sun."

"Sergeant Delvecchio said you took a bad spill this morning. He didn't exaggerate. Feeling any better?"

"What's up, Lieutenant? You didn't come here to pay your condolences."

"Okay. If you insist, I'd like to know why you lied to me yesterday morning." Beaupre sat down on the piano bench and pulled out his steno pad.

"About what?"

"Running. You said when we talked at the Bellemoor" —Beaupre looked into his notebook—"that you didn't run Thursday morning. That you hadn't been feeling well."

"That's right."

"According to your doorman, that's not right." Beaupre again consulted his notes, as if reading from an indictment. "Ramirez says you left the building at your usual time, approximately six-thirty. Dressed to run."

Daniel grappled frantically with the incredible possibility that he had risen, put on his sweats, gone down in the elevator, jogged around the reservoir, and returned to the apartment without remembering any of it. He recalled Luis's coolness of a few hours ago and wondered when Beaupre had questioned him. "There are other runners in this building," he tried.

"Ramirez says it was you. He also says you returned from your run about eight-fifteen. According to what you told me yesterday, that's an hour later than usual. Where did you go?"

Daniel sat down on the sofa and said nothing. He had bantered with Luis almost daily for four years; the doorman could hardly have mistaken him for another tenant. When he looked up from his trap, Beaupre seemed more embarrassed than threatening.

"I know you had some kind of fit Thursday night," he said, avoiding Daniel's eyes. "And this morning. Your friend, Miss Bernstein, told Sergeant Delvecchio it was epilepsy. I had no idea you were an . . . that you had that kind of problem. It must be tough."

"I'll survive."

"I'm not here to pry into your medical troubles. I'm not even here officially. I'm just trying to arrange a little informal cooperation between the media and the forces of law and order."

Daniel suppressed a smile as he recalled how he had tried the same kind of ploy with Rourke, whose contempt he now began to appreciate. Still, Beaupre's request was not so unreasonable. Daniel was not above pooling information with the police when pursuing a common quarry. Nor did he really blame this man for trying to take the quick way around. Whatever their shortcomings, cops had more social refuse to clean up than they could handle. And many, lacking a trust fund, moonlighted to make ends meet. Beaupre covered his alimony payments by driving a cab in Queens on weekends, a revelation the lieutenant had thrown at Daniel during one of their confrontational interviews about the precinct's laissez-faire attitude toward the Bellemoor. This Saturday search for cooperation was costing Beaupre fares, but Daniel's sympathy faded as he realized that Delvecchio's timely appearance in the park might not have been a coincidence.

"Did you have me tailed this morning?"

"Suppose you answer my questions first. Why didn't you tell me you'd run, and why did you come back an hour late? Were you at the Bellemoor?"

"You did have me followed. What's going on here? Am I a suspect?"

"That depends on what you tell me."

"I'll tell you one thing. You can forget about getting any help from me. Why should I throw in with a cop who puts a tail on me before the body is cold?"

"Why shouldn't I suspect someone who lies to me? Someone, by the way, who thought the victim was a scumbag."

"He was. I make no apologies."

"I also think you know where Bledsoe is."

"Maybe I do." Daniel heard his suicidal bravado as if monitoring the conversation through a one-way glass.

"Where?"

"No deal, Lieutenant."

"Okay. Here's another question: Was Bledsoe into coke?"

"Cocaine? Are you kidding?"

"Was he?"

"You must be crazy. That man thinks his body's a temple. He was a goddamn basketball star at Williams and—"

"That was quite a few years ago."

"—can outrun any flatfoot on the force."

"I don't care if he can run a mile in three minutes with you on his back. Half the jocks in the country are juiced up on something. Besides, maybe he was just dealing."

"Dealing? That's fantasy, Lieutenant."

"Perhaps. But the stuff we found taped under Bledsoe's sink at the Bellemoor was real. Almost a kilo, in five plastic bags. And none of it diluted. That's worth more than a hundred grand on the street, maybe twice that if he cuts it with vegetable starches."

This new information tripped Daniel but only for a moment. "Under the sink? How convenient. Why didn't they just put the bags on his pillow? Obviously he's been set up."

"Then why did he bolt?" Beaupre put his steno pad on the piano bench, folded his arms, and leaned against the keyboard. His back mashed out a grating chord.

Daniel turned away and said, "I'm sure he had his reasons."

"So am I. I think he and Rourke were doing business together and had a little disagreement."

"He and Rourke? You're off the deep end. Calhoun was on the tenants' side at that place, in case you've forgotten."

"Coke makes strange bedfellows."

"You think Calhoun killed Rourke in a fight over drug money?"

Beaupre said nothing, and in the silence Daniel recalled Rourke's tirade against the Army for his dishonorable discharge, "just because of some penny-ante dope dealing." That he might still have been at it in the Bellemoor did not surprise Daniel. But he couldn't begin to imagine Calhoun in league with him—pushing cocaine, risking disbarment and prison. And what about the tenants? They were his passion. He would never sell them out.

Daniel looked at Beaupre and said, "Your theory's ludicrous."

The detective shrugged, picked up his pad, rose from the bench, and walked over to the window. With his back to Daniel he said, "Maybe it's more than a theory, Cooper. Maybe I have other facts. But of one thing I'm certain. You're holding out on me, covering for your sidekick." He turned and glared at Daniel. "I suppose you're too high-minded to give us a hand because you might qualify for all that dough Bromley's offering. But you might consider this: I can run you in anytime for obstructing justice."

The bluster was spreading. They both knew Daniel was under no legal obligation to aid in the Rourke investigation. Nor could Beaupre bring him in for questioning against his will, even if he admitted running Thursday morning and did know where Bledsoe was. Daniel could raise hell about the tail too—by airing his grievances in *Tabula Rasa* or even suing for invasion of privacy. He could also simply kick Beaupre out of the apartment at any time. Daniel knew his rights. What he didn't know was how much Beaupre knew, how much of this visit was bluff, and how much a genuine plea for help.

"I've been a bad host," Daniel said. "Is there anything I can get you while you're threatening me? Coffee?"

"No. I've already had too much today. What I need is to get rid of some." Beaupre stuck the steno pad in his jacket pocket. "Could I use the facilities?"

The question hung in the room as Daniel scoured for a plausible reason to put the bathroom off limits. Finally he said, "It's right through there."

As Beaupre disappeared into the bedroom Daniel wondered if he had noticed the pause. Fear and fatigue once more sapped him. He pushed off the sofa and moved through the hall to the bedroom door, straining to hear if Beaupre was actually using the toilet. Daniel prayed that he only had to pee; if he sat on the throne, the hamper would be within easy reach. When at least the flush sounded, Daniel hurried back to the sofa and sagged into the cushions.

"Thanks." Beaupre stayed in the hall after emerging from the bedroom. "I think I'll be shoving off."

This sudden decision to leave confused Daniel. If Beaupre had discovered the gun, the sirens would be wailing already. Or would they? Maybe he'd smuggle it out for lab tests to pin down his case before returning with the cuffs. Daniel joined Beaupre at the apartment door and searched for a new bulge somewhere in the rumpled drape of the detective's plainclothes.

"I'm really not trying to obstruct your investigation, you know." Daniel hoped his accommodating tone somehow would reduce the heat.

"We'll see." Beaupre put his hand on the knob. "Stick around the neighborhood."

"If I go anywhere, you'll know it's me. I'll be on a litter."

"Feel better." He sounded to Daniel as if he meant it.

Out on Central Park West Beaupre looked at his watch. Five-thirty. He headed for the subway entrance at Ninety-sixth Street. If he made quick connections, he could be at the garage in Kew Gardens and out hacking by six-thirty. He'd missed most of the day, but it was Saturday night; he could still pick up seventy-five dollars, provided he managed to stay awake until two or three. He'd sleep late Sunday morning—or at least until Sally came over to deliver Brian for the afternoon and complain that her check was late again. At the corner he stared down into the maw of the IND, then started for the precinct house instead.

In the second-floor squad room Delvecchio was handing five-dollar bills to five teenage boys he had collected on Amsterdam Avenue to make a lineup. They looked eager to leave.

"Gentlemen, you're in luck," Delvecchio said when he spotted Beaupre. "Not all our volunteers get to meet the Twenty-Fourth Precinct's master sleuth, especially on his day off."

"Stow it, Sam." Beaupre sat at his desk and looked up at the anxious group. "Thanks, fellas. We really appreciate your help."

They nodded self-consciously as Delvecchio ushered them out. By the time he returned, Beaupre had taken a small plastic bag from his jacket and placed it on the desk.

"What gives, Frenchie? Why isn't your meter running?" Delvecchio perched on the corner of the desk.

"I decided to have a talk with *TR*'s star reporter instead."

"How's his health?"

"He'll live, I suspect." Beaupre picked up the plastic bag. "I want this sent downtown for analysis. The small pill is phenobarbital, the big one's something called Mysoline. At least that's what the labels read."

"It's probably what he takes for his fits. Did he give them to you?"

"He's not giving us anything. I acquired them when I went to the john. Tell the lab I want to know if the pills are really what the labels say they are. And get these threads checked too. I tweezed them off a washrag full of blood. Let's see how it compares with our samples from Rourke's office."

"Hey, Frenchie, aren't you getting carried away? Cooper was pretty bloody when I brought him back to his building from the hospital at noon."

"This washrag was dry. It hadn't been used today. Any luck with Loring?"

"I'd hate to be one of his patients; he never returns calls."

"Sam, what's the name of the new guy, the one who's always reading thrillers?"

"Spofford."

"Yeah, Spofford. I've got some reading for him. You remember the Torsney case?"

"The cop who shot the black kid. Yeah. In Brooklyn. About ten years ago."

"Right. He shot him unprovoked and got off. His lawyers said he didn't know what he was doing because he killed the boy during some kind of epileptic fit. I want Spofford in the Brooklyn D.A.'s office first thing Monday morning. Tell him to read the trial transcript. They'll have it. I want to know what the hell went on in that case. Who were the expert witnesses? What did they say? The works. Tell him to put together a file of newspaper clippings on the case too. And anything else he can find."

"You think Cooper killed Rourke and just doesn't remember. Come on, Frenchie, what about Bledsoe?"

"What about him? Any leads?"

"Not so far. Or on the gun. But my informants will turn up something. They always do."

"Maybe. But for the time being we work with what we have. Cooper had some kind of epileptic attack that he's reluctant to talk about."

"So I'll bet you would be too."

"Let me finish. He had the attack Thursday night. Friday morning we find Rourke dead and now Cooper, who loathed the guy, is telling me lies about his whereabouts."

"Okay, okay, I'll get Spofford on it as soon as he comes in." Delvecchio uncoiled from the desk. "Coffee?"

"No thanks, I've got to get out to Kew Gardens and start earning a living."

Chapter VIII

THE machine looked more like an instrument to track space shots than to chart brain waves. Surveying the video screen and the profusion of dials and switches around it, Daniel concluded that this computerized electroencephalograph probably didn't miss a bleep and could bring him extremely bad news. He tried to counter this depressing thought by speculating on whether the state of the art had reached a point where it would register his growing enthusiasm for Deborah Beckwith, whose breasts kept brushing his head as she attached strands of blue wire to his scalp.

"We're almost ready," she said. Her delivery, like the rest of her, was relentlessly perky, a red-haired stewardess cheerfully explaining ditching instructions.

"Does that thing have a radio and heater?" Daniel said.

"Practically." The EEG technician laughed as she parted another patch of his hair and pressed down the last of the eighteen electrodes, whose wires now linked his skull to the machine.

"What's that smell?" asked Daniel as Debbie—he could not deal with her as Miss Beckwith—tipped back the reclining chair and raised his feet.

"Collodion. Like ether. We use it to paste on the disks. It washes right out."

"Snakes alive, I must look like Medusa."

Debbie laughed again, dimmed the ceiling lights, and sat down at the console. The screen blinked with arcane digits and glowed eerily in the semidarkness. At her right hand a series of pens began agitating as they recorded the electrical discharges in Daniel's brain. The electroencephalogram, large sheets of computer graph paper with the pens' wavy tracings, slid before her and coiled into an orange collecting tray on her left.

"Are you chilly, Mr. Cooper? Sometimes our air conditioning's too high. I have a blanket if you want one."

"No. I'm fine."

"Good." Debbie examined the screen for a moment, then genially asked where he was from.

"Chicago."

"The Windy City. How old are you?"

"Thirty-nine."

Daniel knew from past sessions that Debbie merely sought to put him at ease with such empty questions. But the exchange thrust him back to Billings Hospital and his first encounter with these ominous decoders. After the fall down the stairs at home Dr. Hermann had called in a neurologist. This dour man, Dr. Pettingill, administered the EEG himself, assuring Daniel that it didn't hurt and would take no more than forty-five minutes. It took almost that long to glue down the electrodes, so convinced was Daniel that the electric box to which they led would fry his head. After several wires pulled off for the third time, Dr. Pettingill lost his patience and ordered, "Sit still!" When Daniel began to cry, the doctor tried to recoup with sour reasoning that now returned in force: "Don't you want to get this over with so we can find out what's wrong with you?"

"I said, 'What kind of seizure did you have?' Are you still with me, Mr. Cooper?" Debbie leaned toward Daniel's chair to see if he had dozed off.

"I'm here. A biggie. Grand mal. Bit my mouth, the works."

"When?"

"Thursday. A week ago tomorrow."

"Where did it happen that you scratched up your face so bad?"

"I had the seizure at home. I got the facial a couple of days later when I tripped jogging. It was my lucky week."

"You a runner? Me too. Three miles every morning along the East River, rain or shine. Don't you love it?"

The vision of a runner's body underneath Debbie's white uniform concentrated Daniel's mind. "Yes, I do."

Debbie brought over a button attached to a wire and placed it in Daniel's left hand. "We're going to test your reaction time now. You know what to do. When you hear the beep, you answer it by pressing the button."

Daniel nodded and set himself for the challenge, as if determined to show this woman that he, too, was in tiptop shape. After he had played Ping-Pong with the beeps for about five minutes, Debbie said, "Okay. If you're a runner, your wind ought to be pretty good. How about taking some deep breaths for me? Through your mouth."

Debbie sounded to Daniel as if she knew he had undressed her and wanted to change the picture. As if to underline his suspicion, she kept urging him to go a little faster as he sucked in and expelled gulps of air. The beeps seemed to be coming faster, too, and he sensed his flagging efforts to sustain the rally. Such hyperventilation constricted the blood vessels and released carbon dioxide, sometimes setting off clinical seizures and aiding in diagnosis. It also caused considerable dizziness, and when Debbie finally let Daniel stop, he felt as if he had just climbed Mount Everest. His hands and feet were numb.

"I think I'll take you up on that blanket."

"Coming up." Debbie tucked a green woolen cover up around Daniel's chin. "Don't worry. It'll pass."

"Yes. I know." Daniel shut his eyes and waited as his breath slowly returned to normal. When he opened them, Debbie had positioned a small light about two feet from his face.

"Feeling better?"

"Yes. Time for the light show?"

"Can't surprise you."

She could surprise him by skipping this particular exercise. Some epileptics suffered seizures upon seeing flickering light. Daniel once joked that this was as good a reason as any for not watching television, but the prospect of such a reflex attack always made him nervous. His one descent into a discotheque ended after ten minutes, not because of the deafening rock, as he explained to his companions, but because of the blinding strobes. As far as he knew, neither Thursday's episode nor those of his youth had been caused by light patterns; nevertheless, gazing into the photostimulator remained the only aspect of the EEG process that still frightened him.

Back at the console, Debbie flipped a switch, and steady white bursts fired into Daniel's eyes. He stretched rigid in the chair, as if willing away the pain of the dentist's novocaine needle. Only after he continued to hear the steady hum of the machine and the plop of the scroll in the tray did he begin to relax. Beaupre and Delvecchio appeared on either side of the chair, dressed in brown uniforms that made them look like generals in a comic-opera junta. The flashing light glinted on their medals. Beaupre scowled, Delvecchio smiled; neither said a word. Then they were gone, replaced by Bledsoe, whose enigmatic grin came at Daniel out of the menacing light.

Daniel thought he might have to settle for these specters. His initial conviction that Bledsoe would surely come in from the cold and clear everything up was waning. Almost a week had passed since the murder, with no word from his friend. Nor had Beaupre come calling again. Daniel assumed the cops were still following him, though he had hardly led them a merry chase. Today's return to the Powell Medical Clinic, where his blood was tested last Friday, marked only the second time he had left the apartment since Beaupre's visit four days ago. On Monday he had gone to New York Hospital for the CAT scan. That evening Kate had come up with a bagful of groceries, leaving after about an hour when it became clear that she could not penetrate Daniel's armored mood. He wanted to be left alone to lick his wounds and struggle with the metastasizing presence of the gun, to nurse a growing feeling that he was the victim of some unknowable conspiracy.

He hadn't heard from Dr. Loring, either—with the results of the blood tests or the CAT scan. And no one had called from *Tabula Rasa* to bring him up-to-date on the Rourke investigation, much less seek his guidance. A few lines yesterday in the *Times*'s police blotter roundup reported no progress. Mostly the papers and television appeared to be ignoring the story. Despite the reward and Bledsoe's suspicious absence, they seemed ready to dismiss Rourke as just another faceless victim with no headline value. Maybe, because of Daniel's involvement, Fosdick had decided to do the same. He would know soon enough; the new issue of *TR* would be on the stands this morning.

"Ready for a short nap?" Debbie stood by the chair, a capsule in one hand, a paper cup of water in the other.

"I guess. Do you really think I need a sedative? I'm up to my eyeballs in medication already."

"If you think you can fall asleep without it, fine. But it's only eleven-thirty. You got out of bed a few hours ago."

She was right. Despite the anticonvulsants he had popped at eight o'clock, despite the blanket and the darkened room, he felt wide-awake, as if hooked up to a booster.

"What's the potion?" he asked.

"Chloral hydrate. You'll sleep for ten or fifteen

minutes and then we'll be done. You'll be a little groggy when you wake up. Did someone come with you?''

''Yes.'' Daniel pictured Kate reading a manuscript in the waiting room and wondered how she would react if she could see his headdress. When he told her on the phone that he had to bring a friend in case he was woozy after the sleep portion of the EEG, she had insisted on taking the morning off. Daniel did not protest. He had no stomach for revealing the week's events to anyone new, and despite the tension that had developed between them, he felt safe with Kate.

''Bottoms up.'' Debbie handed Daniel the cup and capsule.

Twenty minutes later she guided him into the waiting room. With his wobbly gait and sticky hairdo he thought he must look like a Bowery bum on windshield duty. Kate rose to meet them, holding back any display of concern or affection in the face of Deborah Beckwith's obvious command.

''Debbie. Kate. Kate. Debbie. She just measured me for a new head,'' said Daniel, adding, ''You don't happen to have any coffee around while I wait for delivery?''

''Right in that urn,'' Debbie said, nodding to a table in the corner and shaking hands with Kate.

''I'll get it,'' said Kate.

''Thanks.'' Daniel eased into a chair. He felt like hanging a do-not-disturb sign around his neck.

''Dr. Loring told me to tell you that he'd like to see you in his office when we're finished,'' Debbie said. "I'm going to put your tracing in an envelope and you can take it with you. I'll be right back."

"They've only got Cremora. Do you want it?" Kate asked as she closed the spigot on the urn.

"Christ, this head-candling cost two hundred dollars. You'd think they'd be able to afford some real milk."

"Don't be a grouch. Drink it black, it'll perk you up."

"No. No. I hate it black. Put in the gunk, with lots of sugar."

"How do you feel?" Kate handed him the cup.

"Sleepy, but I'll be okay. Are you hopelessly bored?"

"Not at all. I've been reading this." From her shoulder bag she pulled a black volume entitled *Epilepsy—A handbook for patients, parents, families, teachers, health and social workers*.

Daniel frowned as he scrutinized the cover. "It doesn't say anything about lovers."

"I wanted to be a social worker when I was in high school. Doesn't that count?" Kate smiled. "You're certainly in classy company. Alexander the Great. Julius Caesar. Buddha. Napoleon. Even Socrates."

"The Mad Monk Rasputin too. Is he in there?"

"Not that I remember."

"Just the good guys."

"Napoleon was such a good guy?" Kate leaned down and kissed him on the cheek. "It really is a very helpful book."

"I'm sure. Like an owner's manual. The care and

feeding of an epileptic in ten easy steps.'' Daniel grimaced as he sipped the chalky mixture.

"It's not like that. I had no idea, for instance, that seizures and convulsions weren't the same thing, that having a seizure can just mean losing touch for a few seconds."

"Just? Suppose I'm driving a car?"

Kate let the remark pass. "Well, I mean, I didn't know you could have a seizure without having an attack like Thursaday night."

"You can even have them in your sleep. That's why they put me down just now, to see how many abnormal squiggles I could produce while snoozing."

"I know." Kate tapped the book.

"Here we are," said Debbie, returning to the waiting room and handing Daniel a large, thick package. "I just called Dr. Loring. He's expecting you."

"Did I pass?" Daniel noted that Debbie had sealed the package.

"I'm sure the doctor will explain everything."

"They always do, in their wonderful way. Anyway, thanks for the use of the machine."

"Sure. Keep on running."

Kate and Daniel left the medical building in silence. On the sidewalk in front he was anticipating and about to reject her request to come with him to Dr. Loring's when a flash enveloped them. Then another. And a third. Daniel looked up at the leaden sky and waited for the thunder. When it didn't come, he thought for an instant that he was still in Debbie's chair, facing the photo-stimulator. Then he saw Joe Balboni with his camera and the car at the curb with the *New York Mail* logo on the door.

"What the hell's going on?" Daniel walked up to Balboni, a jockey of a man who always wore an ascot and assiduously cultivated what he imagined was the image of a paparazzo.

"I'm taking your picture, chief." Balboni clicked off several more shots, his light meter bouncing off his pink silk shirt as he tarantellaed around them.

"For the paper? Why?"

"Don't ask me. You know they never tell us photographers nothin'. Just get the job done in an hour, no overtime."

"How did you know where I was?"

"The desk knows all, like the Godfather." Balboni snapped two more pictures and ended his dance. "You're not looking your best, Cooper. What happened to your face?"

"None of your fucking business."

"Okay. Okay. Don't get hot. No one out with such a pretty lady should lose his temper about nothin'." He angled his camera at Kate and clicked some more. "Just for my personal file, miss. What's your name?"

Daniel grabbed for the camera, but Balboni nimbly backpedaled out of reach.

"Hey, pal, that's no way to treat a brother in the ranks. Don't you believe in freedom of the press?" He addressed the question less to Daniel than to the gathering spectators.

"Kate Bernstein. Now, you've got your pictures. Could you just leave us alone?"

"Sure. Sure. Just stay calm, everybody." Balboni slipped behind the wheel and slammed the door. Poking his head out of the window, he added, "I never thought I'd see the day when a fellow journalist went bananas like Jackie.''

"Fuck you, Joe.''

"Daniel, take it easy. He's going.'' Kate took his arm and led him away as Balboni drove off.

Daniel felt as if his lunge at the photographer, however feckless, had drained away all his energy. He walked on rubbery legs as they headed up Third Avenue toward Dr. Loring's. All thoughts of sending Kate back to Glossary vanished.

"Do you think the *Mail* wants your picture for a story about Rourke?'' she asked.

"Who knows what that rag wants?''

"Well, it makes sense. You're the expert on the Bellemoor.''

"Newspapers don't generally lavish credit on 'experts' from other publications, especially *Tabula Rasa*. Anyway, we'll find out soon enough. They'll probably run something tomorrow.''

Daniel was not optimistic. He and Kate certainly had not told the *Mail* city desk where to send Balboni this morning. Nor was it likely that Dr. Loring had. That left the police. Since they were tailing him, they could easily have leaked his whereabouts. Yet it didn't make sense. Beaupre was doubtless sore because Daniel had refused to cooperate, but why sic the *Mail* on him? Unless he had obtained a search warrant and found the gun in the last two hours. Daniel envisioned a squad of cops breaking into his apartment as soon as he had left and ripping it apart like cossacks. But that didn't fit, either. If they'd found the gun, they wouldn't be playing footsie with the *Mail*, they'd be on their way to arrest him. Daniel

looked back down Third Avenue, fully expecting to
see a blue-and-white pulsating in the uptown traffic.

Dr. Loring took them right away. As usual he was
running behind and his waiting room was full. Reluctantly he agreed to Daniel's request that he include
Kate. He recalled her hostility on the phone last week
and knew her presence would only prolong a session
he wanted to get through as quickly as possible.
Daniel and Kate arranged themselves on chairs in
front of his desk, and Daniel handed him the EEG.
He set it aside as they sat like legatees waiting for the
unsealing of a will.

Dr. Loring spread open Daniel's chart and said, "I
have the results of your CAT scan. No abnormalities
whatsoever."

"That's good." Daniel said sullenly. He resented
all this probing of his brain, whatever its diagnostic
value. The CAT scan was a medical marvel that
produced a computerized cross section X ray. He
supposed he should be grateful that he didn't have a
tumor and that trepanning hadn't been required to
learn this fact. Yet on Monday, as he lay on his back
and his head had entered the machine, he felt as if he
were being plugged into a huge socket that would
sizzle him to his toes. Daniel looked across the desk
at Dr. Loring, and continued. "All the CAT scan
results really mean is that you've further isolated
epilepsy as the cause of my attack." He eyed the
package.

"I never had much doubt, given your history. As I
told you on Friday, I only ordered the CAT scan as a
precaution."

"What about the blood tests?" Daniel asked.

"They show that your serum level is within the therapeutic range."

"What does that mean?" asked Kate.

"In prescribing anticonvulsant drugs, Miss Bernstein, we try to maintain a certain serum level in the bloodstream. Optimally the right level will prevent seizures without producing toxic side effects."

"The new dosage you've got me on *is* producing side effects. I don't know if they're technically toxic and I don't care. You've turned me into a zombie." Daniel did not wait for a response. Instead he launched into an angry recapitulation of Saturday's running accident, leaving out only the police. "None of this would have happened," he concluded, "if you didn't have me so doped up."

Dr. Loring looked into Daniel's chart. "I did hear about your fall. The Sinai intern who helped you, Dr. Cohen, called my service on Saturday. He didn't say it was urgent, so I didn't call back until Monday, but I missed him. We didn't talk until yesterday afternoon. He doesn't think you had a seizure, either. And neither do I, if you remember everything as clearly as you say you do."

"Then it *was* the medication." Daniel looked for a sign of vindication from Kate, who gave none.

"Possibly," said Dr. Loring.

Daniel started to rise to the maddening cautiousness of this response when the neurologist picked up the package, tore it open, and slipped out the electroencephalogram. He laid it next to the file and, like a Talmudic scholar, began slowly turning the oversize pages, periodically stopping to study a passage and twice doubling back to reexamine a section. It took several minutes to go through the inch-thick readout, during which Daniel stared into the patternless carpet and pulled at his sticky hair. Finally Dr. Loring looked up and said, "The pattern of this EEG is almost identical to your last one five years ago."

He motioned Daniel around to his side of the desk and started going through the pages again. "You see this activity here?" he said, pointing to a frenzy of stalactites and stalagmites on all eighteen lines of the sheet. "They show bilateral spike-and-wave discharges occurring at about three cycles per second. That's the classic measure of absence." He pronounced it *absonce*, as if it were French.

"Isn't that just a fancy word for petit mal?" Daniel asked.

"Yes, it's another word for it."

"Well, I sure as hell didn't have a petit mal attack Thursday.

"Yes, you probably did, at the start. You most likely had an absence seizure that progressed to a generalized tonic-clonic episode. That's not so uncommon. What happens is that the electrical discharges in the absence gradually spread to enough of the brain to cause a convulsive attack. It's an electrical chain reaction from cell to cell."

This doctor has all the cards, Daniel thought as he pictured a Pac-Man gobbling up his neurons. *He knows his subject cold, and I don't even have a brain that's functioning properly.*

"May I ask a question?" said Kate, as if from the audience to a lectern.

"Certainly." Dr. Loring glanced at his watch surreptitiously, without success.

"I thought petit mal seizures—or absence, or whatever you call it—last only a short time. But Daniel's lasted for hours."

"Absence seizures are usually of short duration, even when they culminate in a convulsion like yours." He turned to Daniel. "You may have had thousands of absence seizures over the years that lasted only a few seconds and that you didn't even notice or simply dismissed as woolgathering. Sometimes, however, absence can go on for a long time, like Thursday. We call this absence status." When Daniel said nothing, Dr. Loring continued. "I know this is not what you want to hear, Mr. Cooper, but I want you to continue on the new dose." He checked the chart. "A grain and a half of phenobarb and seven hundred and fifty milligrams of Mysoline."

"But why? Aren't there other drugs? What about Saturday?" Daniel knew from the whine in his voice that Dr. Loring had already won.

"It's not clear to me exactly what happened Saturday, especially since you refused to see a neurologist at Mount Sinai. Even if the accident happened as you say it did, I still want you to stay with the increased medication for now. There are other drugs, but my best judgment is that you should stick with the combination of phenobarb and Mysoline. Maybe you should cut down on your running for a while."

Daniel no longer had the will to express the rage this suggestion triggered. He looked at Kate helplessly, as if for a cue. Her eyes reflected only disgust, for whom Daniel wasn't sure. He said nothing.

"It's a trade-off, Mr. Cooper. You have to deal with a little extra sedation, but please keep in mind the fact that these drugs kept you free of convulsions for twenty-five years. That's a long time, and it's altogether possible that if you continue with them, you may never have another." Without giving Daniel a chance to reply, Dr. Loring looked at Kate and said, "Do you have any questions, Miss Bernstein? Now's the time."

Kate shook her head and reached for Daniel's hand.

"If you don't mind, then, I'd like to speak to Mr. Cooper alone for a moment. Could you wait outside? We won't be long." He came around the desk, looking at his watch as he held out his hand.

Kate took hers from Daniel's, stood, shook hands limply, and went into the waiting room. Dr. Loring shut the door, returned to his desk, and picked up the chart.

"Do you know a policeman named Delvecchio?" he asked.

Daniel had assumed Dr. Loring had ushered Kate out so he could break the real medical news in private. He paused to regain his balance, then answered, "Yes. Twenty-fourth Precinct. He and his partner took me to the hospital Saturday, and brought me home."

"I know. I wondered why you didn't mention it before. He called me on Monday."

"About the park?"

"That, and about the murder of that man at the building you wrote about in *Tabula Rasa*. He also seemed quite anxious to learn all he could about your epilepsy."

"What did you say?"

Dr. Loring sat down. "I told him you were a patient of mine and our relationship was privileged. Still, he pushed rather hard. I thought you'd probably want to know."

"Thanks." Daniel looked away. He felt that Dr. Loring expected some explanation, even had one coming. But he had none to give. "It's probably just a routine part of their investigation because I'm around the Bellemoor a lot. I've already talked to them myself."

"You know the police better than I do, I'm sure of that." Dr. Loring folded Daniel's chart and placed the EEG on top of it.

"Do you have a second for just one quick question?" Daniel asked.

"Shoot."

"All those hours I was in absence status I seem to have behaved fairly normally. I shaved. I dressed. I talked on the phone. I may even have run. Is that really the way it works? I mean, how is it possible to be so out of it and still function as well as I did?"

"I'm sure if anyone had seen you dress or shave, they would have told you you were doing it more slowly than usual. All your verbal responses were delayed too. I definitely noticed that when I spoke to you after Miss Bernstein called me that afternoon, and that's how she described your conversations with her too. And you probably exhibited some uncharacteristic mannerisms, like fidgetiness or prolonged staring. So you weren't exactly functioning as you usually do. But, yes, a person going through a long absence episode can accomplish most of the things he ordinarily does and only someone who knows him well might notice that he was acting strangely. But the big problem is that when it's all over, after you've had your convulsion, you have to cope with retrograde amnesia. No memory. That's what's so disorienting.''

"*Disorienting* is the word, Doctor," Daniel said.

Chapter IX

EVEN after Joe Balboni took his pictures the *New York Mail* remained an abstraction for Kate. She had never been pulled into the tent by the barking headlines on page one and had only the vaguest notion of the hyped-up universe inside. She simply accepted the tabloid's reputation as a noisy compendium of sex, crime, and celebrity and condemned it accordingly, nodding reflexively when the paper came up for derision at literary cocktail parties. Maggie Burke ridiculed the *Mail*, too, but devoured it daily as if it were a bowl of chocolate coffee beans.

"I mean, what are you going to do?" Maggie's voice was almost as shrill as the headline, which read, EPILEPTIC QUIZZED IN SRO MURDER.

Kate stared at the black letters and at the four-column photograph beneath them, the shot snapped as Daniel grabbed for Balboni's camera. It had been enlarged and cropped so that Daniel's scraped face, contorted with anger, appeared directly below the word *epileptic* in the headline. In the grainy background Kate wore a look that now seemed to border on terror. The caption read, "Reporter Daniel Cooper and friend, Kate Bernstein, emerge from an East Side clinic where he underwent treatment for epilepsy yesterday. The *Mail* has learned that Cooper, who wrote a series of articles in *Tabula Rasa,* the left-wing weekly, critical of conditions in a West Side welfare hotel, has been questioned by police investigating a murder in that SRO last week.''

Kate's office was claustrophobic at best, a cramped cubicle with stained wall-to-wall gray industrial carpeting and shelves spilling over with books and manuscripts. The clutter on her small Formica-and-steel desk barely left room to spread out the *Mail,* which Maggie had just breathlessly delivered. Kate swiveled around in her chair, stood, reached behind the piles of books on the dusty sill, and cracked open the window.

"I don't think jumping is the answer," Maggie said, dropping into a canvas sling chair in front of the desk. "Kate?"

"Yes."

"The story says that your friend had an epileptic fit last Thursday. Isn't that the day you left here early?"

Kate continued to look out the window.

"Oh, Kate. You were there. You saw it. It must have been awful."

"I wanted to call you but it was late." Kate took the cushion from her chair, propped it up against the front of the desk, and sat down on the floor facing Maggie.

"I would have come over like a shot, you know that."

"I know, Mag, but there was really nothing you could have done."

"The question is: What are *you* going to do?"

"About what?"

"About what? About seeing him anymore."

"Of course I'm going to see him. Probably tonight."

"Kate, I hate to sound like a maiden aunt, but is that smart? I know you think he's a nice guy and terrific in bed, but how long have you known him?"

"What's the difference? He *is* a nice guy, and as you have pointed out on numerous occasions, they don't exactly grow on trees in this city. He's not married. He's not gay. He doesn't drink or smoke. And as far as I can tell, he doesn't think he's out with his mother every time we're together. I'm not going to cut and run because he's in trouble."

"This is not your garden-variety trouble. This is epilepsy and murder. With cocaine thrown in for good measure."

"Cocaine? Daniel?"

"No. The guy the cops are looking for. The black rent-strike leader. The story says they found a stash of coke in his room at that welfare hotel."

"Calhoun Bledsoe?"

"That's the one. Look, honey, I'm not saying give Daniel up forever; just cool it for a while until you find out how deeply he's involved in all this. For one thing, you don't need the publicity. And, believe me, this is just the beginning."

"Has anyone else in the office seen the paper?"

"Not that I know of. I'm the only one around here with low enough brows to read the *Mail*. It's the closest thing to the stuff we turn out at *Glossary*. But they'll get wind of it soon.''

"I suppose," said Kate as the phone rang.

"Leave it," Maggie urged.

Kate reached up behind her, pulling the phone down onto her lap. "Kate Bernstein."

"Are you the Kate Bernstein who knows Daniel Cooper?"

Kate braced herself for the possibility of obscenities, then said, "Yes."

"Are you alone?"

Kate looked anxiously at Maggie. "No. Not just now. Who is this?"

"I'm a friend of Cooper's. I need to talk to you—privately."

If you give me your number, I'll call you right—"

"No. No numbers. I have to talk to you right now."

"Okay, just a minute." Kate pressed the hold button, stood, and put the phone back on her desk. "Mag, I think I'd better take this. Do you mind?"

"Are you all right?" Maggie pried herself out of the sling.

"Sure. I'll come down the hall as soon as I hang up."

When Maggie shut the door, Kate looked at the flashing button as if it were a detonator, then pushed it again. "Are you still there?"

"Can you get a message to Cooper?"

"Who is this?"

"My name's Calhoun Bledsoe."

Kate wasn't sure how to respond. Finally she said, "How do I know you're Bledsoe?"

"Look, I don't know you from Eve. You're just a face in a newspaper to me, but I'm trusting you because I have to. I haven't time to dick around, so try to trust me. Will you get a message to Daniel?"

"Why don't you call him yourself? He's been waiting to hear from you for a week."

"From me? *He* was supposed to call me. What's going on? I waited four days. Then I called him. Monday morning. And again yesterday. I got his machine both times."

"Why didn't you leave a message? Daniel would have called you."

"Because I had to move on Monday, and there's no phone where I am now. Besides, the cops probably have his line tapped."

The blast of an air horn in the background made Kate realize for the first time that the caller was talking from a pay phone.

"Where are you?" she asked.

"I said I had to trust you, not that I was an idiot. Look, I'm in trouble and I need your help. And if I read today's *Mail* correctly, so does our mutual friend."

Kate looked at the headline and photograph and said, "What do you want me to do?"

"Find out what the hell happened with the gun and why Cooper didn't follow our plan."

"What plan? I don't know what you're talking about. You mean the gun the police are looking for in the Rourke case?"

"Cooper'll explain. And tell him I can't find the girl. The trail's cold."

"What girl?"

"Just tell him. He'll know."

"What's Daniel supposed to do about all this? If you've seen the paper, then you know he has other problems."

"I know. I'm sorry about the epilepsy. But this is more important, believe me. Half the cops in the city are looking for me. Tell Cooper I'll figure some way to get in touch with him—or you—in the next few days. Meanwhile he could help a lot by locating the girl. Can I count on you? Can *we* count on you?"

Kate mumbled yes, and he hung up. She dialed Daniel immediately but put the receiver back on the cradle just before making the connection. She found it hard to believe that the police had actually tapped his phone, but anything was beginning to seem possible. She recalled her promise to come to Maggie's office, then headed out the door for Daniel's. It was just before noon. She hoped Maggie would assume she had a lunch date.

Daniel was still in bed when the Associated Press called at ten o'clock. A young reporter named Rubin worked the phone with the same persistent, sweet reasonableness Daniel had used a thousand times to pry information out of reluctant citizens who suddenly found themselves "news." Daniel fended him off saying he hadn't seen the *Mail* yet and by promising to call him back when he had. He then quickly dressed, turned on the answering machine, and went out to buy the paper at the stationery store on Columbus Avenue. He took it up the block to West Side Storey, sat down at the counter, and ordered coffee and French toast. He told the waitress to soak the bread good; even after a week his mouth still smarted.

He read the article twice, the second time a perverse admiration tingeing his dismay. Whoever wrote it had nimbly walked the tightrope of distortion. The story said only that the police had questioned him in the Rourke investigation, carefully avoiding the word *suspect*. At no point did the piece specifically link his epilepsy to the murder; it simply reported that he had had a seizure on the same day. The rest of the story concentrated mainly on Daniel's journalistic antipathy toward the Bellemoor and Bromley-Keller and on his friendship with Calhoun Bledsoe, "the anti-landlord firebrand in whose room the cocaine was found." The ten paragraphs of telegraphic prose took up less space than the artfully juxtaposed headline and photograph. In all, a masterpiece of crafted truth.

The damning layout reminded Daniel of his own high-wire act three years before at Yale. He had been invited back to his alma mater for a semester to teach a weekly seminar in the politics of journalism, a course of his own devising that skewered the mainstream media as a tom-tom for the established order. One evening he challenged the class with H. L. Mencken's tweaky notion that the hyperbole of yellow journalism was rather amusing, inconsequential titillation, far less damaging to the booboisie than the systematic political mendacity of the so-called respectable press. The students, most of them smooth-edged graduates of elite preparatory academies or suburban high schools, liked the Sage of Baltimore's prose style but found this idea appalling. "Do *you* really believe," one girl had asked, "that the *Times*

is a more dangerous paper than the *Mail*?'' Partly
because he did and partly to keep the kettle boiling,
Daniel said yes—rather glibly, it now seemed.

As he sipped his coffee and took small bites of his
syrupy breakfast, he began to feel as if he were being
watched by his fellow diners. He looked nervously
around the restaurant, half expecting to see the accusing eyes that menaced Prince Myshkin. When this
wave of paranoia passed, Daniel surveyed the *Mail*
layout again and thought, *Well, isn't this what journalists do? Isn't this what I've done for more than
fifteen years, shout to as many people as I can reach
what I think they ought to know? Maybe I have no
right to squirm. If I could, I'd make Steven Bromley
ten times more uncomfortable than I feel now. We all
relentlessly invade people's privacy for a living. Of
course, I do it for the greater good, that high ground
governed by all the ethics that deadlines and the TR
business office will permit. Who knows, maybe the*
Mail *thinks this spread is a public service, too, that
it'll help catch the killer. Shit, maybe they've got him
in a rolltop desk and are about to win the Pulitzer
Prize.*

When Daniel returned to the apartment, the dial on
the Sanyo indicated that five calls had come in. He
rewound the tape and turned up the volume, warily
regarding the machine as the certain bearer of bad
tidings. Rubin, the eager AP reporter, spoke up first
with an afterthought. Did Daniel want him to read
the *Mail* story over the phone? He'd be glad to do it.
''Nice try, kid,'' Daniel said aloud, pigeonholing his
promise to call back. The next person did not wait
for the beep, and the tape ran its thirty-second course

in ominous silence. The deep, disembodied voice of Malcolm Fosdick followed. "Jesus, Daniel, are you okay? Those people at the *Mail* are really pricks. I'm at home. Call me as soon as you can. We've got a lot to talk about." Daniel thought that was it when Fosdick added, "Have you heard anything from Bledsoe?" Then, embarrassed by this business-as-usual question, he added, "Do you have a good doctor?" "I don't think so," Daniel said to the machine, whose fourth message proved another hang-up.

Then: "Hey, cocksucker. I just heard it on the radio. Made my day, pal. It's about time you got yours. Always telling the rest of us how to live. I hope they lock you up and throw away the fucking key and you rot for the rest of your life. You can have lots of fits in the slammer, Cooper; they know just how to handle epileptics there. I know, pal. I've been in. So good luck, asshole."

Daniel sat down at his desk and replayed the assault three times, trying in vain to place the sneering voice. It sounded like a man, but the treble timbre made it difficult to tell for certain. He listened to the words again, rummaging through his personal morgue for a story he had written that might connect with the voice. In ten years at *Tabula Rasa* his reporting had helped send only one man to prison: Bernie Rosenbloom, a state assemblyman knee-deep in garbage-carting kickbacks. But Rosenbloom's Brooklyn accent was as thick and unmistakable as the Horn's cheesecake. He then tried to locate the voice somewhere in the Bromley-Keller domain, again without success.

Like most prominent journalists, Daniel had received his share of such phone calls. More, probably, since he rejected an unlisted number, the advantages in tips outweighing the occasional obscenities. But he'd always answered himself and managed a cathartic "Fuck you" before the person hung up. Coming out of the Sanyo, the anonymity and hostility seemed far more threatening, as if someone had commandeered the public-address system at Yankee Stadium and announced that a man with a rifle was loose somewhere in the stands. Daniel knew, too, that if some version of the *Mail* story were now on the radio, he could expect a lot more calls. He considered unplugging the modular phone and sealing himself off for a while but could not resist the instinct to eavesdrop on his own travail. He recocked the Sanyo with the volume up and sought refuge at the piano.

His fingers moved into the chords of a close-harmony arrangement of "Over the Rainbow" that he had written for the Wiffenpoofs at Yale. He tried to sing, but his mouth refused to cooperate, so he threw himself into the playing. Despite his persistent fatigue and anxiety, he stayed at the keyboard for forty-five minutes, summoning up one tune after another and wrapping himself in their warm sentimentality. In dissonant counterpoint, a half dozen more calls came in: Fosdick again, this time more urgent and less solicitous; the AP man, more determined than before; Faith, saying a friend had called her at the store with the news, and it was awful, and could she help, and filling up every second of her thirty with the kind of nonstop, do-this efficiency that had driven Daniel crazy in their marriage; two more hang-ups in a row; and, finally, Lucien Jay, the only reporter on the *Times* Daniel counted as a friend. He wondered if Luke were phoning in that capacity or on assignment, which forced him to grapple with a vow he had confidently made in the abstract long ago: that as a journalist he would not dodge other journalists when they came calling.

Daniel rose from the piano bench and moved toward the phone, then detoured into the bedroom and turned on *News at Noon*. Art Flaherty and Cindie Benson, the twin pretties, flickered into view chatting up a Queens dentist who sculpted busts of the famous out of ice cream. He had a chocolate-swirl Ronald Reagan in his basement freezer. Opening, rather than closing, the fifteen-minute program with this kind of light touch was the major innovation of *News at Noon*.

"Down to serious business now, Cindie," said her teammate, wiping the vanilla smile from his mouth.

"Right, Art." The camera closed in on Cindie's earnest face, leaving enough room for a shot of Daniel in the upper right-hand corner of the screen. "Our top story at this hour is about one of our own, a well-known New York reporter who may be involved in a murder on the West Side. Daniel Cooper . . ."

Her monochromatic delivery of the *Mail* story squeezed it dry of sensationalism, lacquering the details with a sheen of smarmy objectivity. Daniel sat on the edge of the bed and thought, Christ, this is their lead item. It must be the slowest news day in history. Well, at least their picture doesn't make me look like a crazed killer.

Flaherty's ruddy features now appeared on the screen, and a photograph of Robert Torsney replaced Daniel's. "The Cooper investigation, Cindie, recalls a similar case of several years ago involving a New York policeman named Robert Torsney. He shot and killed a teenage boy in Brooklyn, without provocation. At his trial his lawyer argued that Torsney had a psychomotor epileptic seizure at the time of the murder and could not be held legally responsible. The jury agreed, acquitting him by reason of insanity."

"I remember the case, Art." Cindie shook her head just perceptibly, more than enough to register her view that justice had not been served.

There the playlet ended. The actors moved quickly to their next drama, an oil-tank explosion in Bayonne. Daniel sat transfixed by the flames when the bell rang. He switched off the set, went into the hall, and opened the door on Kate.

"So you know," he said.

"And then some." She brushed by him and, when he had shut the door, said, "Calhoun Bledsoe knows too. He called me this morning."

"You? Where?"

"At the office. At least he said he was Bledsoe."

"What did he sound like?" A rush of adrenaline purged Daniel's lassitude.

"Suspicious. For one thing, he didn't sound black."

Daniel suppressed a sarcastic response and said, evenly, "Neither does Cal. What did he say?"

"May I come in?"

"Of course. Sorry." They entered the living room and sat down on the sofa.

"How do you feel? You look much better."

"Never mind that. What did he say, Kate?"

By the time Kate finished recounting the phone conversation, Daniel felt desperate. For days he had counted on Calhoun to reappear and explain everything. "Where was he calling from?"

"Somewhere in the city, I think. He refused to tell me. Do you think it really was him?"

"Yes."

"Then what did he mean about the gun and you two having a plan? And finding the woman? What woman?"

Daniel put his fingers to his temples and forehead and literally squeezed his brain, trying for the hundredth time to force his memory. "I don't know. It *sounds* as if I may have seen him at the Bellemoor the morning of the murder. But I just don't remember. I don't think I ever will. Loring says I have retrograde amnesia." As Daniel said this he realized that the doctor had made the explanation after asking Kate to leave the room. He looked at her now, convinced that she didn't believe him.

"Even if you can't recall all the specifics, you must have some inkling of what Bledsoe was talking about. He's your friend. You worked together on the series. What woman is he talking about?"

"I told you, I don't know. Didn't he tell you her name?"

"No."

"Jesus, didn't you ask?"

"Yes, Daniel, I did. He said you'd know and then he hung up."

"Well, I don't."

"You must. Think."

He grabbed her hand. "Come here, I want to show you something." He led her into the bathroom and opened the hamper. "That's a 45-caliber automatic you see in there. It's the murder weapon. I found it in this bathroom when I got back from the blood tests last Thursday. I don't have the slightest memory of bringing it here, but I doubt that the tooth fairy dropped it off. So don't talk to me about inklings." He was shouting, his eruption echoing off the tiles.

Kate stared into the hamper, then at Daniel. "You mean it's been here all week?"

"All goddamn week. Right."

"Why didn't you tell me? Why didn't you call the police?"

"Would you have?"

"Are you serious? The minute I saw it."

"And tell them what? That I just don't know how it got here? It probably has my fingerprints all over it. They'd never believe me. Even without the gun they're on my ass because they know I sympathize with Cal and hated Rourke."

"Did you?"

"Did I what?"

"Hate Rourke."

"You mean, enough to kill him?" Daniel sat down on the edge of the bathtub. "I may have knocked him off a couple of times in my fantasies. He was despicable. But in reality? Kate, I couldn't have." He buried his face in his hands.

Kate came over and held his head. "Daniel, you've got to go to the police, today."

He looked up at her like a frightened child. "I can't, not yet. Not until we hear from Calhoun again.

I've got to get *him* to explain what the hell happened Thursday. I don't know about any plan or woman. He thinks I know, but I don't.''

"How do you know it really was Bledsoe on the phone this morning? And even if it was, how can you be sure he'll call back? And what about the cocaine, Daniel?"

"That stuff was planted. I'm certain. He's being framed.''

"By whom?"

"I don't know. Maybe by Bromley-Keller. All I know is that Calhoun is no pusher or cokehead.''

"Daniel. Daniel. Lots of people who take drugs can fool you. They're like seemingly happy couples whose breakups surprise all their friends. It happens all the time. How well do you really know the man?''

"I know him, Kate." Daniel stared up at her.

She stepped back. "I don't know much about the law, Daniel, but hiding evidence in a murder investigation surely must be a criminal offense. You could go to jail for that alone.''

"As well as for murder.''

"I didn't mean that.''

Daniel wasn't so sure, but as he stood, his eyes fell on his medication and he was distracted by the realization that he had yet to take his midday dose. Anger again overwhelmed him, not just at Dr. Loring's prescription but at rage itself, which now seemed lodged permanently in his malfunctioning brain. He swallowed the pills with a slug of water from the red plastic cup, looking at Kate like a patient determined to show a stern nurse how really sick he was.

"Who's that?" Kate turned toward the bathroom door.

Daniel set down the cup and hurriedly closed the hamper lid. He listened hard, but the voice was inaudible. Then he smiled. "It's the machine. I left the volume on." By the time they returned to the living room the message had run its course. Daniel rewound the tape and set it on its slow forward crawl. An aggressively chipper woman joined them in the room:

"Hi, Daniel. It's Marilyn Constantine. We met at the Habersteins' a couple of months ago. I'm Jack's cousin. I'm also supposed to be a liberated woman, so I thought I'd give you a call. If that's too threatening, then just think of me as a party invitation for a week from Saturday night. It's a really fun group of people. Hope you're free. It would be great to see you again. Give me a call at 641-9093. Bye."

"A *fun* group," Kate said, grinning.

"At least someone in town doesn't know yet."

Chapter X

ANIEL gave himself an extra half hour to get to midtown by bus. A wave of unseasonable heat had arrived in the night, and the late-morning sun parched him as he stood waiting on Central Park West. The subway offered shelter of sorts only two blocks away, but he realized weeks ago that he had unconsciously stopped riding the trains. Last spring he had twitted his parents when they plugged their ears as the express racketed through the Ninety-sixth Street station. Soon after they returned to Chicago he began doing it himself, conceding his father's contention that traveling underground in New York was like being trapped beneath a fingernail scraping down a blackboard. Daniel eagerly anticipated the air conditioning as the bus pulled up to the curb, but the machinery that produced it had already broken down. They headed south, a sarcophagus on wheels.

Daniel wondered if Kate had read this morning's *Times* story yet. Unlike the *Mail*'s opening salvo and the TV crossfire that followed yesterday afternoon and evening, the *Times* piece was altogether discreet: six paragraphs tucked away on page B5, no picture.

Daniel had expected much worse. Most *Times* editors
sniffed at *Tabula Rasa*, royalty eyeing the rabble
from the parapets. He had taken many shots at this
smug castle on Forty-third Street over the years and
had assumed that the paper would not miss this opportunity to embarrass him, especially after he
agreed—at Lucien Jay's urging the previous afternoon—to talk with the reporter assigned to the story.
But the piece proved a model of conventional even-
handedness, recapping the murder and recording the
cocaine discovery. It then simply relayed Daniel's
confirmation that, yes, Beaupre had questioned him,
and yes, he had suffered an epileptic seizure on the
day of the murder. The account carried no speculation, no mention of the Torsney case, and ended with
the obligatory quote from Beaupre saying that the
police were pursuing several leads. Daniel appreci-
ated this quiet objectivity but knew it mattered less
than the fact that his predicament had now been
validated in the paper of record. The Sanyo would
doubtless have collected many more messages by the
time he returned home.

The comic relief provided by Marilyn Constantine's invitation yesterday had faded quickly, replaced
by Kate's renewed and adamant demand that Daniel
turn in the gun to the police. He tried to mollify her
by insisting that Calhoun was certain to make contact
again very soon, but she rejected this faith as wishful
and irrelevant. "You are breaking the law, Daniel!"
He finally promised to go to the police on Monday
whether or not he heard from Bledsoe, a timetable
Kate accepted only after she saw she could extract
nothing better. They had eaten lunch in silence, and

when Kate left for Glossary afterwards, Daniel knew his purchase of three days had been costly. He also had begun to suspect that Kate's skepticism about Bledsoe might prove justified.

When it came right down to it, how well *did* he know Calhoun? He had made several attempts to extend their relationship beyond running and the Bellemoor, inviting Bledsoe to dinner or suggesting they grab a bite together along Broadway. Each time he declined, vaguely pleading too much work or a previous commitment. He never proposed an alternate date or made a social overture of his own. True, he had asked Daniel up to the Adirondacks last June, but even in that isolated setting he remained oddly detached, had not shown even the slightest curiosity when Daniel revealed his epilepsy after their first swim. Only when Bromley-Keller came up did Bledsoe shed his reserve, railing against the company's rape of the poor. Daniel shared this passion, had enthusiastically devoted many weeks and thousands of words to it with Bledsoe's eager cooperation. But in the last forty-eight hours he had come to fear, against all contrary instincts, that Calhoun may have used him.

The cocaine would not go away, like a mound of snow that refused to melt in the glare of a hot spotlight. Daniel's conviction that the powder had been planted in Bledsoe's room was weakening. That he snorted the stuff still seemed incredible given his consistent ability to outsprint Daniel on the reservoir track. But Beaupre's cynical contention that Bledsoe and Rourke had been dealing together at the Bellemoor, and had fallen out, now seeped into Daniel's head like so much coke itself. He loathed himself for this suspicion yet could not shake it. Why had Calhoun fled if the cocaine had been planted? He was a streetwise, Harvard-trained lawyer, not some panicky pusher. It didn't make sense. Nor did his phone call to Kate, with its cryptic references to the gun and a "plan," and to a woman he said Daniel must find but whose identity he had not supplied.

Bledsoe's disturbing new visage claimed only part of Daniel's dismay. He felt besieged from all quarters: by Beaupre, whose investigation kept lapping at him; by Mac Fosdick, whose support he had begun to question; by Loring, who came up with no satisfactory explanations; by the press, which would doubtless nag increasingly; by Kate, whose angry disapproval of his stalling over the gun was not ameliorated by the fact that he understood it. Alone after she left yesterday, he felt his life slipping out of his control, like his brain on the verge of seizure. Just before five o'clock he decided to call Steven Bromley.

Now, roasting in his plastic seat, Daniel wondered if Bromley had ever taken public transportation in his life. Probably, he concluded reluctantly, conjuring up the adolescent scion pranking with his blazered classmates on the Madison Avenue bus. These days he went everywhere behind the smoked windows of his Mercedes limousine, license number BK-1. Daniel pondered the vanity plates he might order if he owned a car. SLEUTH, perhaps, or MUCK. No, too predictable. He toyed with AEROPAGITICA and rather liked it, however pretentious. But it was far too long; besides, no one read Milton anymore. He ran through and rejected several others, then settled on HILDY, the hero of *The Front Page,* a reporter fed up with his trade. If that was taken, he'd ask the Department of Motor Vehicles for BURNS, Hildy's cynical, manipulative editor. Both fit; either would do.

Daniel got off the bus at Broadway and Fifty-seventh Street and walked east to the new Bromley-Keller pylon near Fifth Avenue. His shirt matted to the moisture on his back as he collided with the arctic air in the lobby, a glistening glass cage that vaulted five stories and dripped with greenery. The frigid atmosphere did not dry his perspiration as the elevator rose to the thirty-fourth floor. He went into the men's room, turned on the cold water, cupped his hands under the tap, and splashed his face. He risked this chilling shock, hoping it would somehow banish the sedation for the next two hours. He let the drops linger as he ran a comb through his hair, then sopped away the water with a paper towel, gently blotting at his healing wounds. He stepped back and examined his reflection, unfamiliar in the bow tie and seersucker jacket he had put on for this mission.

"Good morning." The receptionist looked at her watch and, with a plastic smile, corrected herself. "Actually, afternoon, right?"

"Right. My name is Daniel Cooper. I have an appointment with Steven Bromley."

"Yes. He's expecting you. He told me to bring you right up."

According to the nameplate on her desk, this high-heeled ornament was Wendy Graham. She led him to a stairway that made one spiral up to the thirty-fifth and top floor. The reception area had been standard corporate chic: gray sectional sofas, glass coffee table bearing a full complement of business magazines,

Wendy Graham's semicircular sentry post, and dark green wall carpeting imprinted with the gold B-K colophon. Upstairs, antiques lined the oak-paneled corridor that led to Steven Bromley's office. In muted secretarial bays, Selectrics clicked quietly, operated by women who looked like variations on Mary Worth. Personnel departments at these places must have formulas, Daniel thought. "Sorry, your skills and references are excellent, miss, but we only have an opening on the executive floor and you're simply not grandmotherly enough." Here was a whole new area for affirmative action. All typing ceased momentarily as Miss Graham trotted down the hall before him.

They entered Bromley's open door without announcement. Had she signaled their coming with a hidden button on her desk downstairs, or tripped an electric eye in the grandfather clock at the top of the spiral? Bromley stood with his back to them, uncorking a bottle of wine at a dining table elegantly set for two. Daniel fastened on the wide-screen window that looked north over the vast rectangle of Central Park, summer-brown in the hot September sun. Daniel wondered if he, too, would forget about the people who lived down below if he worked in such an aerie every day. He was still locked into the view when Bromley turned around.

"How rude of me. How long have you been standing there?"

"We just came in, Mr. Bromley. This is Mr. Cooper."

"Of course, Wendy. I didn't think it was William Safire."

Cute, thought Daniel. He wondered if Bromley

was nervous, too, or if he felt invulnerable here on his home court. Certainly he appeared calm. He looked as if he had just showered and dressed after three sets of hard singles at his club and was now about to lunch on the terrace. He wore spit-polished cordovan loafers, white socks, charcoal-gray slacks, and a sharply pressed blue Levi work shirt. Daniel wondered if he always dressed so informally at the office or if this was the camouflage of the day.

They had never met. Bromley had declined to be interviewed for the Bellemoor series, sighing over the phone that *he* had no objections whatsoever but, alas, the company lawyers advised otherwise. He looked far less formidable than his newspaper photographs, which usually froze him in business uniform at a meeting or on a podium, capitalism congealed in his eyes. He seemed shorter now, and his hard-set public face beamed with an almost dandified innocence. As he walked across the room to shake hands he looked about as lethal as a fraternity pledge, and as eager to please. He told Miss Graham to shut the door on her way out and, when she had gone, said, "There. Now, what can I get you to drink?"

Daniel did not drink at all. He had been warned early on that the combination of alcohol and anticonvulsant drugs could cause more trouble than epilepsy itself. But from years of experience he knew that few things upset a host or hostess more than a refusal to participate in so hoary a custom. They all seemed to take it as an indictment of their own drinking.

"That wine looks fine," he said.

Bromley poured two glasses and handed one to Daniel, whose attention had turned to the floor-to-ceiling bookshelves opposite the window. The several hundred volumes had the textured look of value.

"All George Bernard Shaw," said Bromley. "Either by him or about him. Do you know Shaw?"

"I know he was a socialist."

"True enough, but one who loved money. He made a fortune from his plays. I've been collecting these books for almost fifteen years, ever since I wrote my honors thesis on him at Princeton. Some are really quite rare. Would you like—"

"Did Shaw say, 'Property is theft'?" Daniel knew he had not; Pierre somebody, a French socialist, had. As a gag he had proposed to Mac Fosdick that they use the phrase as a rubric for the Bellemoor series.

"No, I don't think I ever came across that line in Shaw. He did say, 'The test of a man or woman's breeding is how they behave in a quarrel.' Bromley raised his glass slightly and smiled.

Daniel did not return the toast, submerging his anger in the thought of how archaic the word *quarrel* had become.

Bromley took a sip of wine and continued. "I was sorry to read of your medical difficulties. Are you better?"

"I'm fine."

"I'm on the board of Uptown Hospital, you know. We have an excellent neurology department; the best in the city, I'm told. If they can be of any—"

"I'm fine."

A knock at the door sounded, like a bell ending round one.

"That will be lunch," Bromley said. "I hope you don't mind eating up here. There are several first-rate restaurants in the area, as I'm sure you know, but even the best of them tends to be crowded and noisy at lunchtime. And, of course, none of them has my view.''

A black waiter in a white jacket entered and pushed a tinkling service cart across the thick pile to the dining table by the window. The two men abandoned Shaw.

"Ah, *salade niçoise*. Perfect for a day like today, don't you think? I never know what the menu will be. I like surprises. Isn't that right, Edward?'' The waiter nodded and stood at respectful attention as Bromley inspected the meal in its polished wooden bowl. "Good. No anchovies. I hope you don't mind. I think they ruin a good salad. Too salty.''

Daniel loved anchovies, but the salad looked more than satisfactory. As Edward deftly tossed and served it Daniel reflected on how much he relished such epicurean dining: the feel of the snow-white napery, the sparkling silverware, the promise of fine food expertly prepared and impeccably presented. This gastronomic lust did not square with his journalistic crusade on behalf of those New Yorkers who were lucky if they saw the inside of a Burger King once a year, but he could not—did not want to—kick the habit. As he sat down he pushed his bitten tongue against the roof of his mouth. For the first time in a week it no longer seemed an obstacle to enjoying his food.

"Thank you, Edward. I'll buzz when we're ready for dessert and coffee.'' When the waiter withdrew, Bromley looked across the table and said, "I must confess that I was surprised to get your call yesterday afternoon. But delighted, of course. I've found that it's often quite useful for adversaries to get together like this; often they discover that their differences aren't nearly as great as they imagine."

"Did Shaw say that too?"

"You may not believe this, Mr.—may I call you Dan?"

"Daniel."

"You may not believe this, Daniel, but I'm all for a free press, even when it criticizes me. I just wish you journalists understood business a little better. Your articles on Bromley-Keller and the Bellemoor were quite inaccurate and unfair."

Daniel started to respond, then decided this lecture came with lunch.

"Sure some dislocation takes place when we convert a property or put up a new building, I don't deny that. It's inevitable. It was inevitable when they built Rockefeller Center. But do you really prefer the West Side the way it was fifteen years ago? You couldn't cross the street without getting mugged. You didn't mention that in your articles. Or the fact that the work we and other real estate firms have done—are *doing*—has stabilized the neighborhood and greatly increased the tax base. And you didn't see fit to mention all the construction jobs we've provided. Worst of all, you didn't talk to anyone other than the residents of the Bellemoor and Calhoun Bledsoe.

"Let me tell you a story. There's a secretary downstairs in our rental department, Connie Maddox. Terrific worker. She has a great future here and she's black." Bromley paused to let this fact sink in. "She lives on Amsterdam Avenue, a block from the three buildings we want to tear down for the Dickinson co-op. She came up here a couple of months ago and literally begged me to find a way to get around Bledsoe and his rent strikers so we could begin demolition. It's not just the garbage in the streets and the ghetto blasters at all hours. It's shootings and knifings and drunks in the doorways. She told me that one evening she and her young daughter were walking back from Broadway when this man staggered out holding himself. Why didn't you talk to people like Connie about gentrification? They don't think it's a dirty word.''

"Maybe you should have invited her to lunch.''

"Maybe so.''

"The issue is not whether gentrification is a dirty word. The issue is your treatment of people who live in the Bellemoor and other places like it. That's what I set out to write about and did. But I do concede that I may have gotten too close to Calhoun Bledsoe. I had no idea he and Rourke were dealing cocaine.''

"What makes you think Rourke was involved?''

"He told me himself he did it in Vietnam.''

"I know all about that. But he was clean when we hired him, and he stayed clean. I keep an eye on my employees, Daniel. I hate drugs. Anyone messing with them gets fired on the spot. Rourke knew that. I think you have things a little mixed up.''

"Meaning?''

"It's pretty clear to me that Bledsoe murdered Rourke because Billy discovered he was dealing out of the Bellemoor and was about to expose him. Not the best kind of publicity for the champion of the people.''

"That's not what Lieutenant Beaupre thinks. He thinks they were operating together."

"He's wrong. I've already told him that Billy called me the day before he was killed to say that he was going to the cops about Bledsoe." Bromley held up the bottle of wine, then noticed that Daniel's glass was still full. "Not to your liking? May I have Edward get you something else?"

"No. I'm not much of a midday drinker."

"How about some Perrier and lime?"

Daniel shook his head. "Frankly, it doesn't really matter to me whether they were in it together. Coke or no coke, Rourke was a two-bit bully. Besides, he's dead. But I'm feeling more than a little embarrassed about my involvement with Calhoun. If he killed Rourke, or even if he's just been pushing drugs, I'd obviously like to see him caught."

"So would I. For one thing, I don't share your view of Billy. He had a few rough edges, but he was a loyal employee. I meant what I said about him when I offered the reward."

"I'm interested in that too."

"In what? The reward?" Bromley put a forkful of tuna back down on his plate. "I'm surprised. I didn't know reporters at *Tabula Rasa* were interested in money."

"We're certainly more interested in it than management. Besides, I'm not exactly the fair-haired boy at *TR* anymore."

"So I've heard. I'm sorry. When our lawyers went to see your boss—what's his name, Fosdick?—their intention was not to get you fired, only to call atten-

tion to what we felt was a certain overzealousness on
your part.''

Daniel wondered if Bromley knew of his rampage
with the baseball bat. Probably. The media grapevine
snaked through the gossipy underbrush all over town.
How much else did he know? Had he purposely
misstated Daniel's current status at *TR*, or did he
actually believe his guest had been sacked instead of
suspended? Daniel suppressed a defensive urge to set
the matter straight. His pitch for the reward would
hardly be strengthened by calling attention to the fact
that his paychecks, such as they were, continued to
arrive. Daniel also beat back a sudden desire to test
his host's reaction to the principal target of his
''overzealousness'': the Wilder bribe. Now that the
bag man, Rourke, was dead, did Bromley feel
untouchable?

Daniel was enveloped in a fantasy conversation on
the subject when Bromley said, ''You know, we
really did get a number of complaints from the tenants about the prying you did at the Bellemoor last
July.''

Daniel found this impossible to believe. ''From
whom?'' he said acidly.

''For one, from a man who said you threatened to
take his daughter away from him.''

''That drunk.'' Daniel recalled instantly his encounter with the wretched child in Rourke's steamy
office and his subsequent visit to her father's foul,
wine-drenched apartment on the fourth floor. ''I told
him that I'd see that *he* was locked up for child abuse
if he didn't stop beating his daughter. You should
have seen her.''

"I can understand your feeling. I have three children myself, two girls. But you were on private property. We can't permit people to go barging into our buildings telling our tenants how to run their families."

"You don't seem to have many qualms about barging in and throwing them out on the street."

"We don't throw them out," Bromley said evenly. "We try our best to relocate them. You didn't write about those efforts, either."

"Because I couldn't find any evidence of them. But we're getting off the subject."

"Which is?"

"The twenty-five thousand you're offering for information."

"If you have such information, why don't you go to the police? I'm just putting up the money. It's up to them to decide who provides the most useful leads."

"Beaupre thinks I'm hip-deep in this thing myself. You've seen the papers. I'll go to the police eventually, but for the time being, I plan to work on my own. I'm interested in more than twenty-five thousand."

"Sorry, I have no plans to increase the reward."

"Not more money. I want the story. For *Tabula Rasa*. I need it to get back into Fosdick's good graces, and I think I can get it. I know Calhoun's habits, who his friends are, how he thinks. If you're right and he did murder Rourke, I think I can pin him down. But I want the story exclusively. If I work with the police, every newsroom in the city will be in on it."

"I admire your competitiveness. But I don't quite see how you can find Bledsoe when the police have failed—at least so far."

"Because I know the man; they don't. I know the places he might try to hide. And I also have an idea where the murder weapon might be."

"Rourke's gun?" Bromley leaned forward and ran his index finger around the base of his wineglass. "Where?"

"I'm not sure, but I've a strong lead. Twenty-five thousand dollars would provide considerable incentive."

"As I said, that's up to the police. To Beaupre, probably. It's his investigation."

"Not to put too fine a point on it, bullshit. If Steven Bromley wants the reward to go to Dick Tracy, I suspect that's where it would go."

"Why should I want you to have it?"

"You want Calhoun corraled. So do I. Our motives differ, but so what? Adversaries with something in common is how you put it earlier, I believe." Daniel smiled and now raised his glass. "And think of the public relations: 'B-K and *TR* Team Up To Catch Killer.'"

"Are you finished?"

"That's pretty much what I have to say, yes."

"No. I mean with your salad."

"Yes."

Bromley leaned back in his chair and pressed the intercom on his desk. Edward reappeared with the cart and cleared away the plates, then set ricotta cheesecake and coffee before both men.

"Try it with honey," said Bromley, pushing a small, ceramic pot across the table.

"The coffee?"

"You've never had it that way? Better than sugar and better for you. Much."

Daniel stirred in the honey and took a long sip. The sweetener cut the drink's bite, made it too smooth.

"I agree with you, Daniel, that we may have found an area of common interest. And I'm certainly glad we could get together today. But I'm afraid I can't make any commitment. Not because of the police, mind you. Of course, you're right. I can steer the money to anyone I choose. But I'm a business-man. I don't make deals with people unless I'm pretty sure they can produce. You haven't convinced me you can."

"Suit yourself." Daniel finished his coffee and began folding his napkin.

"I will say this. Since the police don't appear to be getting anywhere, you certainly would seem to have the inside track on both the story and the re-ward. If, of course, you really can locate Bledsoe—and the gun. So, by all means, let's keep in touch." Bromley took a card from his pocket and wrote on the back. "Here's my private number. It rings both here"—he pointed to the white phone on his desk—"and at my town house. Call anytime."

"We'll see," said Daniel, rising from the table. "Thanks for the lunch."

"I respect your willingness to admit you were wrong about Bledsoe. Not many reporters would be willing to go after a story that would make an earlier one look foolish. If it's any help to you, I assure you our conversation today will go no further than this room.''

''I'd appreciate that, at least for the time being.''

When they reached the office door, Bromley said, ''By the way, I meant what I said earlier about Uptown Hospital's neurology department. If you think they can be of any help to you, I'll put in a word. Today.'' He held out his hand.

Daniel shook it, again declining the offer, and headed for the grandfather clock and the stairs. Wendy Graham bid him a cheerful good-bye as he passed her desk. The knot in his stomach slowly began to unravel as he descended in the elevator to the marble lobby. But out on the hot street fatigue slapped him hard, as if in punishment for pumping up the adrenaline for the encounter upstairs. He wanted to walk into the park and curl up on a bench. It was time to take more medication too.

Chapter XI

"WELL, look who's here. Mike Hammer," said Delvecchio from his perch on Beaupre's desk.

Lewis Spofford ignored the remark. A trim ex-marine, he had arrived at the precinct just three months ago, shortly after his promotion to detective third-grade. He read two or three books a week, mostly thrillers, but resented the nickname Delvecchio laid on him. He thought the hard-boiled antics of Mike Hammer almost as silly as the cutting up of his fedoraed creator, Mickey Spillane, in the Miller Lite Beer commercials. Spofford preferred Hammett, Chandler, MacDonald, LeCarré. He took his reading seriously and had private contempt for his fellow cops, most of whom never ventured beyond the sports pages. He took his work seriously too. He did not like most white people and trusted none. He addressed Beaupre almost formally.

"You asked for background on the Torsney case. Here it is."

Beaupre looked at the envelope, then at Delvecchio, who shrugged. "I was beginning to wonder what had become of you," the lieutenant said. "What's the bottom line?"

"Whose bottom line? Torsney's or his victim's?"

"You've got the envelope. Suppose you tell it any way you want."

Spofford pulled a chair over from an adjacent desk and sat down. "Okay, let's start with the verdict. An all-white jury found Torsney not guilty by reason of mental disease or defect. That was in November, 1977, about a year after he shot the Evans kid in the head. The usual hired guns testified. Torsney's main psychiatrist said he was in the middle of a psychomotor seizure when he killed the boy and didn't know what he was doing. The prosecution's man, a psychiatrist from Columbia–Presbyterian, said this was bullshit."

"In court?" Delvecchio laughed.

"No, he put it in shrink talk." Spofford reached into the envelope and pulled out a spiral-bound pad. He leafed through the pages until he found the notes he had taken on the trial transcript. "The guy's name is Spiegel. He found no evidence that Torsney had epilepsy, in the past or at the time of the murder."

"Homicide," Beaupre said.

Spofford let the correction pass. "Spiegel said Torsney 'had the capacity to understand . . . the nature and consequences of his act' and at worst suffered from 'a neurotic personality disorder . . . and a proneness to hysterical dissociation.' "

"What the hell's that?" asked Beaupre.

"I don't know, but it isn't epilepsy." Spofford consulted his notes again. "Next he went to Creedmoor, and by the middle of 1978 a special com-

mittee of doctors there said he didn't suffer from a
psychosis, a psychiatric disorder, or organic brain
damage.''

"Where the hell did you get all this," Delvecchio
challenged.

"It's in the appeals court decision."

"What did this committee recommend?" asked
Beaupre.

"That he be released. They said he wasn't a danger to himself or anyone else. The DA fought the
decision, but the appeals court ruled two-to-one in
favor of the Department of Mental Hygiene. He was
sprung in 1979." Spofford tipped back in his chair.
"They said he shouldn't carry a gun."

"Yeah, I remember," said Beaupre. "The department wasn't too eager to have him back. He even
lost his pension."

"He even did, Lieutenant."

"So if Torsney wasn't having a fit when he killed
the kid, why did the jury buy the epilepsy pitch?"
Delvecchio said.

"You tell me, Sergeant," Spofford replied. "Maybe
the boy was browner than he should have been."

Beaupre jumped in before Delvecchio could respond. "Lewis, the fact is that at least one psychiatrist testified that Torsney was having a seizure when
he killed the boy. Am I right?"

"Correct."

"Then let's not be so quick to swallow Mental
Hygiene's findings. You know as well as I do that
they don't like to warehouse a guy if they can find
any excuse for letting him out. Why do you think

half the people on Broadway are talking to themselves?''

The phone on the desk rang. While Beaupre took the call Delvecchio ambled off to refill his coffee mug and returned dragging a chair. Spofford remained seated, pretending to sift through his notes.

When Beaupre hung up, he looked at Delvecchio and said, "Cooper just paid a visit to the Bromley-Keller building."

"To see Bromley?"

"Jerry's not sure. He didn't make it into the elevator, so he doesn't know what floor Cooper got off at. But he did use the bank that goes to the company offices. He went up just after noon and came down a little before two."

"Too long for a session with the dentist. Do you want me to call Bromley?"

"Can't hurt, Sambo. Do it."

Delvecchio moved off to his desk on the other side of the squad room.

"Is this guy Cooper really a suspect in the Rourke case?" Spofford asked Beaupre.

"Along with Calhoun Bledsoe, yes."

"Because of his epilepsy?"

"Among other things."

Spofford leaned forward, fished into the envelope, and pulled out a paperback book. "Ever hear of *The Terminal Man*?"

A man wielding a pistol—his head shaved and hooked up to EEG wires, his eyes heavy with menace—stared out from the cover. Beaupre looked at it and shook his head.

"It's a medical thriller by Michael Crichton. I read

it in Vietnam, and when I was going through the Torsney transcript, I remembered it. It's about a homicidal nut who's a psychomotor epileptic.''

"So?"

"So listen to this. It's from the postscript." Spofford found the underlined passage and read: 'Since the publication of this book in its hardcover edition, several neurologists have advised me that the syndrome of psychomotor epilepsy is incorrectly portrayed in significant ways. These professionals emphasize that psychomotor epileptics are no more prone to criminal behavior than other individuals in society. They also agree that a psychomotor epileptic in the midst of a seizure is unlikely to injure anyone, except by accident. They regard complex, purposeful aggressive behavior in the course of a seizure to be either extremely rare, or nonexistent.' There's more. Do you want to hear it?''

"I'll take your word for it," Beaupre said, deflecting the book like a goalie turning away a loose puck. "I don't think we need the help of some guy who earns his living making things up.''

"Crichton's not just a writer. He went to Harvard Medical School.''

"I don't care if he wrote the Hippocratic Oath. I'm old-fashioned, Lewis. I like facts. That's the way we solve most of the mysteries around this place. Look, maybe you're right about Torsney. Maybe he did get off because the jury was lily-white and didn't want to nail a cop. But maybe, just maybe, he really did kill the kid in the middle of a fit. His psychiatrist said he did. Let's say Torsney really hated blacks, hated 'em like a Klansman. He'd shoot 'em if he could. But he can't. Then one night he has this freak thing, and for an instant, whatever it is that keeps us all from going haywire breaks down. And the poor kid just happens to be in the wrong place at the wrong time.''

"You think that's what happened with Cooper too?''

"Maybe. He certainly had in it for Rourke. And I know he had a fit just before the man was killed. And he's lied to me about his actions at the time.''

Spofford started to press his case when Delvecchio returned. "Cooper did have lunch with Daddy Warbucks,'' he said.

"Who'd you talk to?'' Beaupre asked.

"Bromley himself. He said it was a date they made a long time ago.''

"What the hell for? They're mortal enemies.''

"He wouldn't say. I only managed a couple of questions before *he* started grilling *me*. 'Do we have any leads on Bledsoe? Have we found the murder weapon? Has anyone tried to claim the reward?' ''

"Didn't you push him? Their meeting's a little coincidental.''

"What do you want me to do, threaten to cuff him around? He's not some two-bit pimp. He's Steven Carter Bromley, Junior. You know what he said? Would we like him to call the mayor and get some extra men assigned to this case? Not ask to get, *get*. Nice, huh?''

"He asked if anyone had tried to claim the reward?'' Spofford said.

"Yeah,'' replied Delvecchio, as if it were none of the black man's business. "Why?''

"Not sure. But maybe he wants to know if there

are any other candidates, because that's what Cooper came up to discuss.''

This possibility had not occurred to either Beaupre or Delvecchio; they glanced at each other with a flicker of embarrassment.

"That son of a bitch," Beaupre said. "If he's trying to arrange a private deal with Bromley, I'll have his ass.''

"If he is, that would seem to rule him out as much of a suspect," Spofford said.

"Bullshit. He's a prime suspect until he stops jerking us around. Your theory about the reward is interesting, but it's only a theory.''

"Get your hands off me, you motherfuckers." The shrill demand pierced the squad room as two sweating patrolmen entered struggling to contain an immense black woman. Handcuffs bit deep into her fleshy wrists, shackling her trunklike arms behind her back. Her screamed obscenities reverberated off the tile walls as her captors pushed and shoved her toward the lockup.

"Five will get you ten that they can't get her through the cell door," Delvecchio said.

With some effort the patrolmen did, and clanged the gate shut. The three detectives watched like theatergoers at a familiar drama, the meaning of which they were no longer inclined to discuss with one another.

"What do you want me to do with this material?" Spofford asked.

Beaupre looked at the envelope wearily. "Leave it, Lewis, I'll get to it. Meanwhile, you got anything else? The gun, perhaps. Or just something that doesn't require a lot of reading.''

''Not much. I did talk to a couple of people at the West Side Tenants Council. One of them said it seemed as if Bledsoe had a lot of extra cash to throw around in the last few months. This person said that one afternoon he told everyone in the office to go home early and get dressed up and meet him for dinner at the Terrace Atop Butler. About a dozen people.''

''The place where the Columbia University brass hangs out?'' said Delvecchio. ''Très expensivo.''

''Yeah, my person said the tab came to something like six hundred bucks, which Bledsoe paid with cash.''

''Drug money,'' Delvecchio decreed.

''Maybe. But my person said Bledsoe never showed the slightest sign of messing with drugs.''

''What the hell do you expect them to say at the council? He's their goddamn saint.''

''Cool it, Sam,'' Beaupre said. ''When did this outing take place?''

''Late August. My source says Bledsoe did it because no one was getting any vacations.''

''That doesn't explain where the money came from.'' Beaupre thought for a moment. ''Lewis, try to find some more evidence of big spending. Start with the restaurant. Maybe Bledsoe developed a taste for eating there. Check his bank account. Find out how he's been using his credit cards. You know what to do.''

As Spofford moved off, Beaupre called after him cheerfully. ''Hey, don't come in here next week and hand me a chit for eating at that restaurant. There's a perfectly good coffee shop around the corner, Mama's Place. Tell them I sent you.''

Delvecchio waited until Spofford was out of earshot and said, ''Do we really want him on this case?''

''Yes, Sam, I do. He's okay. Just a little too serious. He won't go easy because Bledsoe's a brother. If anything, he seems more eager to get Cooper off the hook. Besides, what have *you* got for me, white man?''

''The dried blood you tweezed off Cooper's washrag is type AB. According to his Army records, that's his type. Rourke's is type O, and that's the only kind we've found at the scene so far.''

''Keep looking.''

''We are, Frenchie, but that rat hole's not very big. If any other type was splattered around, I think we'd have found it by now.''

''Keep looking. What about the pills?''

''Legit, according to the lab report.'' Delvecchio pulled a folded sheet of paper from his shirt pocket. ''Mysoline's the trade name for something called primidone. Phenobarb is phenobarb. Both are anticonvulsants; they keep epileptics from flipping out. There's a lot of chemistry here. You want it?''

''No. Anything about side effects?''

''Yeah. It says primidone sometimes aggravates an epileptic's behavioral problems. Mostly in kids, though. And both drugs cause drowsiness. Maybe Cooper did it in his sleep.''

Beaupre permitted himself a half smile.

"When you talked to Jerry before, did he say where Cooper was now?" Delvecchio asked.

"Back at his apartment."

"Why don't we bring him in for a Q and A?"

"Come on, Sam. And give *Tabula Rasa* a chance to tell the world we're the Gestapo? Besides, what's the charge? Having epilepsy?"

Chapter XII

"SLOW down." Daniel craned around and looked out the rear window.

"I'm only doing fifty."

"I know. I want to see if the green car back there will pass us."

Kate lifted her foot from the accelerator, and the rented Cavalier coasted down to thirty-five. The car behind maintained its distance. Kate glanced into the rearview mirror. "He's been there at least since we got on the Saw Mill."

"Terrific."

"Hey. I thought we decided on the phone yesterday that we didn't care if we were followed. He's the one who has to sleep in the car. That's what you said. We've got the whole house to ourselves. Wait till you see it."

When they had talked yesterday after Daniel returned from his encounter with Bromley, Kate had come on like a slightly overeager country real estate dealer. She was determined to sell this big red converted barn: four bedrooms, modern kitchen, vast living room with a cathedral ceiling and two fireplaces, sliding glass doors, and a wooden deck on three sides that looked out on more than a hundred acres. It belonged to a Barnard classmate and her husband, an architect who had designed the renovation himself; they were in Europe for all of September and had given Kate the key. "It's heaven, Daniel, just what you need. And it's only about three hours—at the end of the Taconic, near Chatham. There's a spring-fed pond too. Cold, but a great way to wake up."

Daniel had not mentioned his aversion to such chill morning dips. Nor had he protested Kate's proposal that she rent a car and pick him up the next day at noon. He knew he shouldn't drive, that even if he didn't have a seizure at the wheel, he was still a menace because of the drugs. If he couldn't break a fall while running, his reflexes would hardly respond in time to brake a car in a sudden emergency. He had not owned one since moving from Washington to New York ten years ago. Even back then he had the proper disdain of a well-trained liberal for the hairy-chested romance of the American automobile and made do with a 1965 Rambler whose succession of ailments often seemed the biggest running news story at *The Washington Post*. The choke and snarl of Manhattan's traffic had only deepened his contempt for cars and the sex-bait that sold them. But now, relegated to the passenger seat next to Kate, he felt emasculated, as he had at seventeen when his parents finally relented and reluctantly allowed him to apply for a driver's license. He got it with no trouble, but neither Ben nor Betsy Cooper permitted him to drive when they were in the car.

"We'll need to get gas," he said.

"There's a station soon, just after we cross into Westchester." Kate turned and gave him a confident smile.

Her competence charged him with a rush of affection through which resentment streaked like the staccato of white dashes that divided the lanes of the parkway. Her obvious command as she steered their course north and her alert eyes on the winding road made Daniel feel helpless. He gazed at the sun combing through the soft hairs on her arms and at her breasts, where the seat belt pressed against them, and wanted to put his head in her lap. Instead he looked away at the reddening foliage flashing by and realized he had begun to distrust her. In the middle of the night he had awakened convinced that she had informed Beaupre of their weekend destination, a suspicion that faded by morning but now revived each time he looked behind them. At the very least, he decided, she was relieved that Beaupre had assigned one of his minions to keep watch.

He also questioned her motives for this trip. She had enthusiastically billed it as a way for him to escape for thirty-six hours from the telephone siege at his apartment. He suspected, however, that only the possibility of hearing from Calhoun Bledsoe really concerned her. Daniel knew she was determined to make him keep his vow to turn in the gun on Monday and that she feared he would push to postpone that deadline if Bledsoe did get in touch again. She was right. He planned to stall for more time even if Calhoun didn't make contact by Monday morning. He remained convinced, for all Beaupre's initially disturbing talk of cocaine, that Calhoun could—and eventually would—explain what the hell happened at the Bellemoor ten days ago. Despite Kate's fears, he was unlikely to do so by calling Daniel at home this weekend since he already thought that the line was tapped. So why not go to Chatham?

Daniel needed to get away, however briefly, however monitored by trailing cops. By the time he had gone to bed last night, the telephone seemed permanently clenched in his fist. Faith, with maddening efficiency, had tipped off her former in-laws, who called from Chicago and stayed on the line for more than an hour trying to persuade Daniel to let them fly in and help him. His mother, who more and more seemed to merge with Faith now that he lived with neither one, was all practical advice: "Have you talked to a lawyer? Have you gotten a second medical opinion? Do you have your mittens, Dan-Dan?" Ben Cooper said very little. Daniel pictured him on the extension upstairs, slumped on the bed, his face a field of anxious perplexity. When he did speak, he sounded like a baffled football coach who could summon no encouragement for his injured star. "Have you been taking your pills?" he said more than once. It was less a question than a plea.

Marilyn Constantine had phoned again, clearly hoping to get the Sanyo, and tongue-tied to find herself voice-to-voice with the subject of the *Times* story she had just read. "Oh, Daniel, it's you. About the party . . . I'd completely forgotten I have to go to Philadelphia that weekend. I'm really sorry. Will you take a raincheck? I'll, um, call." After fending off WCBS all-news radio, Daniel had dialed *Tabula Rasa* and, while waiting for the receptionist to put him through to Fosdick, considered discussing his lunch with Bromley. A few minutes of conversation convinced him not to. Fosdick remained solicitous about Daniel's health but cooled when the Rourke investigation came up. "Frankly, I'm not too happy about that little item in the *Times* this morning," he said finally.

"Well, fuck you, Mac. I'm sorry I've become such an embarrassment," Daniel shouted into the empty apartment after hanging up. At seven o'clock he brewed some tea, scrambled three eggs with onions, and switched on the Sanyo.

He left the volume up. There were calls he needed to get, voices he wanted to hear. Like Norman Werner's. Surely he must have seen the *Times*; he read the paper like holy writ each morning. They had been friends since Fort Leonard Wood where they discovered their common love of show music and had boosted each other's morale during basic training with boisterous renditions of the songs from *Call Me Mister*, a revue about getting out of the army after World War II. Norman now worked in Wall Street managing pension funds (and, as a favor, Daniel's relatively modest stash). They rarely talked about their disparate occupations. Norman always seemed completely indifferent to what people did for a living. As a topic of conversation it simply did not interest him, even if the subject was tax-exempt bonds or the latest SEC investigation. When anyone tried to take his measure with "What do you do?" he invariably fixed a poker face and replied, "About what?" He thrived in political debate and on the exploration of ideas and, unlike most men, did not cower at the prospect of discussing personal problems. On the contrary, what increasingly attracted Daniel over the years was how sympathetically and perceptively Norman dealt with the emotions. Why hadn't he called?

Daniel strained against his seat belt and reached for the radio.

"No." Kate pushed his hand away from the dial. "Sing."

"Sing? What?"

"Anything." She radiated an encouraging grin. "No. Not anything. Make it something I've never heard before, something funny. I've never told you this, but I think most soupy show tunes sound dumb. I mean, 'Like a lark who is learning to pray.' Yuk."

"I have it on the best of authority that before Oscar Hammerstein wrote that he actually taught a lark to pray. In Bucks County. Schubert's 'Ave Maria,' I believe it was."

Kate shut her eyes for a moment and hunched up her shoulders. "Sing," she ordered.

"Okay, you asked for it. I hope you can take this one. It's all about my checkered past." Daniel loosened his seat belt, cleared his throat ostentatiously, and ran his baritone up and down the scale with feigned pomposity. Angling toward Kate, he announced, "And now, by special request, here's Daniel Cooper himself with one of Cole Porter's little-known gems, 'They Couldn't Compare to You.'" As he began the introduction he feared his still sensitive tongue would stumble over the tripping diction of the verse; but he reached the breakaway point easily and, with growing confidence, sprinted into the patter.

After playing the local sirens
Who resided in my environs,
I decided to learn the art of Cupid's trickery,
So, at once, I started cruising,
Found the Muses so amusing
That I even got a kick outa Terpsichore.
After her, I met Calypso,
Who was definitely a dipso,
Then I fled to big Brunnhilde, she was German.
After snitching Eve from Adam,
I attended Call Me Madam
And shortly began to nestle Essel Merman.

"*Essel* Merman." Kate laughed. "That 's not fair."

"If you're Cole Porter, baby, anything goes." Daniel gathered enthusiasm and velocity as he continued the catalog. By the time he reached the end, he was clipping off the lines like Danny Kaye.

There was Melisande,
A platinum blonde
(How I loved to ruffle her locks).
There was bright Aurora,
Then Pandora,
Who let me open her box!

" 'Open her box'? Why, that naughty man."

"You don't know how naughty. It's from a show called *Out of This World* that Porter wrote in 1950. I was only four when the record came out, and I wowed 'em even then on Kenwood Avenue. But 'box' was a no-no in those days. After that last line the chorus comes back in with, 'They couldn't compare to us.' I never saw the show, but on the record they enter a beat early to cover up Pandora's box. As it were. For years I went around singing, 'Who let me open her *they*.' Eventually I figured out that 'they' didn't exactly rhyme with 'locks' and then I read about Pandora's box somewhere. But I didn't put the double entendre together for a long time.''

"It's an incredible lyric. A long way from 'Orgasm Addict.' ''

"That's a song?''

"Sure. By the Buzzcocks. Where've you been?''

"The Buzzcocks?'' Now Daniel was laughing. "Let's look up *risqué* as soon as we get to a dictionary. I'll bet the word isn't even listed anymore. 'Orgasm Addict' by the Buzzcocks. I can't believe it.''

"Are all Coopers Broadway aficionados?''

"Crazed. Especially my Dad. He buys the record and piano score of every show the minute they come out. He's one helluva sight reader, and we used to have these great sessions around the piano when I was a kid. Dad. Me. My mother. My Aunt Katherine, sometimes. Also the beauteous Caroline Farwell. She lived next door and I was always deputized to get her. She was blond and a terrific soprano, your dream ingenue; stacked, too, as we used to say in those days. I loved her madly, but she was four years older and always wearing some jock's Hyde Park High School varsity jacket. Still, *I* got to sing all the love duets with her. 'People Will Say We're In Love.' 'If I Loved You.' Dad would assign everyone parts and we'd sing through entire shows, sometimes three in an evening. I know almost every song Essel Merman ever sang, including all the verses to 'You Can't Get a Man With a Gun.' ''

Daniel grimaced, and they drove in silence for a few moments.

Finally Kate said, '' 'They Couldn't Compare to You' is amazingly clever. But don't you think a lot of show tunes are awfully sentimental? I mean, really corny?''

"Of course. That's why I love 'em. Why do you think they're so popular? Moon-June makes an unexamined life worth living. If Socrates had seen *The Sound of Music*, he never would have taken hemlock, and the whole course of Western civilization would be nothing but one long happy ending.''

"*I* have it on the best authority that he *did* see *The Sound of Music* and that's *why* he drank hemlock.''

Kate tugged on Daniel's shirtsleeve and, when he bent toward her, kissed him gently on the cheek. He nipped her nose and then swiveled his head for another look behind them.

"You know," he said, "there's a song from *Fiorello!* called 'I Love a Cop.' Before we go to bed tonight, let's serenade that guy.''

"It's a deal. You can teach it to me after we get gas. There's the station up ahead, and not a moment too soon. My bladder's bursting.''

"Pull up to the self-service island. I'll fill 'er up while you empty.''

"Don't be vulgar.''

"My deah, I'm not being vulgar. I'm being risqué.''

The Cavalier rolled to a stop by the pumps, and Kate bolted for the great unknown of the ladies' room, shouting "unleaded" over her shoulder. Daniel got out, steadied himself on the open door, and stretched his cramped joints with several deep knee bends. They came slowly against the glue in his bloodstream, but the fresh air countered his depression over the drugs. He looked forward to trying a short run as soon as they arrived at the barn. And for the first time since the seizure he felt capable of making love to Kate.

He unhooked the hose nozzle, setting the pump's motor running. After cranking the digits of the previous sale back to zero, he unscrewed the gas-tank cap, inserted the snout, and started the flow. The pump's escalating numbers hypnotized him for a moment, and he did not notice the green car when it parked behind him next to the station's wrecking truck. The driver stepped out, quickly surveyed the area, and walked over to the Cavalier.

"Cooper?"

Daniel jerked around, released the trigger, and faced the stranger.

"No scenes," the man said, looking hard at Daniel. "If the woman comes back before I split, I'm simply asking you how to get to Mt. Kisco. Just tell me to stay on the Saw Mill. I can't miss it."

"It won't work, Officer," said Daniel, spotting the green car. "The woman, as you call her, has been on to you for miles. How's Beaupre?"

"I'm no cop. I'm here for your friend Bledsoe. He needs to see you, as soon as possible. *Comprende*?"

Reflexively Daniel restored the hose to the pump, silencing the motor. Fumes from the gasoline rose around the two men, preserving the revelation like formaldehyde.

"Who are you?"

"I'm a friend of Calhoun's. Like you."

"Where is he?"

The man's eyes swept the station again, making sure Kate was not returning and that the attendant remained in the office, transfixed by the television set beside his feet on the desk. Satisfied, he pulled a map from his rear pocket and hurriedly spread it on the hot roof of the Cavalier.

"Right here," he said, his index finger hovering over a tiny rectangle of green. "Just off Saratoga Park in Bedford-Stuyvesant. It shouldn't take you much more than an hour to get there."

Daniel stared at the crosshatch of blocks on the detailed map of Brooklyn. The man jabbed his finger down.

"You see Kimbark Street?"

Daniel nodded, caught in the wind tunnel of his curiosity.

"He's at 482, in the block off Howard Avenue. Most of the brownstones on the street are occupied. Number 482's empty. But the door's not locked. You can go right up."

"Are you with the tenants' council? I've never seen you there."

"No, I'm a friend, like I said. A friend who thinks Calhoun is being framed for Rourke's murder."

"By whom?"

"Let him tell you that." His radar tracked nervously.

"How long have you been following us?"

"Too fucking long. You're a hard man to get alone. I thought you'd never stop for gas. Where the hell are you going?"

"To the country," Daniel said with the embarrassment of someone confessing disloyalty.

"Do it another day. He needs you." The man folded the map and returned it to his pocket. "Number 482 Kimbark Street. Near the park. You got it?"

"Yes."

A dozen questions formed behind Daniel's tentative reply, but the man had already started back to his car. When he reached the door, he took one fast look around again and, without meeting Daniel's pursuing eyes, got in and drove off up the parkway. Daniel watched until the car curved away, then found himself focusing on the $18.40 registered on the pump, as if seeking refuge in the mundane transaction. He screwed the gas cap back on and walked across the apron and into the office, where he handed the attendant a twenty and asked for something to write on. The young man stayed plugged into his movie while he worked the money changer on his belt and pointed to the notepad below the girlie calendar on the wall. Daniel took the stubby pencil strung beside it, wrote down the address, tore off the piece of paper, and folded it into his pants pocket. When he emerged from the office, Kate was rounding the corner of the garage. Pretending not to see her, he moved at a half trot toward the Cavalier and took the wheel.

"Hey, fella, slide over. You've got a song to teach me," Kate said, leaning in the driver's window.

"Get in." Daniel started the motor.

"Whoa. You're not driving. Not today. Move over."

"Please, Kate, go around and get in. I'll explain everything."

"Explain what?" She put her hands on her hips and backed off a step.

"Just get in."

"No, I won't. What's going on?"

Daniel switched off the ignition. "*Now* will you get in?"

Kate walked around the front of the car, piercing the windshield with her irritation, then slammed herself into the passenger seat. Without a word Daniel revved up the engine and pulled away from the island.

"Daniel!"

"Just listen."

He edged the Cavalier into the northbound traffic and recounted his meeting at the pumps.

When he finished, Kate nervously clicked in her seat belt. Cinching it tight, she said, "What did this masked man look like?"

Daniel paused for several seconds. He had been so stunned by the message, he had paid little attention to the messenger.

"He had a crew cut."

"What color? And his eyes? How tall was he? What was he wearing?"

"Both his hair and eyes were brown." The unspoken "I think" fell between them. "He was wearing slacks and a sport jacket."

"Gray slacks? Plaid? Polka dot? What material was the jacket?"

"Sort of tweedy. I don't remember the pants. He was big and beefy, about six-two. In his late twenties or early thirties. He had very rough hands. I noticed that when he spread out the map for me."

"What map?"

"Of Brooklyn. To show me exactly where Calhoun is."

"Where's the map?"

"He kept it."

"Kept it? Why would he do that? You're the one who's supposed to need it."

"I don't know. Maybe he doesn't want us to have it if we're picked up by the police. He kept it." Daniel edged over fifty-five as they continued north.

"Was he black?"

"No."

"At least you remember some colors. What kind of car was it? Did you get the license number?"

He had bobbled both facts, like a shortstop blanking on the fundamentals in the middle of a double play. He wanted to blame the drugs for these errors but knew it was more a matter of his involvement. He had not been a coolly observant reporter back there at the pumps. He considered lying to Kate, fabricating a model and plate for the mystery car, but his silence had already condemned him.

"I don't suppose he told you his name," Kate said, eyeing the speedometer.

"No."

"Did you ask?"

"Kate, he didn't give me a chance. The whole thing took about three minutes, maybe four."

Kate looked out the window and said nothing.

"You think I'm making all this up? Look behind us. The car's gone."

"You're the one who decided he was following us. For all I know, he's on his way to his Saturday golf game in Chappaqua."

"This guy was no golfer."

To Kate's relief the traffic light ahead was turning red. "Pull onto the shoulder and let me drive."

Instead Daniel slipped the Cavalier into the left lane and came to a stop.

"What are you doing?"

"We're going back."

"*No*. No, we're not."

Daniel buckled his seat belt and waited for a pickup truck to cross in front of them. Then, to beat the line of cars poised in the southbound lanes, he gunned a sharp U-turn against the light and headed back down the parkway, picking up speed like a luge in its run.

"You're insane. You can't do this. I'm responsible for this car." Outrage and fear combusted in Kate.

"We'll be okay." Daniel floored the sluggish four-cylinder compact.

"I can't believe you're doing this. Don't you care about anyone but yourself? For a week now it's been nothing but 'I love you, Kate; I need you, Kate; I can't get along without you.' Now you're ready to kill us both."

"We'll be okay, I said. I've driven all my adult life and never had an accident."

"Stop it. That kind of rationalization's unworthy of you. Please pull over. Or at least slow down."

Daniel shaved their speed back to fifty-five, less to mollify Kate than because he didn't want to invite arrest. He wondered if she knew that his mutiny was more than merely ill-advised. To drive legally in most states, New York among them, epileptics generally had to be seizure-free for at least a year. In the meantime all insurance bets were off. Should he maim or kill anyone, including himself or Kate, he or his estate would be liable for every penny of any judgment against him. The Saw Mill suddenly seemed too narrow, a tollway designed for horse-drawn wagons. The metal median rail looked thinner than tinsel. Daniel's hands began to perspire on the wheel.

"Where are we going?" Kate said.

"Brooklyn."

"Bedford-Stuyvesant? Now?"

"Yes, now. I'm sorry. I really wanted to go up to Chatham. The house sounds wonderful. But I just can't sit in front of a fireplace all weekend now. In another couple of hours we might be able to clear this whole thing up."

"How do you know? How do you know this isn't some kind of trick?"

"Like what?"

"I don't know. Something."

"Kate, when Calhoun called you at the office, what did he say? That he'd find a way to get in touch again soon, right? Well, he's done it."

"You have no idea who that man is."

"Why is that so important? You make it sound as if Calhoun's in a position to pick and choose who he sends. He's a fugitive."

"And you're not Clint Eastwood. You can't simply swagger in and solve this case by yourself. It's Bedford-Stuyvesant."

"What's that supposed to mean?"

"You know."

"No, I don't know. You tell me."

"All I mean is—"

"That it's a ghetto full of blacks waiting to plunge a knife in your back. Have you ever been there?"

"No."

"I have. Many times. Including at night. And here I am, unscathed, to tell the tale. Bed-Stuy is full of middle-class *people* and some of the best-kept brownstones in the city. On a Saturday afternoon like this everyone will be out of the stoops. You'll see."

"No, I won't, because the first time you have to stop this car, I'm getting out."

"Kate."

"I mean it. Okay, so I don't know Bedford-Stuyvessant. And if you think I'm a racist, fine. But I'm not going. I mean it, Daniel."

He looked at her and knew she did. He knew, too, that his decision to meet Calhoun carried more danger than he pretended and that he had no business dragging Kate along, car or no car. After fifteen minutes of silent standoff they entered the North Bronx, slicing through the playing fields of Van Cortlandt Park. Daniel abandoned the parkway at Broadway and continued south along the park until he reached a Burger King. He turned into the lot and parked the Cavalier between two cars.

"Thank you." Kate sighed. "Let's go in and have one of those awful hamburgers and talk."

Daniel killed the engine but did not respond. A dozen cricketers milled about, just emerged from a post-game feast. Their dark West Indian faces and spanking whites evoked lawns and tea, not asphalt and Whoppers.

"Cricket in the Bronx?" Kate said, trying to break the tension.

Daniel looked at the smiling squad but ignored Kate's observation. He pulled the keys from the ignition and, handing them to her, said, "One Cavalier. Returned in good condition." He met her eyes. "And I don't think you're a racist."

Kate touched his arm. "Let's go in and get something to eat. I'm starving."

"I can't. I'm still going to Brooklyn." He pointed to the el station across the street. "Do you know how to drive back from here?"

"Yes. But don't do it, Daniel, please. Let's go in and talk about it."

Daniel was already out of the car and bending in the driver's window "We already have. Slide over here and give me a kiss."

Kate moved behind the wheel and looked up at him. Their eyes connected again and he kissed her. Several of the cricketers began applauding

"I do love you and I do need you. Now go home and don't worry. I'll call you later tonight."

"Daniel. Don't."

"I'll be fine."

He grabbed his sweater from the backseat and headed for the stairway to the el platform.

Chapter XIII

DANIEL pushed three singles through the aperture in the bullet-proof glass and scooped up the three tokens and change shoved back by the automaton caged in the booth. He thanked her and she nodded impassively. Graffiti covered almost every inch of the wooden walls of the antique terminus and of the train idling at the platform. Clicking through the turnstile was like entering a finger painting entitled *End of the Line*. Gallery status, in fact, had long ago been bestowed on the city's ubiquitous hieroglyphics, expunging them having proved far more difficult than declaring them art. Well, why not? thought Daniel. The smears certainly were no worse than the pristine car cards plugging the heroic properties of Preparation-H or the benefits of spring-fresh Salems. Advertising won awards and occasionally hung in museums. Did graffiti deserve any less just because the rogue artists didn't ask permission before firing their spray cans?

Daniel picked out a car in the center of the train and stepped in. The teenage Hispanic couple across the aisle gave him a quick once-over and resumed necking. Daniel tried not to watch, to honor the unwritten New York prohibition against eye contact in public places, but the boy's black shoes each bore a Playboy bunny decal on the toe. When the wearer caught Daniel studying these decorations, he glared a laser beam of hostility. Daniel instantly turned away and refocused on the car's only other passenger, a man stretched out asleep on the hard plastic seat that ran the length of the car. His denim cutoffs and striped dress shirt were soiled, but not as befouled as the clothing of most derelicts who rode the rails. From where Daniel sat he looked young and healthy, as if he might simply have decided to take a nap after a strenuous outing in the park—except that he wore no shoes. He lay on his stomach, his head resting on his left arm, his right arm hanging down into flakes of discarded newspaper on the floor. As the train jerked out of the station an empty Diet Pepsi can began rolling erratically around the grimy, gum-matted linoleum, caroming about like a runaway billiard ball.

The number 1 Broadway Local rattled south out of Van Cortlandt Park like the Toonerville Trolley, stopping every seven blocks or so, as if the internal combustion engine had yet to be invented and ladies still carried parasols. The car grew more crowded and hot with each stop, and by 125th Street, anyone who boarded had to stand. At 116th Street two Columbia University students, both bearded and well pressed, got on and began politely hawking a radical newspaper. "Help dump Mayor Koch. . . . Stop racist gentrification on the Upper West Side. . . . Return New York to the people. . . . Buy the *National*

Alliance.'' Eyes were averted as the earnest reformers threaded their way through the straphangers. Even the three or four passengers who purchased their broadsheet seemed tentative and embarrassed as the train began its run beneath the offending terrain, where Saturday afternoon shoppers were spreading their discretionary income like beluga on a toast point.

At Columbus Circle Daniel shouldered himself out of the train and transferred through the cavernous labyrinth to the IND. From the Pakistani manning the kiosk on the platform he bought a package of Planters Peanuts, two mouthfuls for forty-five cents. He was still struggling to unwrap his purchase when two uniformed Transit Authority cops ambled to a halt less than ten feet away. Their intense discussion of the relative merits of foreign versus domestic cars struck Daniel as transparently staged, and instantly he decided that Beaupre had managed to pick up his scent down here. It really wasn't that hard. Traveling in these entrails only gave the illusion of anonymity and escape. Most cops, including the two auto analysts, carried hand radios; keeping tabs on a suspect was mostly a matter of good relay work, especially if someone cued things from the start. Daniel imagined Kate angrily watching him climb to the Van Cortlandt Park station and then, fed up, going into the Burger King and calling the Twenty-fourth Precinct, telling Beaupre he was headed for a lunatic rendezvous with Calhoun Bledsoe in Bedford-Stuyvesant and that the police had to save him from himself.

Daniel felt the blast of stale air that signaled a train pushing toward the station. He faced the tracks again, straining to hear if the auto debate was continuing behind him, until the arriving A express obliterated all other sound. When the doors opened, he checked the impulse to look over his shoulder and boarded the train. He pulled his sweater tighter around his shoulders against the air conditioning and moved to get his bearings from the pastel map above the seat. The purple IND stripe ran down the spine of Lower Manhattan, tunneled under the pale blue East River into Brooklyn, and beneath Fulton Street into Bedford-Stuyvesant.

Daniel sat down and conceded he had overstated the case for the area when deriding Kate's fears back at the Burger King. True, a hard core of middle-class blacks had purchased and renovated many brownstones with the help of cheap loans cajoled from reluctant banks by the Bedford-Stuyvesant Restoration Corporation. But these hardy pioneers, and the corporation itself, squatted in a great urban outback of decay, population more than 300,000; a land where unemployment, crime, drink, and drugs swirled about the homesteaders like choking dust storms. Daniel had not come to this place on several occasions, as he had loudly proclaimed to Kate, but only twice—as a reporter for *Tabula Rasa* covering upbeat press conferences at Restoration Plaza, the redbrick shopping center that housed the corporation's headquarters. Both times he had taken cabs each way.

Daniel stepped out of his capsule at the Utica Avenue Station and caught his reflection in the token booth as he headed for the stairs. He had dressed for the country, and his lightly starched khakis, navy Izod polo shirt, pricey Adidas, and summer tan made him look dangerously prosperous. As much to mod-

ify this image as to cool off in the sweltering cata-
comb, he undraped the maroon cashmere sweater
from around his neck and tried to carry it unobtru-
sively at his side. For the first time since setting out
he seriously contemplated the possibility of getting
mugged and attempted to recall how much money he
carried. Norman Werner insisted that cash provided
the surest defense against physical harm in New York
and always kept five hundred-dollar bills tucked in
his wallet, what he called his urban hedge fund.
Daniel guessed that he had no more than twelve
dollars on him, having been assured by Kate last
night that he could cash a check at the Finast when
they got to Chatham.

At the top of the exit a familiar thwocking noise
sounded behind him; when he turned around, he saw
several earnest tennis games in progress on the courts
of Boys and Girls High School. This benign sight
shamed him for allowing so much paranoia to accu-
mulate on his subterranean ride. But the broad inter-
section of Fulton and Utica proved an oasis. Every
step away from it took Daniel deeper into a desert of
despair, his path strewn with broken glass glittering
in the afternoon sun. Kids, some of them barefoot,
scrambled over the sharp rubble of a vacant lot while
at the curb their elders dismantled the motor of an
abandoned or stolen Buick Skylark with the concen-
tration of dedicated surgeons. On Howard Avenue,
house after house stared at him through empty windows as he passed.

A hymn Daniel had never heard declared its desperate hope from inside a white-brick African Meth-
odist Episcopal Church, the neon cross on its steeple

long ago broken. Baking on the sidewalk, a few people sang along halfheartedly as they waited for free cheese in a dispirited line that stretched for almost a block. Daniel wondered what kind it was and how much each person got, then began savoring the heaping portions of Kraft Macaroni & Cheese he used to consume at Jenny Mae's apartment in Chicago. Jenny Mae, the Cooper family's cook and maid, knew better than anyone how much Daniel liked the bland porridge and always made a point of serving it when he and his mother came to visit. They crossed Cottage Grove Avenue into a black neighborhood Daniel had never heard called a ghetto and did not fear in the slightest.

"Hey, honky. You lost or somethin'?"

Daniel smiled weakly at his challenger, one of four teenage boys draped in front of a run-down corner grocery.

"You don't need that sweater in this heat," said another. "Let me hold it for you." He feinted toward Daniel, who dropped the sweater as he fumbled to switch it to his street-side hand.

"Dropped somethin', honky," the first boy said, to a chorus of derisive laughter.

Daniel picked up the sweater and hurried on. Like Prince Myshkin, he sensed all eyes burning into him, searing his differentness. He locked his own eyes into the pavement and, almost as a diversion, summoned his epilepsy to center stage. It danced there like some taunting mime, signaling that whatever he might learn from Calhoun Bledsoe in the next hour— about the gun, about the mysterious woman, about the cocaine, about Billy Rourke's demise—the epilepsy would remain. And with it the possibility—likelihood—that he faced seizures for the rest of his life. Or, if he were really lucky, merely day after day of the drug-induced semi-stupor that he felt even now. Once again this trade-off inflamed Daniel, setting off a shouting match with Dr. Loring that reached its silent apex as he arrived at Saratoga Park.

People jammed the block-long rectangle, seeking refuge from the unseasonal September heat in a forest of ancient elms. Daniel scanned the area. Almost anyone in his sweep could have been a cop: the sweating jock at the drinking fountain with the basketball under his arm, the drunk propped in the doorway across the street, the cornrow hairdo on the corner seemingly lost in the headphones of her transistor radio. With the forced confidence of someone operating on the edge, Daniel decreed that he had shaken any tail with his sudden U-turn on the Saw Mill and subsequent underground slither into Brooklyn. Besides, what did it matter? Calhoun needed him, had risked sending a messenger to get him to come as soon as possible. Calhoun certainly understood the gamble.

Daniel walked into Kimbark Street, which appeared exactly as described. On both sides most of the three-story row houses had been affectionately restored. Their steep stoops rose to polished, hand-carved wooden doors and freshly painted grillwork and gave the scene a turn-of-the-century placidity belied only by the cars lining the curbs bumper to bumper. In the middle of the block stood a house newly painted bright white, like a lone naval officer in dress uniform who had stepped into an army formation by mistake. A neatly stenciled sign underneath the first-floor window read: IT'S NICE TO BE IMPORTANT, BUT IT'S IMPORTANT TO BE NICE.

Number 482 was across the street. It looked like most of the other refurbished houses, except that no one appeared to live there. Neither curtains nor shades hung in the windows on any floor. Daniel started to look up and down the block before mounting the stoop, then decided that would only call more attention to himself. He climbed the stairs, opened the heavy front door, and entered the marble vestibule. Two brass mailboxes flanked the inside door, each name slot vacant. The ghostliness of the dwelling began to unnerve Daniel, even though he realized it made sense for Calhoun to seek a deserted hideout. What was he supposed to do, move in with his mother? Daniel tried the knob, which was unlocked, as Green Car had said it would be, and pushed into the hallway.

The transient coolness of the vestibule gave way to a stifling mustiness, and Daniel sensed that no windows had been opened for weeks. The absence of furniture in the living room and the dust marks on the walls where pictures had once hung made it clear that no one had lived here in a long while. Calhoun couldn't possibly be holed up in this part of the house; he'd suffocate. Instinctively Daniel started up, hoping the central stairway would lead to air and his quarry. But the second-floor landing proved equally claustrophobic and opened into three furnitureless bedrooms, like ovens. Of course, Daniel realized; heat rises. Try the cellar.

The basement door was right next to where the

refrigerator had been in the now barren kitchen. Daniel opened it and peered down into the blackness. "Cal?" he whispered. "Cal? It's me. I'm alone, so you can come up. Or should I come down?" Getting no response, Daniel found the light switch and started slowly down the stairs. With each step the dankness grew more pungent. "Christ, Cal, I came as fast as I could. Where are you?"

Daniel waited in vain for a reply, then stood at the bottom of the stairs and looked around in the half-light cast by the single ceiling bulb. The area had once been a den or game room, and the Beaverboard paneling had begun to pull away from the walls. Nonetheless, unlike the rest of the house, this room was sparsely furnished with chairs, a table, and a built-in pine cabinet that ran the length of one wall. In the dimness the glass pieces on top at first looked like glistening *objets*. But on closer inspection Daniel recognized the globes and pipes as freebase extraction kits—four in all. A butane torch sat among them like a missile poised to blast a cokehead into outer space. A digital gram scale rested nearby.

Daniel bent down and opened the cabinet's sliding doors. Red Contact paper neatly lined the single shelf, on which lay a pharmacopoeia of escape: cocaine ready for sale in foil packets; Quaaludes and glassine bags of heroin to cushion the crash and depression when the coke wore off; Perks; amyl nitrate capsules; amphetamines; more drugs than Daniel had ever seen in any one place. And the paraphernalia to go with them: coke spoons, hypodermic needles, syringes, toilet paper, cotton, rubbing alcohol. As he stared at this poison Daniel saw that the cabinet originally had been made to hold records, and his head suddenly filled with the taunting tenor of Sportin' Life tantalizing Bess with promises of happy dus'. This absurd intrusion of *Porgy and Bess* faded quickly, but not before the villain Crown appeared, looking exactly like Calhoun Bledsoe.

Okay, Daniel said to himself, closing the cabinet doors and standing up, let's take the worst-case analysis. Let's suppose that Calhoun *is* the bad guy in this enterprise, that he has been taking and pushing drugs, that he was more than an innocent bystander in Rourke's murder. *Then what the hell am I doing in this cellar?* If Calhoun was leading a double life— Robin Hood by day, King John by night—he certainly wouldn't have dispatched Green Car to point the way to this house. Who did? Beaupre? Daniel pummeled himself for suspecting everyone he had seen on the subway and street of trailing him but not once, until now, figuring that the gas station tipster just might have been a plainclothesman, after all. He reeled at the possibility that the cops—and even Kate— had enginered his trip.

It all began to make perfect sense. Who better to uncover the duplicitous dealings of Calhoun Bledsoe than his stanch ally Daniel Cooper, spokesman for the downtrodden and fearless reporter for *Tabula Rasa*? Beaupre knew Daniel would see it as a major scoop, even if writing it would require a certain amount of mea-culpa prose to explain how Bledsoe had managed to take him in.

Daniel now assumed the basement was bugged to record the damning conversation that would take place between the two men when Bledsoe arrived—if he ever did. He began to work his way around the room to see if he could confirm his suspicion. When he got to the entrance to the boiler room, he entered and groped along the wall and then above him but found no light; the room grew black as he moved in deeper. The furnace bulked in the dark like a dormant fire-beast. Daniel was still feeling for a light string when his foot struck something soft. He jerked his leg away, then pushed it tentatively forward again. Slowly his running shoe traced the contours of an arm, then a shoulder, a head.

Daniel ran out the doorway and across the den. He found matches on the cabinet top, lit the butane torch, and carried it back to the furnace. The body lay facedown on the dusty basement floor, white painter's pants incongruously clean. The man wore no shirt, and Daniel could see in the flickering light the skin discoloration that left no doubt that decomposition had begun. A rubber tourniquet remained knotted just above the elbow of the left arm.

Daniel bent down and set the burner beside the body, as if the flame could magically restore life, or at least reveal that he had made a mistake. But the face was clearly Calhoun's, a trace of his smile frozen at the corners of his mouth like an epitaph. Or was it instead the blissful countenance of a junkie, the sardonic legacy of the needle marks that tracked across Bledsoe's arm? The airless room became a crypt, the guttering flame casting shadows that smothered any effort to think rationally about the enormity of Calhoun's death. Daniel was trying to break through this suffocation when he heard steps in the hall upstairs. He could not decipher the muffled voices, but they carried an unmistakable tone of urgency and command. For the first time since discovering the gun in his apartment, Daniel welcomed the possibility of seeing a policeman.

"If you and Bledsoe are in the basement, Cooper, show yourselves at the bottom of the stairs. Both of you."

Daniel recognized Delvecchio's Bronx cadences. "Bledsoe's dead, Sergeant. You'd better get down here."

Delvecchio appeared on the stairs followed by a ruddy-faced, nervous young cop. They came down in a wary crouch, almost Keystone except for the .38s each held out before him. The guns locked on Daniel the second their bearers spotted him.

"Against the wall," Delvecchio ordered.

"For Christ sake, I told—"

"Do it, Cooper. Now."

Daniel looked at the weapons and turned around, taking a step back and spreading his feet. He then leaned forward and placed his palms against the Beaverboard.

"Search him," Delvecchio barked.

Ruddy-face holstered his gun and earnestly patted Daniel down. "He's clean."

"You sure?"

"Of course he's sure. Didn't you hear what I said before?" The whine Daniel detected in his voice angered him.

"Why don't you repeat it?"

"Dammit, Bledsoe's dead. Look in there." He nodded toward the furnace room door.

"Keep him on the wall," Delvecchio told the

young cop, and entered the vault. The butane flame continued to burn beside the corpse, as if a demonic rite were in progress.

"Get some flashlights down here," Delvecchio shouted. "And call an ambulance."

"What about this guy?"

"I'll take care of him."

"Do you mind if I sit down now?" Daniel said as Delvecchio reappeared and his gofer started back up the stairs.

"In a minute, pal. First it's time for your Mirandas."

"My Mirandas? What for? You've obviously been tailing me, so you know I just got here. How could I have anything to do with this? Besides, what's the charge?"

"Aggravated coincidence, maybe. I'm sure Lieutenant Beaupre will think of something. He's good at that."

Daniel stayed at his humiliating tilt as Delvecchio droned that he had the right to remain silent and have an attorney, and cautioned him that anything he said could be used against him. Though Daniel had always regarded the Miranda warnings as a bulwark of civil liberties, hearing them at this angle and in this dungeon did not prove reassuring. When Delvecchio finally let him stand up straight and turn around, it was only to snap on a pair of handcuffs.

Chapter XIV

BEAUPRE read Daniel his Mirandas again, with an edge that seemed to dare him to make trouble. On the ride in from Brooklyn, siren shrieking of the prize fettered in the backseat, Daniel considered phoning Henry Spott once they delivered him to the Twenty-fourth Precinct. Henry was his lawyer, if engineering one routine divorce conferred such status. They had been friends in high school, splashing about in Hyde Park's placid pool of noblesse oblige. That was the trouble. Henry now labored in New York for the American Civil Liberties Union, whose enthusiasm for most police practices was measured at best. He also tended toward sarcasm, which issued from behind dense facial foliage. Introducing him into this squad room would be like dropping William Kunstler into the Burger court. Daniel knew other lawyers but was not persuaded that these relative strangers would eagerly embrace his cause once he revealed his epilepsy.

Beaupre unlocked the manacles. Daniel rubbed his wrists and looked around the squad room, whose denizens seemed to regard him as something of a celebrity.

"You certainly have a genius for fucking up my weekends." Beaupre snapped a cassette into a tape recorder on the desk.

"It's not such a great one for me . . . or for Calhoun. Has anyone told his family?"

"Someone from Brooklyn's taking care of it."

Daniel imagined an anonymous cop—Ruddy-face, maybe—standing in the doorway of Mary Bledsoe's apartment, shuffling his feet and announcing that her son was dead, his eyes zooming past hers into the apartment and inviting himself in. Can I ask you a few questions? Was your Hunter-Williams-Harvard basketball star son a cokehead, Mrs. Bledsoe? Was he pushing the stuff with Billy Rourke? Did they have a falling-out? I know this is difficult, ma'am, but do you have any reason to suspect that your son might have killed Mr. Rourke? Did he ever speak to you of someone named Daniel Cooper, a reporter? Maybe the department now sent women on such missions. They could comfort the hysterical mother, embrace her, kiss her, even. Then ask the questions.

Delvecchio arrived with a meatball hero that he unwrapped on the desk. He set down his coffee and pulled up a chair.

Daniel looked at his watch. Just after six. He scanned the squad room in a vain search for a vending machine, then said, "Do only you white hats get to eat? I haven't had any food since breakfast."

"I hope the rest of your statements are more accurate than that one," Beaupre said.

"What the hell does that mean?"

"Actually you had a bag of peanuts on your way to Brooklyn. At the Columbus Circle station."

"Not bad, hey, Cooper?" Delvecchio laughed through a mouthful of meatball.

Daniel realized he had been in the cross hairs of a telescopic sight all day and felt as if someone were now about to pull the trigger. "I'm impressed, but I'm also still hungry."

Beaupre pushed his phone across the desk along with a food-stained menu from the Amsterdam Coffee Shop. "Order anything you want. It's on us. They deliver."

"And you're gonna deliver now too," Delvecchio said.

"More than you know," Daniel replied, and dialed the coffee shop. He ordered a BLT on whole wheat, an extra side of cole slaw, and a double-thick chocolate milk shake. Then, as if to purge himself utterly for the meal to come, he told the two detectives that the murder weapon was in his hamper. Their undisguised astonishment rewarded him with a flush of power that quickly faded when Delvecchio volunteered to go poke through the laundry. At Beaupre's strong urging Daniel uneasily relinquished the key to his apartment. After the sergeant departed, Beaupre appropriated the remainder of his hero and clicked on the tape recorder.

"How long have you been holding out on us?"

"Since the day after Rourke got it. Look, can't you shut that thing off and just listen to what I have to say for a minute?"

"More special privileges for the media. Okay, go ahead." Beaupre stopped the recorder, grabbed Delvecchio's coffee, and tipped back in his chair.

"I found the gun under my running clothes on the

floor of my bathroom when I came back from the doctor the day after the murder.''

"We talked at the Bellemoor that morning. You said you burned your mouth on pizza. A lie. You said the doctor's visit was just routine. A lie. You said you hadn't run the day before. A lie. Three strikes.''

"I did lie about the pizza and Dr. Loring, but not really about the running. This is hard to believe, I know, but I'm still not sure whether or not I ran the morning Rourke was killed. And I don't know how the gun got into my apartment, either.''

"No wonder you don't want me to record this. The tape would probably come out blank.'' Beaupre sipped at the coffee. "Go on.''

Like an aerialist working without a net, Daniel grabbed the bar and swung out into the void. He sketched his early history of epilepsy and described in nervously excessive detail his recent attack and memory loss.

Beaupre absorbed this information with mounting skepticism and discomfort, a hard-nosed cop faced with an implausible story but embarrassed to challenge the teller's illness. When Daniel finished, Beaupre drained the container, restarted the tape recorder and said, "Why didn't you come to us right away when you found the gun?''

"Because I was reeling from the seizure, because Rourke had barely been taken to the morgue, and here I was with the murder weapon and no explanation.''

"Just like now.''

Daniel looked at the rotating eyes of the cassette.

"Yes, Lieutenant, just like now, if that makes you happy."

A frail Puerto Rican man approached the desk, his eyes flooded with apprehension. He was about fifty and walked as if he had wandered into an operating room and feared the doctors might strap him down and remove his liver if he made one wrong move. Beaupre grunted an indifferent greeting and paid for the brown paper bag the nervous caterer deposited on the desk. Daniel reached in and pulled out the sandwich: mayonnaise oozed from between two slices of stale white bread, a bad omen.

"Reporters like to speculate," Beaupre said as the delivery man backpedaled away with his tip. "How do *you* think the gun found its way to your apartment?"

"I don't know. I really don't. I was sure Calhoun would eventually show up and explain everything. That's why I held out, especially after he got in touch the first time."

"He called you?"

"No." Daniel wondered where Kate was at the moment, what she was thinking, what her reaction would be when she heard about Calhoun. He balked at naming her, at sucking her any deeper into this maelstrom. Yet Beaupre would hardly settle for some vague response. "No. He called my friend Kate. At her office."

"And said?"

"Something about the two of us having a plan."

"You and Bledsoe? What kind of a plan?"

Daniel shook his head. "I simply don't know. Whatever it was, he asked Kate why I hadn't followed through on it. And he also told her it was urgent that I track down some woman. He implied to Kate that this person could explain a lot, maybe everything. She asked who it was, but Calhoun assured her that I'd know, and then hung up.''

"Who is this woman?"

"I haven't a clue, Lieutenant."

"Or to what this so-called 'plan' might have been?"

"Right. No idea."

"Had Miss Bernstein ever met Bledsoe?"

"No."

"Or heard his voice?"

"Not until that day."

"So we're not even sure it was Bledsoe who called her—if *anyone* did."

"Hey. I'm here. I'm cooperating. I haven't complicated your life by making waves with a lawyer. I've told you about the gun. Why would I lie about the phone call?"

"Please. You sound as if you just showed up here today to deliver a lecture on how we can improve our relations with the press. In case you've forgotten, you're here because we collared you in close proximity to another corpse. You've lied before, so you'll pardon me if I don't rule out the possibility that you're lying now about the phone call. Okay?"

Daniel started to challenge Beaupre to put the question directly to Kate, but he didn't want to drag her into this den. More than that, he was beginning to lose confidence in himself. He had tried not to let the seizure's shock waves drown him: by resuming his running, by probing Dr. Loring for hard answers, by bearding Steven Bromley in his rookery to prove to himself that he could still muster his faculties in a

tough situation. Even after Delvecchio nailed him
with Calhoun's body, he remained convinced he could
somehow maintain the upper hand, that he could
extricate himself with the same skills that had served
him so well over the years as a reporter. *Just use
your bean, Daniel; keep boring in with the right
questions.* Only he was beginning to think his head
might really be on the fritz. And even if it wasn't,
what did it matter? They now commanded the tape
recorder and were asking all the questions.

"Let's concede it was Bledsoe who called her.
You say that was his first contact. When did he get in
touch again?" Beaupre asked.

"Today, for God's sake. You know that. You just
finished telling me how you've been on my ass since
I brushed my teeth this morning."

"I'd like to hear your version, if it's not too much
trouble."

Daniel listened to the faint whir of the recorder as
he described his encounter with the man in the green
car on the Saw Mill River Parkway. He told the truth
with the desperate sincerity he had once used to try to
win over Miss Broctl, the guidance counselor at Ray
Elementary School, when she confronted him with
some now forgotten recess transgression. She had
seemed doubtful too.

"You never laid eyes on this guy before?"

"Never. We assumed he was a cop from the minute we spotted him following us."

"And your friend just happened to be in the ladies'
when he made his cameo appearance?"

Daniel nodded and reluctantly took another bite of
his cardboard BLT.

"Someone must have seen you. What about the station attendant?"

"I used the self-service pump. He was in the office." Daniel censored "watching television," then looked into the floor and said the words, hoping that by volunteering this further piece of inconvenient information he would persuade Beaupre he was not lying.

"We've got a pretty good TV show here ourselves. Two stiffs. Lots of drugs. A mystery voice. A mystery woman. And now a mystery man." Beaupre frowned, then looked evenly at Daniel. "Plus a gun you claim traveled the better part of a block all by itself. Maybe it's time to call in Cagney and Lacey for help."

"What about the tail you had on us? They must have seen me talking to the guy."

"Those TV ladies probably would have. We real-life types tend to be less efficient. Hanging back out of sight on the shoulder when you pulled into the station. Amateur stuff like that. Our boys did manage to stay with you, though, when you burned that illegal U-turn on the parkway and cracked seventy getting back to the Bronx. That's two moving violations right there. Useful for openers if we decide to keep you around for a while." Beaupre suddenly stood. "Keep an eye on this guy," he said to a plainclothesman sifting through a bureaucratic mound at the adjacent desk.

Daniel watched his inquisitor move off and wondered if he knew he had broken the law by driving in the wake of his seizure. He looked across the room at the lockup as other "useful" charges came to mind, not the least of them withholding key evidence in a criminal investigation. Two sullen black men in their early twenties gripped the bars and stared him down. He rummaged through his conscience for the reflexive sympathy he usually found for such victims of the skewed criminal justice system. But all he saw when he sheepishly returned their gaze were two toughs in head rags who looked as if they would like nothing better than to have a honky to toy with in their cage. From the doorway of the squad room two other sets of eyes fixed Daniel. Delvecchio had returned from 329, and as he spoke to Beaupre they both observed their catch with what seemed like new hostility. Daniel began to think more seriously about calling Henry Spott, fearing now that he had delayed too long and would not be able to reach him on this Saturday evening.

Beaupre disappeared down the stairs, and Delvecchio walked back toward Daniel, inspecting the few remains of his hero as he parked himself on the edge of the desk.

"This weapon you say you found—what did it look like?" he asked, as if firing the question from a gun himself.

"I don't know. Bulky, sort of. With a bluish finish. And the grip had some kind of diamond design."

"What kind was it?"

"I told you before. A .45."

"How do you know? You don't strike me as much of a gun fancier."

Daniel suppressed a strong impulse to say "Fuck you." "I saw it on Rourke's permit. He showed it to me when he showed me the gun, during an interview at the Bellemoor.''

"When was that?"

"When I was working on my series about the building. In July."

"He just presented the gun and permit for your inspection?"

"He liked to show people what a tough customer he was. Especially if they were weak and he had the drop on them. But that never seemed to interest the police."

"We're not in the real estate business. How do you know the gun you found is Rourke's?"

The question irritated Daniel, but he knew it was part of the game. He had spent enough time around cops to know that playing dumb was a chief trick in their bag of amateur psychology. He forced out a dollop of patience and said, "Because, Sergeant, I recognized it."

"Maybe it was another gun, same model."

"And maybe it was a cap pistol. But it's not, so stop jerking me around. You know that 45-caliber bullets killed Rourke, and Beaupre's been speculating right from the start that they were from his own gun. Well, now you've got it. So just get ballistics—"

"It wasn't there, Cooper."

"—to match them up . . . what?"

"The gun. It wasn't there. Just undies in the hamper." Delvecchio removed himself from the corner of the desk and sat down in Beaupre's chair.

"Bullshit. It has to be there."

Delvecchio leaned back, folded his arms across his chest, and shook his head.

More cop psych, Daniel thought. But to what end? What did they hope to learn by pretending the gun wasn't there? He was leveling with them, revealing all secrets—except, of course, those still hidden behind the epileptic shroud that descended eight days ago. He strained yet again to penetrate those lost hours; he would now gladly spread them on the desk for Delvecchio, some winning cards at last. But his hand remained a bust.

"When did you last see it?" the sergeant asked.

Daniel realized he had not bothered to check the hamper since showing the gun to Kate two days ago.

"Thursday afternoon," he said.

"What about this morning? Did you check before you left for the country?"

"No."

"Why not?"

"I don't know. Who the hell could have gotten in? Had the door been forced?"

"Not a chance."

"Then someone must have used a key."

"Like who?"

"I don't know. The only extra set of keys I have is on the board in the package room off the lobby. The board's kept locked, but the doormen have a key."

"So someone just waltzed up to your doorman and asked for the key to your apartment? Come on, you can do better than that."

Yes he could. Maybe during his attack he had simply handed over his door key to someone who then went to the hardware store on Columbus Avenue and had a copy made. He could have had the original back in half an hour. Daniel did not offer up this scenario.

"Did your lady friend have a key?"

Kate floated by like a spar, and Daniel realized that this time he had to grab hold. "No, she didn't. But she saw the gun in the hamper. I showed it to her."

"When?"

"The last time I saw it. Thursday. She was furious and made me promise to turn it in, which I planned to do on Monday." Daniel paused, then suggested, reluctantly, "Ask her."

"We already have." Beaupre had materialized behind Daniel, who swiveled his head around as the lieutenant added, "She's downstairs."

"Here. Shit. She's an innocent bystander. Did you have to yank her in?"

"Bystander?" Delvecchio scoffed. "More like an accomplice, if you—"

"We didn't 'yank her in,' " Beaupre interrupted. "She came of her own accord. She actually seems rather worried about you."

"About me? What about her? She has no business in this mess."

"You should have thought of that before showing her the gun," Beaupre said.

"Then she told you. So now you know the gun was there," Daniel said.

"We know you both *say* it was there," Delvecchio said.

Daniel deflected the remark and instead began worrying about what else Kate had told these men. He loved her for her lack of guile, her determination to see things clearly and honestly. He now envisioned her isolated downstairs in some tacky, neon-lit chamber, easy—even willing—prey to these detectives' fake friendly routine. He pictured her frank eyes and heard her troubled voice telling the truth: about the fears he had expressed that he might have killed Rourke himself; about his growing suspicion that Calhoun might not have been the unblemished hero he had exalted in *Tabula Rasa*. Doubtless there were other incriminating areas they had explored with her, but in his sudden fatigue he couldn't get his brain to focus on them.

"How long are you going to keep her here?" he asked.

"She's free to leave now, but she wants to see you," Beaupre replied.

"Is that okay?"

"Your choice." Beaupre raised his eyebrows and spread open his hands.

Daniel descended the stairs in lockstep between the two cops, assuming angrily that they would insist on sitting in on this reunion. But when they reached the first floor, Beaupre gave a nod of consent toward Kate, who stood alone a few feet in front of the desk sergeant's high oak dais. She had replaced her country jeans and sweatshirt with a maroon skirt and yellow silk blouse; her smile embraced him and combined with her familiar perfume, pushing him to the point of kissing her. But he held back, aware that any emotion in this display case would only bind him closer to Kate in the eyes of his interrogators. In a forced avuncular fashion he curled an arm around her waist and guided her to a bench against the wall.

Delvecchio waited until they were out of range, then turned angrily to Beaupre. "Why are you treating those two like little lost lambs, Frenchie?"

"Calm down, Sam. They're cooperating."

"Some cooperation. He tells us where to find the gun, only it don't happen to be there when we look. I know you feel sorry for the guy because of this epilepsy stuff, but I'm not sure I buy it. He says he had a fit the morning Rourke was killed. How do we know? His doctor, what's his name, Loren, Lawson—"

"Loring."

"Yeah, Loring. When he finally agreed to talk to me, he mostly claimed doctor-patient privilege. All he'd say is that Cooper had a *history* of epilepsy and that it was well controlled. Did Cooper tell you this was the first attack he'd had since he was a kid?"

"No."

"Well, according to Loring it was. Pretty convenient, don't you think?"

Beaupre started to interrupt, but Delvecchio had no intention of yielding the floor.

"I'll tell you something else," he said. "The good doctor admitted that short of witnessing a fit, there is no way even a neurologist can prove it took place."

"If he didn't have the attack, where did he get the bloody lip and the limp I saw when he came to the Bellemoor?"

"Fighting with Rourke before he killed him?"

"And Miss Bernstein is in on all this? She says she was with him when he had the attack."

"Maybe she was, maybe she wasn't. Come on, Frenchie, you didn't see her performance on the running track last Saturday, screaming epilepsy this and epilepsy that after Cooper took his spill. Only trouble was, neither the intern who happened to be on the scene or the doctor who patched him up at Mt. Sinai thought he tripped because he had a fit. Besides, even if she actually was at Cooper's apartment, she didn't get there until after three in the afternoon, by her own admission. Rourke was murdered early that morning. And how do we know Cooper took those pills you snatched for epilepsy? Phenobarb has lots of other uses, as you know. I think all of 'em were into drug action: Rourke, Bledsoe, Cooper, *and* the broad.''

Beaupre looked across the room at the two surviving members of the foursome. ''I think you may be right, that Cooper did shoot Rourke,'' he said. ''But for the moment, at least, I'm inclined to believe his epilepsy story. I think he just may have killed him without realizing it. The way Torsney shot that kid.''

Delvecchio started to protest, then shrugged. ''Okay, boss, like Torsney. But either way, Cooper's our man. I can feel it in my corns.''

Beaupre laughed. ''What do your corns tell you about the elusive gun?''

''That Mr. Lambykins over there on the bench knows exactly where it is right now. So don't let him wander too far this time.''

Daniel now sat holding Kate's hand.

''Not exactly a weekend in the country,'' he said.

''Was it awful?''

''They told you about Calhoun?''

Kate nodded. He shut his eyes and watched, as if from a helicopter, as he and Calhoun circled the reservoir on their morning run. Then the black man disappeared, at last transmuting the body in the furnace room from the police blotter to the death of a friend.

"He was a rare man. Not an ounce of bullshit." Daniel pushed aside the possibility of drugs and added, "Are you okay?"

"Yes. They've treated me very well. Lieutenant Beaupre even sent a car for me."

"How gallant. Did *you* call them?" Daniel instantly regretted the question.

"Yes I did, Daniel. Not right away. After I got home. I felt helpless. I was frightened for you. I thought you were getting in way too deep by yourself." Kate dropped his hand and edged away slightly. "I also told them about the gun."

Daniel laughed. "So did I. And guess what?"

"What?"

"Our hosts tell me it isn't there anymore."

Kate tilted her head back. "They didn't tell me that."

"Delvecchio just went and looked, after I fessed up."

"And it wasn't in the hamper?"

"That's what the man said."

Kate looked less astonished than skeptical, of whom Daniel was not quite sure. Did she share his view that their captors might have staged a disappearing act for some reason, or did she suspect that he was the prestidigitator? "You moved that gun yourself," he imagined her accusing. "You were afraid I'd tell the police where it was before you could wrap up this case yourself."

Instead she said, "Daniel, I know this isn't something you want to hear, but isn't it just possible that you had another attack and put the gun somewhere else without realizing it?"

"That's fucking ridiculous," Daniel shouted. "Whose side are you on?"

"Yours, but—"

"But nothing. I know *some*thing about epilepsy. You don't have a seizure without realizing it afterward. Petit mal blinks, maybe. A second or two. But more than that you know something's cockeyed when you come out of it."

"But you were the only one who could get in the apartment."

"How do you—"

"Daniel, calm down."

"—know? I've been away all day today and was out several hours yesterday when I went to see Bromley." Daniel glanced across the room to see if his tantrum had attracted Beaupre. It had. He lowered his voice and shifted down.

"I'm sorry," he said. "I'm just exhausted. But your theory's wrong. If that gun really is missing, I had nothing to do with it."

"Who, then?"

"I'm not sure. But I'd like to explore some possibilities."

"What possibilities?"

"We can't go into that now. Will you do me a favor?"

Kate started to say "Of course," then scaled down her response to the barest nod.

"Beaupre says you can leave here. Go. And when

you get home, sit down at your typewriter right away and try to reconstruct your telephone conversation with Calhoun."

"I've already told you everything." She paused. "And the lieutenant too."

"Not necessarily. Start with the moment the phone rang. Go after every detail. The sound of his voice. The background noises. Everything. You'll be surprised at what you've retained once you start concentrating. I do this all the time after an interview when I don't take notes. Believe me, it works."

"Daniel, you're a professional reporter."

"We're no smarter than anyone else, only nosier. Do it, Kate. Try to remember every syllable he uttered about the plan he said he had and this woman I'm supposed to find. Don't leave anything out, even your speculation. The tiniest shred may help us."

"I really don't think I'll come up with anything new."

"Just try, Kate, that's all I ask."

"What should I do with it when I'm finished?"

"Hang on to it. They can't keep me here forever."

"They won't put you in jail, will they?"

"Overnight, maybe. Don't worry, I'll be fine."

"Won't you need your medicine?"

Don't forget to take your pills. Daniel seethed as his father's persistent reminder unfurled. "If they can send a car for you, they can send one for my medicine," he said sharply.

Kate recoiled, then offered, "I don't mind bringing it."

"Please, I don't need a nurse. I need your help on the phone call."

"Okay, I'll try." Kate rose from beside him.

Daniel wanted to apologize for this second outburst but could not summon the energy. He ached to lie down and, if it came to that, was prepared to spend the night on a lockup mattress if Beaupre and Delvecchio would just leave him alone for a few hours. Maybe he'd even get lucky and the two present tenants would be sprung by the time they tucked him in. He walked Kate back to the oak rostrum.

"Are you ready to go, miss?" Beaupre said.

Kate nodded and looked apprehensively at Daniel. "Does he have to stay?" she said to the assembled authority.

"I'm afraid so," the lieutenant said. "Sergeant Delvecchio will take you home."

Daniel no longer cared if these men witnessed his affection for Kate, but his move to kiss her good-bye came an instant too late; her escort had abruptly started ushering her out to his patrol car. Daniel watched them disappear, then looked up at the anonymous desk sergeant, a robeless judge on his high seat. Beaupre, the prosecutor, pointed to the exit.

"You can go out that door tonight too," he said.

"Downtown, you mean?"

"No, home. In fact, let's take a stroll now and talk it over."

The ploy was no less effective for its obviousness. Once on the sidewalk in the orange dusk, Daniel felt the sights and sounds of freedom eroding what little resistance he had left. Even the racket of competing street radios, which he usually loathed, lifted his spirits.

"Let's walk toward the park," Beaupre said.

"Aren't you afraid of getting mugged, Officer?"

Beaupre smiled. "Okay, comedian, here's the deal. One, we want to search your apartment tomorrow morning. First thing. We don't want to waste a lot of time getting a warrant. You just cooperate. I say, 'Cooper, we need to search your apartment for the gun and any other clues that might prove helpful.' You say, 'Why, of course, Lieutenant, be my guest.' "

"Why not? I'll serve brunch. How do your men like their eggs?"

"Two, I've arranged for you to have a complete examination up at Columbia–Presbyterian. At their Neurological Institute."

"Not a chance. You can snoop around my apartment tomorrow, but butt out of my medical problems."

"Whether you like it or not, I'm afraid your medical problems have become my medical problems for the moment. Or have you forgotten that you just told me you can't account for some rather important hours on the day Rourke was killed?"

"So ask my doctor to tell you about my epilepsy."

"Loring? He's insisting on doctor-patient privilege. Anyway, I want an independent opinion."

"Independent? How is someone you guys bring in independent?"

"This neurologist—a Dr. Havighurst—was recommended by the New York State Epilepsy Association. I'm not trying to set you up, I'm trying to get some information."

They had reached Central Park West. Daniel could see the bright blue canopy of 329 six blocks to the south. Whatever fury he felt at this cop's outrageous invasion of his privacy dissipated in the tantalizing proximity of his piano, his kitchen, his bed, the enveloping texture of his home. He also found himself suddenly drawn to the idea of seeing a new neurologist. He had sensed Kate's antipathy to Dr. Loring from the beginning and had now lost confidence in him himself.

"When am I supposed to see this doctor?"

"As soon as possible next week. You call to set up the appointment. Here's the number." Beaupre pulled a phone slip from his billfold.

"You know, you have absolutely no right to make me do any of this."

"I'm asking, Cooper, not making. You can call your lawyer anytime. I'll give you the quarter."

"And if I go along with the exam?"

"You get to sleep in your own bed tonight. And because tomorrow's Sunday, we won't be around until at least nine A.M."

"How could I possibly resist such a generous offer?"

Beaupre started down Central Park West. "Come on, I'll walk with you. It's a nice night. I don't get outside much."

Chapter XV

"THERE'S some real estate I'd really like to get my hands on." Steven Bromley leaned against a naked I beam and gazed into the harbor.

"Governors Island? Don't that belong to the Federales?"

"I'm afraid so, Juice; it used to be an Army base, but now the Coast Guard's got it. Ever been over there?"

Frank Brennan shook his head, shifted the Skoal in his cheek, and spattered his nickname on the newly laid concrete of the twenty-first floor.

"You should. Take the family. They hold open house on Armed Forces Day. I went last spring. It's the greatest piece of land in New York. Half the place is like a New England village. You see that fort in the middle of the island?"

"Yeah."

"All that grass around it is a nine-hole golf course. Just a ten-minute ferry ride from Wall Street. Turn those redbrick barracks into condominiums and renovate the Victorian houses around the common and, presto, Governors Estates; call Bromley-Keller for an appointment. There's an old officers' club too. Perfect for a first-class restaurant. I'd have them swimming out there to sign up.''

"I hear Reagan has deficit problems. Maybe he'd sell you the island cheap.''

"What would I do with the Coast Guard?''

"Put 'em in a welfare hotel. They don't do nothin' important.''

Bromley smiled and moved toward the open edge of the floor. Below, a Circle Line boat began curving around the tip of the Battery, its deck awash in sunlight and Sunday tourists. He would have preferred to be out on the water himself, sailing the *Pygmalion* on Long Island Sound. But the Lighthouse, Bromley-Keller's first monument in the business precincts of Lower Manhattan, was six floors behind schedule—despite hundreds of thousand of dollars in overtime for weekend crews. Bromley turned into the wind, which blew through a labyrinth of wood shoring and electrical conduits. A dozen hard hats sat eating their lunch amid acetylene tanks and uninstalled aluminum ducts. They pulled on beer cans and eyed Bromley cautiously as he stepped around a giant spool of yellow wire and confronted his—and their—superintendent.

"Don't try to con me, Juice. Are we going to make it?''

"Have I ever let you down, Mr. Bromley? The skin'll be up on this baby before the snows come. You can count on it.''

Bromley looked around at the idle diners.

Brennan spat again. "Hey, it's lunchtime. You want me to get in trouble with the union?''

"What I want is the skin up on this building by the middle of December. If it isn't, I'll install you as head of the carpenters' union."

Brennan laughed. This was one of their running jokes. Three officials of that union had been murdered in recent years, including a president charged with conspiring with organized crime to rig bids and extort money from contractors.

"I appreciate the offer, Mr. B., but I think I'll stick with Bromley-Keller, if you don't mind."

"Then make sure these guys get off their butts after lunch. At the bell." Bromley turned up the volume to make sure his audience knew the heat was coming from the top. He didn't want the men souring on Brennan; he was a good superintendent, especially at maintaining smooth relations with the assorted hoods who milked the construction trades. His contacts in the mob seemed to like his beery Irish blarney, and buildings did not go up in New York City without such diplomacy.

"Come in, Top Hat, this is security; come in, Top Hat."

Brennan squatted and picked his radio off the concrete. "Yeah, security, this is Top Hat. What's shakin'?"

"Some guy down here wants to see Mr. Bromley."

Brennan looked up at his boss to see if the message had pierced the static and wind.

"Find out who it is," Bromley said, bending closer to the radio.

"Identify visitor, security," Brennan ordered.

"Says his name is Williams and that he has some information on the Rourke killing."

Conversation among the hard hats subsided as Bromley replied, "Tell him that's police business. Lieutenant Beaupre at the Twenty-fourth Precinct."

Brennan relayed the message.

"Negative. He'll only talk to Mr. Bromley."

"What's this guy look like?" Brennan shot back.

"Pretty shaky. A bottle baby's my guess."

"Jesus, a Sunday drunk. I'll go down and kick this guy's ass, Mr. B. Don't worry."

"No, Juice. I'll go. Maybe he actually knows something. You never can tell."

"What if he—"

"He sounds harmless enough. If he's not, then the security guard can earn what I pay him." Bromley stepped into the hoist that ran outside the construction's skeleton. "I'll be right up again; we still have a lot of ground to cover this afternoon. I want to see that luncheon club hard at it when I get back too."

"Like Trojans, Mr. B. The skin may even be up by then." Brennan grinned and juiced again, as the hoist jolted into its descent.

On the ground, Bromley threaded his way through more lounging workers to a temporary wooden security shack near the half-finished lobby. As he entered, the guard jumped to attention from behind his desk, a military response subverted by his coffee-stained uniform, the week's worth of takeout debris that littered the room and the hard rock blaring from twin speakers on a massive Panasonic. He shut it off like a private caught goldbricking by the post commander and pointed nervously to the man seated next to the blueprint table.

"Mr. Williams?" Bromley said.

The man nodded, the forward tilt of his head threatening to pull the rest of him off the chair and onto the floor. He braced trembling hands on his knees and pushed himself back, revealing eyes so bloodshot that they seemed incapable of sight. Despite the warm weather, he wore a brown leather cap, which gave an incongruous measure of swagger to his otherwise sad and sagging countenance. He began running his hands down his emaciated frame, as if washing his clothes and body to make himself more presentable. He stared up at Bromley for several seconds, clearly confused to see a man wearing boots, a blue denim work shirt and a hard hat. Finally he said, "You're the boss of this place?"

"Yes. Steven Bromley."

"The one the TV said is giving out all that reward money?"

"For the right information. How did you know you could find me here today?"

"That new man at the Bellemoor tol' me."

"Ross?"

"I don't know his name. He runs us, like that dead one use to. Mr. Rourke."

"You live in the Bellemoor?"

"Uh-huh."

"Now?"

Williams nodded, again righting himself with quivering hands. "Would you really pay all that money to me?" he asked, his voice thick with the plea.

"That depends on what you tell me and what the police think of it."

"What I mean is, if my fac's is good ones, would you give the reward to somebody like me?"

Bromley smiled faintly, then caught the guard sniggering at his black brother's obsequiousness. "What's your name?" he asked, swinging around.

"Davis, sir."

"Do you have the keys to the model apartment, Davis?"

"Yes, sir." The guard pointed to the wall hooks behind his desk.

"Well, hand them to me. Mr. Williams and I will finish our talk over there while you clean up this pigsty." After pocketing the keys Bromley added, "Tell Mr. Brennan that I may be longer than I thought and that when I do get back up there, I want to go over the delays on the cooling tower."

"Yes, sir, Mr. Bromley." The guard swept a half-eaten Danish and its wrapper off the edge of the desk into a wastebasket.

Bromley turned back to Williams. "Of course someone like you can have the reward. Anyone can have it if he really helps us catch whoever killed Mr. Rourke. So let's go hear what you have to say."

Williams gripped the arms of the chair and pushed himself up, struggling to balance on unsteady legs. Outside, the workers slowly returned to their tasks and paused in collective perplexity as their patron crossed the site and entered the model apartment with a wobbly black derelict.

"Hey, looks like Mr. Bromley's getting into the numbers," said one hard hat.

"Don't be stupid, you candy ass. He's in there buying up Harlem for a case of Thunderbird."

"You're the candy ass. Thunderbird don't come by the case."

"Okay. For a couple of bottles. That nigger looked like he'd settle for anything."

The men's laughter filtered into the living room as Bromley slid open the windows to let in some air. A Bloomingdale's Japanese screen covered the wall opposite, a tapestry of people and animals in brightly lacquered blacks, reds, and greens. A beige sectional sofa anchored one corner of the room, strewn strategically with a half dozen pillows covered in red or black Oriental silk. A delicate porcelain Chinese ashtray rested in the center of a smoked glass coffee table. Thick beige carpeting stretched to all walls, themselves covered in beige paper patterned with silver Japanese characters. A potted ficus tree sat catercorner from the sofa and coffee table.

"You lives here too?" Williams said, hanging back in the narrow hallway.

"No, this is just for show." Bromley tossed his hard hat into the corner of the sofa and sat down. "This model gives perspective buyers an idea of what their apartments could look like furnished." Bromley patted the cushion. "Come on in and sit down."

Williams took several hesitant steps forward, then peered anxiously through the doorway opening on the dining room. Another glass table, this one surrounded by bamboo chairs, was set for six, the black plates handpainted with gold peacocks. Black napkins fanned out next to fluted champagne glasses at each setting.

"Relax, Mr. Williams. No one's coming to dinner. We're alone. That's why I came here. Now what have you come to tell me?"

Williams moved uncertainly toward the sofa. "If I

wins that twenty-five-thousand reward money, I could get me an apartment like this, ain't that right?''

"Absolutely," Bromley said, seeing no point in deflating his guest with the two hundred and fifty thousand dollars starting price for one-bedroom apartments. "But you don't have the reward yet, and you don't stand a chance of getting it unless you start talking. Do you know who killed Mr. Rourke?''

"I ain't too clean. You sure it's okay if I sits down?''

"Yes, yes, you're fine. Please."

Williams eased himself onto the edge of the sofa farthest from Bromley and shook his head. "No, I don't know who shot Mr. Rourke, but I think my chil' knows.''

"Your child? What do you mean?''

She began acting very strange-like after that morning, like she know'd something.''

"The morning Rourke was killed? Like what?''

"I don't know. I tried to beat it out of her, but that girl's real stubborn. Like her slut of a mother. She know'd something, though; I could tell.''

This cast of characters—the drunken father who beat his daughter, the whoring mother—suddenly came into focus for Bromley. He pushed the pillows aside and slid closer to Williams.

"Do you remember a reporter named Daniel Cooper?'' he asked.

"A reporter? You mean like them people on TV?''

"No. He writes for a paper called *Tabula Rasa*. Mr. Rourke told me he gave you and your daughter a hard time at the Bellemoor last summer. A thin man, about six feet tall. Dark hair.''

Williams strained to embrace the description. Finally he said, "I remembers. But I didn't think he was no reporter. He acted more like from the welfare office, comin' in the apartment and ordering me how to treat Bernice. He said he'd get the police on me."

"Do you think your daughter—Bernice, is it?—do you think Bernice saw Cooper the morning of the murder?"

Williams shrugged. "Could be. She surely saw something, I knows that."

"How old is Bernice?"

"About seven. Old enough to always make trouble."

"I know what that's like. I have daughters myself, Mr. Williams; what's your first name?"

"Jones."

"Jones, I'd like to talk to Bernice. Would you mind? If she really did see something, as you say, that could provide the break the police are looking for."

"And I'd get the money?"

"Since your daughter's a minor, you certainly would."

Williams thrust his hands between his thighs to stop their shaking and, for the first time, looked directly at Bromley, helplessly.

"She's gone," he said.

"She's not back at the Bellemoor? Where is she?"

"With my sister."

"Well, I'll talk to her at your sister's."

"I don't know where they is."

"You don't know where your own sister lives?"

Williams shook his head and stared into his lap, where his hands remained locked. "She used to be at the Bellemoor on the same floor with me, but Mr. Rourke, he put her out. Her two kids too. They all prob'bly in some other welfare hotel now, but I don't know which one.''

"You're sure Bernice is with her?''

"Most likely. She came and got her about a week ago. Says I don't know how to take care of my own daughter.''

"What's your sister's name?''

"Carrie. Carrie Williams. She's had a couple of husbands, but she keeps Williams.''

"And her kids? How old are they, what are their names?''

A tug horn sounded on the river as Jones Williams squirmed under this interrogation. He looked into his lap again and said, "The boy, he's about fourteen; they calls him Jimbob.''

"Is that his real name, or is it James or Robert?''

Williams looked blank.

"Christ, well, what about the other one?''

"Clara. I knows her name is Clara, after our mother.''

"How old?" Bromley demanded.

"Younger.''

"By how much?''

"Two years, 'bout, I guess.''

Bromley cursed under his breath and got off the sofa. He went into the dining room, picked up two goblets from the table, and entered the streamlined kitchen. He hoped someone had stashed a few cans of beer in the refrigerator, but it was empty. He slammed the door and tried the sink tap, which produced no water.

"I'm sorry," he said, returning to the sofa: "I wanted to offer you something to drink, some water at least; but the plumbing hasn't been hooked up yet."

"That's all right. I's used to it. We ain't had no water at the Bellemoor for a long time now."

Bromley scrutinized his guest for irony but found none. He sat down again and said, "We've got to locate your daughter as soon as possible."

"Then I gets the reward?"

"Yes. Yes. Now the first thing tomorrow morning I want you to go to the welfare office and start looking for your sister. Be there when it opens. Do you know where to go?"

Williams nodded. "But they don't likes me there."

"Why not?"

"They say I don't treat Bernice no good. But I say a chil's got to be kep' in line if—"

"Tell them it's an emergency. You don't want her to move back in with you. You just need to know where she is. Tell them her mother wants her to visit her."

"They don't give a shit. . . ." Williams looked at Bromley apologetically for this lapse. "They don't care about no one like me at that place. But if an impo'tant man like you tol' them to find Bernice, they'd find her right off."

"No, Jones, you're her father. You have to do it. And right away. Tomorrow morning."

"Maybe if I tol' them the police wanted to talk to Bernice, that would—"

"No, not yet. If you want the reward, I have to talk to Bernice first. Then we'll all go to the police.

That's how these things work. Do you need any money now?'' Bromley reached into the pocket of his work shirt and pulled out a silver B-K money clip thick with bills.

''Well, I—''

Bromley unfolded five twenties and handed them across the sofa. Williams grasped them eagerly but found it impossible to put them in any crevice of his foul clothing, as if doing so would deflate their value.

''Remember, that's not for booze. If you want the reward, you've got to stay away from the bottle. The welfare people aren't going to help you find Bernice if you show up drunk tomorrow.''

''You're surely right 'bout that.'' Williams tightened his grip on the money.

''As soon as you've talked to them in the morning, I want you to call me. This is my number at the office.'' Bromley extracted a card from his other shirt pocket and handed it over.

Williams examined the tiny rectangle as if it were a passport with which he could at last cross over into the white man's world. He wrapped the bills around the card and shifted the damp wad to his other perspiring fist.

''I'll stay sober. No way am I gonna get drunk now.''

''Good. Now I've got to get back to work up top. But I'm counting on you to call me tomorrow.''

Bromley stood up and watched with embarrassment as Williams, trapped in the soft cushions of the sofa, struggled without success to rise. Finally he reluctantly took Williams's sweaty hand and pulled the man to his feet. Out in the bright afternoon sunshine the hard hats now energized the site. But Bromley did not notice as he guided Williams to the sidewalk and watched him waver toward the subway, the passport clutched in his hand.

Chapter XVI

D ANIEL awoke from the sleep portion of his EEG to find Debbie Beckwith bending over him, her titian hair falling into his face. She smiled and met his mouth, tracing his lips with her tongue and, like a sorceress, magically exorcising his drug-induced grogginess. She turned off the machine, locked the door, and slowly unzipped her white nurse's uniform. Even in the darkened room he could see that her runner's body was everything he had imagined: long, muscular legs rising to a taut stomach, beneath which more red curls interlaced the frilled edges of black satin panties, erect nipples punctuating her matching bra. He tried to reach around and unhook her, but she gently pushed him back into the reclining chair. Caressing his face with one hand, she pulled away the blanket with the other and loosened his belt. She did not speak, but her touch seemed to say, "You deserve this, Daniel." And then he was arching his hips as she took him lovingly in her mouth, liberating him with an orgasm of miraculous duration. Only in its final tremor did Daniel reconnect with Kate, in whose bed he lay.

He reached down, took her head in his hands, and pulled her up toward him, still quivering as her naked breasts pressed against his chest. He felt he should confess his fantasy, which seemed cruelly disloyal in the heat of her unselfish ardor. He wanted to return her lust in kind, too, to fuck her silly, as she had pleaded at the apogee of their first night together a month ago. But already his troubles began crowding out any further thoughts of sex, with women real or imagined. He kissed her and cradled her face against his neck, looking up at the ceiling fan as it stirred what little night air came through the window. Four candles flickered in the room, enveloping the hanging plants in a forest of shadows and shimmering in the tarnished mirror set in the bed's antique oak headboard. "My sanctuary," Kate had said when she ushered him in. Daniel hugged her tightly but did not feel safe.

"If you're a very good boy and promise not to obsess about Topic A for the rest of the evening, we can do that again when you recuperate. You sounded as if you liked it." Kate rolled over onto her side and ran a finger down his belly.

"You are the best. Just incredible." Tears welled in Daniel's eyes as he turned and began kissing her nipples.

"Relax, sweetie." Kate cushioned his head against her. "I'll settle for some of your patented back scratching."

"You're sure?"

"Yes. I love it, you know that." Kate presented her back.

Daniel spooned around her, moving his lips up her

spine and burying his face in her sweet-smelling hair. With the index finger of his left hand he spelled out "I love you" across her smooth, pale shoulder. Kate wriggled her warm body deeper into his as a siren sounded down the street and the details of that morning's search came flooding back.

"What's up there?" Delvecchio pointed to the closet shelf.

"Just my tax records," Daniel replied.

"Get 'em down."

Daniel brought the stepladder into the bedroom from the kitchen and did as ordered, handing the two heavy cardboard boxes to the sergeant, who summarily dumped their dusty contents on the bed. Several ancient, frayed rubber bands snapped, pieing checks and receipts across the quilt. Delvecchio pawed through the material, jumbling it further, then motioned Daniel off the ladder and mounted it himself to explore the upper reaches of the closet. Daniel started for the living room to tell Beaupre he'd had it, but the lieutenant had problems of his own. His ex-wife had tracked him to Daniel's phone and wanted to know just when the hell he planned to pick up his son for their Sunday outing.

Beaupre and Delvecchio had arrived just after nine, two fingerprint men in tow. While these technicians began dusting in the bathroom the detectives started poking into every corner of the apartment. Daniel prepared no eggs but did serve coffee, which Delvecchio sloshed onto the strings of the sounding board while probing the Steinway's innards for the gun. With a perfunctory "Sorry," he moved on to an invasion of the desk. While Daniel cleaned up the spill Beaupre crawled about inspecting the undersides of the living room furniture, after which he removed the sofa cushions and shook them out of their slip-covers. When he walked swiftly into the kitchen, Daniel fully expected him to return with a knife to slice open the pillows. But he had only shifted his hunt, rattling through cupboards, the stove, the dishwasher, the refrigerator. By the time the former Mrs. Beaupre called, it was almost noon, and Daniel felt as if he had been gang-raped.

"Did you guys find any whorls that weren't mine?" he asked as the fingerprint cops packed up their kits.

"You're not here as a reporter, Cooper," Delvecchio cut in, "so let's skip the questions."

Daniel reconstructed the sofa and sat down, steeling himself for further interrogation now that the search was apparently over. In particular, he expected some curiosity about his visit to Steven Bromley on Friday, a subject that had come up only briefly last night. No questions of any kind followed, however, whether because Beaupre's fatherly duty called or for a more threatening reason Daniel could not be sure. He wondered if they had tightened the case against him overnight, if this visit was aimed at cinching matters with evidence Beaupre knew was in the apartment when he arrived. Had he found it? The lieutenant thanked him for his cooperation and the coffee—too politely, Daniel thought—and the four policemen left.

Daniel stared at the fat Sunday *Times* on the coffee table. His guests had arrived so early, he had not had a chance to read Marvin Hinkler's story about the discovery of Calhoun's body. Nor was he sure he had to bother; the page-one shot of himself standing in front of the Bellemoor looking impossibly smug said more than enough already. He had asked Denise Gold, *Tabula Rasa*'s staff photographer, to take it on her last afternoon of shooting pictures to art his series. Had she sold the photo to the *Times* or had Fosdick made it available in the spirit of journalistic fraternity? It hardly mattered. Either way he was the hot topic of Sunday brunches all over the city. Wearily he picked up the section and began reading when the phone rang.

"I figured I'd be hearing from you before the day was out," he said when he heard Henry Spott's stern hello.

"Is the *Times* stuff true?"

"Probably. I haven't read all of it yet. I've been entertaining the police."

"There? What for?"

"They wanted to search my apartment."

"And you just let them? Jesus, why?"

"Because I got the distinct impression last night that if I said no, I'd wind up in the slammer." Daniel started to add that, besides, he had nothing to hide; but he wasn't so sure.

"You're not going to like the *Times* piece. It's full of the Gospel According to Cops, everything neatly attributed: police say this, police say that, police say they are—and I quote—'investigating the possibility that Mr. Cooper may have killed Mr. Rourke while in some form of epileptic seizure.' "

"It says that?" Daniel turned to the continuation and began combing for the passage.

"Yes. And drags in all that Torsney bullshit from ten years ago, plus a few other cases."

Daniel found the passages but could not focus on them, leaving him in the clutches of his interpreter, who said, "Hinkler writes that he tried to reach you. Did he?"

Daniel stared at the blurry type. "Yes."

"Did you call him back?"

"No. When I got back here last night, I didn't feel like answering any more questions. What the hell would I have said, anyway? I did have a seizure, Hank; there's a whole day I can't account for."

"Okay, I'm sorry. I didn't mean to lecture. You know me. Would you like me to come over?"

Before Daniel could answer, Spott covered the phone, then came back on.

"Great idea. Annie suggests you come over here. You can use Dorian's room. She never comes down from Bard these days, the ingrate. You'd have your own bathroom. For as long as you like."

"Thanks, both of you, but I think I'll tough it out here."

"You're sure?"

"Yes, positive."

"Do you want me to represent you?"

"Let me think about it. I'm not convinced that putting a lawyer between me and Beaupre is the best strategy right now. After all, he hasn't charged me with anything."

"No. He just plants innuendos in a newspaper with a Sunday circulation of a million and a half. You've got to stop rolling over for these guys. They're not on your side. I can't believe you let them sack your apartment. I'd like to come over."

"No. I'm exhausted."

"Tomorrow, then, at my office?"

"Maybe. I'll call you."

"Suit yourself. You know how to reach me."
Spott's irritation sizzled over the line.

After hanging up Daniel tried again to read the
Hinkler piece, but the vision of other people doing so
over their coffee kept intruding. Daniel assumed the
story had moved on the The New York Times News
Service. The players were all local, of course, but
one of them had epilepsy, a titillation factor most
national editors around the country would love. *The
Chicago Tribune* subscribed to the *Times* wire, and
Daniel imagined his parents reading a truncated version of the lines before him even as he sat there. The
prospect of a call from them, or anyone else, persuaded him that he needed to put more than his
answering machine between him and the outside world,
and he sought refuge in Kate's sanctuary.

He burrowed closer to her and suddenly recalled
how he had bragged about his enthusiasm for basic
training. "You are walking with a trained killer; I got
straight A's in death," he had joked after the first
visit to Dr. Loring's.

"Kate?"

"Yes."

"You read the *Times* story this morning. I think
Beaupre really thinks I killed Rourke."

Kate kissed his arm.

"I know it must be awful not to remember, but
you're not a murderer. You know it, I know it, and
I'm sure the police know it. Beaupre's just being
thorough."

Daniel gauged her words, as if with a Geiger
counter, for any lethal rays of doubt.

When he said nothing, Kate continued, "You let them search your apartment, you've agreed to see their neurologist, you're telling them everything you know."

"Somewhat tardily, as you'd be the first to point out. And why should they believe me? I still can't believe most of it myself: the seizure; Rourke; Mr. Green Car, whom no one happened to see but me, telling me to go to Bed-Stuy where I find Cal; a gun that wanders in and out of my apartment like Topper. I'm surprised you let me come over here."

"Scratch." Kate guided his hand to her back.

Daniel's renewed agitation had extinguished any sexual afterglow. He turned and faced her. "Did you reconstruct your phone conversation with Calhoun?"

"Oh, Daniel, now? I thought you came over to get away from all this for a few hours."

"Did you do it?"

"Yes. This morning."

"And?"

Kate threw off the sheet and stalked out of the bedroom. She returned with a piece of paper and thrust it at Daniel.

"Hey, I didn't mean to—"

"I'll be in the kitchen." Kate put on her robe and angrily blew out the candles.

Daniel started to protest further, then turned on the table lamp and rolled up onto his elbow. The neat typing ran almost to the bottom of the page, single-spaced, and began:

Man claiming to be C. Bledsoe calls at office late Thursday ayem, 9-18. Voice cultured, not like black. Traffic in background. Pay phone? Caller alternately desperate and hostile. Refuses to disclose whereabouts. Claims you were supposed to call him. Says he finally called you but got machine. Didn't leave message, afraid of tap. (??) Asks why you didn't follow "plan." Exact word. I push him about plan. He says: "He'll know." (??) Then he said you had to locate some woman, because "the trail's cold." Exact phrase. He wouldn't say what woman, only "he'll know" again (??).

Daniel read the rest of the page, which ended with the caller's promise to get in touch again followed by two more of Kate's not-so-parenthetical question marks. Like a prospector panning for the faintest sparkle, Daniel sat up against the headboard and reread the brief document. Then he got out of bed and pulled on his pants.

"Do I win the Pulitzer Prize?" Kate said as he entered the kitchen.

"And the Nobel, just for putting up with me." He kissed her on the head and pulled up a chair next to her at the table. "This is fine," he said, spreading out the page.

"You don't have to pretend. I know there's nothing new in it. I sat at the typewriter and racked my brains, as per instructions, for more than an hour; I kept coming up with the same stuff over and over."

Daniel began worrying the pepper shaker. "You're not at all convinced it was Calhoun, are you?"

"I never have been. His voice just didn't sound right."

"You'd never talked to him before. He didn't speak like Stepin Fetchit; I've told you that."

"Don't you think it's a little odd that he didn't try harder to get through to you?"

"What do you mean?"

"I mean exactly what you just said. *I'd* never heard his voice. But you had hundreds of times. You would have spotted a phony right away. So he called me, with his song-and-dance about your phone being tapped."

"Maybe it is."

"Maybe. Daniel, you told me to speculate. I think whoever called me was posing as Bledsoe to set you up so that when the man on the parkway told you to go to Bedford-Stuyvesant, you'd go like a shot. And it worked."

Daniel stared into the holes of the pepper shaker.

"If it had really been Bledsoe," Kate continued, "why wouldn't he have told me what the so-called plan was, or who this mystery woman is?"

"Maybe he was afraid to trust you."

"No. I don't think there ever was a plan, and I don't think this woman exists. They were simply bait to hook you."

"What about my epilepsy? He knew about that."

Kate removed the pepper shaker and took Daniel's hand. "It was in the paper, sweetie, remember? Maggie Burke had just showed me that awful *Mail* story when he called."

Daniel looked at Kate, then down at her question marks.

"Has there been an autopsy report on Bledsoe yet?" she asked.

"Too soon."

"You said the body had begun to decompose when you found it yesterday. Maybe the autopsy will show that he died before the phone call."

Daniel tried to view Calhoun as a moldering piece of evidence, to calculate if his friend's flesh and bones had been decaying more than fifty-five hours when he discovered them in the furnace room. But he was no pathologist, and as he contemplated the dark dungeon, he realized he had become so preoccupied with his own survival that he had made no effort to find out when Calhoun's funeral was. He wondered if anyone would be at the West Side Tenants Council office on a Sunday evening and was about to ask to use the phone when he shouted, "Hilda Purvis. That's the woman, Kate. Hilda Purvis. It's got to be." Daniel stood so quickly, he knocked over his chair.

"Who is—"

"How could I be so stupid?" You're wrong, Kate. There is a woman. I've been right about the Wilder bribe all along."

"The Wilder bribe? What's—"

"The phone? Where's the phone?"

Kate pointed to the wall and picked up the chair. In his haste Daniel misdialed twice before getting the council number correct. It produced a recording, a somber woman's voice that announced: "A memorial service for our director, Calhoun Bledsoe, will be held in the St. James Chapel of the Cathedral of St. John the Divine at eleven A.M. on Wednesday, September twenty-fourth. If you would like to leave a message, please wait for the tone." The beep came instantly, permitting no time to compose a coherent response. Daniel started to stammer that Hilda Purvis should call him as soon as possible, then hung up; his voice on the council's tape was something he could live without for the moment.

"Calhoun's funeral is Wednesday."

"Who is Hilda Purvis?"

"She worked for him at the council. A secretary. She witnessed Rourke passing money to Frank Wilder."

"The city councilman?"

"None other."

"For what?"

"To get the health department to condemn some buildings Steven Bromley needs demolished so he can throw up another pleasure dome."

Daniel boosted himself up on the counter and, gaining renewed conviction with every syllable, spilled out the story of Calhoun's efforts to stop the Dickinson condominiums by organizing the tenants at the three Amsterdam Avenue properties. At a considerably slower pace he also recounted the visit by Bromley-Keller's lawyers to *Tabula Rasa* and Mac Fosdick's subsequent refusal to include the bribe material in the Bellemoor articles for lack of hard evidence. He left the baseball bat out of the account.

When he finished, Kate said, "Do the police know about this?"

"From me? No."

"Why not?"

Daniel started to answer honestly, then censored himself. He would only infuriate her by telling the truth—that he was holding back because he wanted the bribe story all to himself for *Tabula Rasa*, that despite his predicament, visions of Read-All-About-It danced in his head, that at thirty-nine he still had not shaken the scoop mentality. He sidled down the counter and picked up a package of Famous Amos chocolate-chip cookies.

"May I?"

Kate nodded. "Why haven't you told Lieutenant Beaupre?"

"Because I don't have the goods on Bromley now any more than I did when Fosdick killed the stuff back in August."

"Then tell him what you suspect. All of it. They may be working on it already; your leads may be just what they need."

Daniel edged off the counter, got a carton from the refrigerator, and poured himself a glass of milk—less to wash down the cookies than to stall his response.

"Because I want to talk to Hilda Purvis first."

Kate stood up and cinched the belt on her robe. "This is idiocy. Two people are dead, you're up to your neck in trouble, and you want to sally forth again like King Arthur. Enough, Daniel! Leave it to the police. It's their job. Tell them about this Purvis woman, please. They'll follow you every step of the way, anyhow."

"Where's the phone book?"

"In the bedroom." Kate dropped back into her chair as he drained his glass and left the kitchen.

Chapter XVII

"HOW long have you had epilepsy?"

"What's it feel like to have a fit?"

"Mr. Cooper, I'm Melanie Bart, WABC. Can you tell me why you've agreed to be examined at the Neurological Institute today?"

"Are there tests that can prove you didn't kill Rourke?"

"Do you think you did?"

"Does anyone else in your family have epilepsy?"

Daniel jerked his head around. "Yes, everyone—all the way back to Genghis Khan."

As cameras clicked and whirred, the pack moved in on its prey. Daniel had proposed avoiding this assault by slipping out the service entrance and meeting Delvecchio at the Twenty-fourth Precinct, but the sergeant perversely insisted on coming to 329, in front of which his patrol car lights now flashed.

"Why don't you turn on the siren too?" Daniel said when he reached the curb.

"Get in."

"The back?"

"The back. Or you can sit up front with cuffs on.

Take your choice.'' Delvecchio held the door open like a hostile chauffeur.

"Do you plan to make an arrest after the examination, Sergeant?" someone asked as the door slammed.

"Talk to Lieutenant Beaupre." Delvecchio got behind the wheel.

Daniel looked out the window at his colleagues jockeying on the sidewalk. He didn't see Hinkler and imagined him interviewing Beaupre at the precinct, accumulating new and incriminating details for tomorrow's *Times* instead of standing around with these panting wolves. *That's what I'd be doing,* Daniel thought as he glared out the window. Joe Richards, the soap actor who lived on the fourth floor, had just returned from his morning tennis in the park. Pushing the handle of his racquet into his chin, he contemplated the strange Tuesday morning scene and then fell into conversation with Jerry Orlofsky, the super. Daniel watched both men shake their heads in dismay as Delvecchio pulled away and the reporters dissolved, racers sprinting for their Formula Ones.

Rides in this cramped backseat were getting to be a habit, Daniel thought: to Mt. Sinai and back to 329 after his running accident; from Bedford-Stuyvesant after Delvecchio found him with Bledsoe's body; and now again. Each time Daniel marveled at how much it felt like being cooped up in a cab, barely able to move your body as you careened through traffic you could hardly see, the two-way radio squawking incomprehensibly. Of course, there were a few differences: Delvecchio's backseat doors had no handles, and the partition between him and Daniel offered no slot through which to push bills at the end of the ride.

The blue-and-white could also run red lights with impunity, but Delvecchio seemed to be stopping for every one as he crawled up Broadway toward the Columbia Presbyterian Medical Center at 168th Street. This law-abiding pace convinced Daniel that his antagonistic driver was determined to make sure his pursuers got another crack at him when he entered the Neurological Institute.

At 145th Street Daniel looked east into Harlem. Hilda Purvis lived only a few blocks away, on St. Nicholas Avenue, a fact he had learned along with her phone number from the Manhattan directory at Kate's Sunday night. To his surprise he had reached her on the first try, an encouraging breakthrough that her fear quickly erased. He had barely formulated his first question when she anxiously demanded to know what he had been doing in the house where the police found Calhoun Bledsoe. Her voice sounded as if she were looking over her shoulder on a dark ghetto street, and Daniel realized that she, too, had read the papers and thought she might be talking to a killer— Bledsoe's as well as Rourke's.

"I was Calhoun's friend, Miss Purvis, you know that; you know what I wrote about his work and the council's. I went to that house because someone told me he'd be there. I didn't expect to find—"

"Who?"

"—him dead. A man. I don't know his name. That's one of the things I'm trying to find out, and I think you can help me."

"Why?"

"Because a couple of days before I found Calhoun, he called a friend of mine and said I should find a certain woman, implying that she could help solve the Rourke murder. He said I'd know who this woman was, and it makes sense that it's you. Is it?''

"Why does it make sense?"

"You saw Rourke give the money to Frank Wilder. I—"

"How do you know that?"

"Calhoun told me at the time. Are you the woman?"

Hilda Purvis said no—so emphatically that Daniel simply assumed she was lying.

"I'd like to ask you a few more questions," he said.

"No. I can't afford any trouble."

"Only for background. You won't get into any trouble. I don't want to put your name in the paper. You can trust me."

"No. I have to hang up." She did.

Daniel redialed and got a busy line, either because she had taken her phone off the hook or was sending out signals of her own.

"Maybe she's talking to Mr. Green Car, mystery woman to mystery man," Kate said after Daniel's third try.

"What's *their* connection?"

"Drugs?" She said it tentatively, adding, "Could Wilder be involved too?"

"Frank?"

"Yes. Fifteen thousand dollars doesn't sound like much of a bribe these days, more like a smoke screen."

Daniel said nothing.

"Isn't it at least possible that this Purvis woman and Mr. Green Car and Frank Wilder and Rourke were dealing drugs for really big money?"

"And Calhoun?"

Kate let the question evaporate between them, then said, "Are you going to tell the police about Hilda Purvis?"

"No. Not yet."

Now, trapped in his mobile prison heading up Broadway, he again angrily rejected Kate's scenario and began to wonder if, in fact, Hilda Purvis had been calling the police herself Sunday night, adding further to his dossier, a file he sensed was growing daily with increasingly damaging information.

The press swarm had only just begun to regroup when Delvecchio double-parked in front of the Neurological Institute and released Daniel from his cage. Both made it into the building before the stinging could resume.

"Dr. Havighurst," Delvecchio told the security guard inside the entrance.

"Yes, sir, Sergeant. Second floor. Turn left down the corridor at the top of the stairs."

"Are you going to hold my hand during the examination too?" Daniel said as they walked down the hallway.

"Maybe." Delvecchio pushed open the doctor's door and announced their arrival to a secretary, who told them to take a seat in the waiting room just across the corridor.

It was large, a carpeted lounge already full of patients and their relatives, some trying to read magazines but most staring into space and wondering what verdicts the institute's white-coated judges would render in their cases. The appearance of Daniel and his armed, uniformed keeper distracted them briefly, but they soon returned to their anxious speculations, as did Daniel, until he heard his name called. He and Delvecchio looked up, then at one another, their mutual animosity suspended for a blink while they shared the fact that Dr. Havighurst was a woman. The two men stood awkwardly, as if the ground had started shifting beneath them, and ran the gauntlet of waiting-room eyes until they faced her in the doorway.

She introduced herself and shook their hands with a firmness that belied her small frame. If she was amused by their ill-disguised surprise, it did not show. On the contrary, the corners of her mouth seemed permanently turned down, producing an earnestness that masked her agreeable face. "Sergeant, I believe Mr. Cooper and I will need about an hour together. There's a cafeteria in the building across the street if you'd prefer to wait there."

Delvecchio looked at Daniel. "No, I think I'll stick around."

"He's afraid your windows may not be locked," Daniel said, testing the mask.

Dr. Havighurst's expression remained fixed. She opened the door to her anteroom, and Daniel moved through, past two preoccupied secretaries and into a small, plain office that had no window at all. His medical file and EEG lay on the desk, released by Dr. Loring; he had required his patient's permission and got it after Lieutenant Beaupre made it clear to Daniel that refusal would only suggest that he had something more to hide. Delvecchio had picked up the records yesterday, and Daniel now pictured the two detectives reading them at the precinct, running off copies for themselves and maybe for Hinkler and other reporters, before neatly resealing them for delivery to the Institute. He imagined his spikes and waves appearing in the *Times*, like a business graph charting some frantically active stock.

"How are you feeling?" Dr. Havighurst sat down at the desk and bid him do the same in a hard, wooden chair facing her.

"Somewhat beleaguered, actually."

"I mean, physically."

"Okay, I suppose. Except for the extra medication. I feel wiped out a lot of the time."

"We can discuss that later if you want. First I'd like you to tell me about your seizure. According to Dr. Loring, the episode began sometime late Wednesday, September tenth. Is that correct?"

"Yes."

"What's the last thing you remember?"

Daniel didn't like the question. It struck him as much less a medical probe than one designed to catch him in some further lie, just as the claustrophobic room now seemed less a neurologist's office than an interrogation cell in which this benign-looking woman in her white coat served as Beaupre's paid surrogate. Daniel started to challenge her allegiance but realized that, whatever her response, he could hardly waltz back into the waiting room and tell Delvecchio he had changed his mind about the examination. Besides, despite his suspicions, he wanted to know what this doctor could tell him, however widely the news might spread.

"Johnny Carson's monologue," he said.

"What time was that?"

The pendulum of distrust swung back a little as

Daniel insisted to himself that no person could be all bad who didn't know the hour of the Carson show.

"Eleven-thirty."

"Do you watch the program often?"

"Just the opening monologue. It lasts about ten minutes, then I usually go to bed. It's my Ovaltine."

Dr. Havighurst unlocked an indulgent smile, then clicked the corners of her mouth back in place. "Are most of these monologues pretty much the same?"

"A string of topical gags, yes."

"Can you remember any from that night?"

Daniel conjured up Carson's corn-fed Nebraska grin, but no one-liners followed. "No, I can't. Why is it important?"

"I want to make sure your episode began when you think it did and not earlier in the day. Are you certain the show you're recalling took place that night? Could you be confusing the monologue with a previous one?"

The pendulum swung wide again. "No. It was definitely that night. If I can't remember any of the jokes, it's because they weren't memorable, that's all. They usually aren't. I was lying on the sofa. I got up, turned off the set and the lights in the living room, and that's it. I don't remember leaving the living room or going to bed or anything else until after my convulsion the next night. Certainly—"

"Do you have a clear memory of the day's events before the Carson program?"

"Yes." Daniel ticked them off defiantly. "I ran when I got up and then made breakfast for myself. Spoon-size Shredded Wheat with milk and bananas. I didn't measure the slices, but they were about a quarter of an inch thick.''

The corners cracked again. ''And then?''

''I took my shirts to the laundry and ran some other errands in the neighborhood.''

''That still leaves a lot of time until eleven-thirty.''

Daniel could account for all that time but was embarrassed to describe how he used it. As usual, since Mac Fosdick had furloughed him, he had filled the day with make-work projects at his desk, long walks in the park, and sessions at the piano.

''I practiced my singing for a couple of hours. Mostly stuff from *Sunday in the Park with George:* ''Finishing the Hat'' and ''Children and Art,'' to be specific. Would you like to hear them?''

''Did you talk with anyone?''

Another cop question, Daniel decided, barely controlling his anger. ''Will Mr. Lee do? You can check with him at the laundry. In fact, you can check right now; I've got the dated ticket in my wallet.''

He started to reach into his back pants pocket when Dr. Havighurst released another fleeting smile and said, ''I believe you, Mr. Cooper. Could you step into the examination room and take off everything but your shorts.''

Over the next twenty-five minutes she put Daniel through all the neurological exercises he had performed ten days ago for Dr. Loring, and more. Her thoroughness did not reassure him, did not produce the salutary flush he usually experienced when doctors examined him. Walking the invisible tightrope again, listening to the tuning fork, watching his Babinski reflex, sitting almost naked on the leathery, paper-lined table answering her enigmatic questions, he felt like a convict in solitary confinement facing the prison doctor. When she left for a few moments to take a phone call, the isolation tightened as he looked down at his bare chest and recalled curling up against Kate on Sunday. The evening had ended badly, Kate furious at his unwillingness to tell Beaupre what he suspected about Hilda Purvis. Her sanctuary had become a den of hostility and he had gone home at ten o'clock. Now he anguished over whether he would ever see her again, and when Dr. Havighurst at last told him he could get dressed, he realized he had sleepwalked through her questions and instruction for the last ten minutes. As he pulled on his shoes he feared that his preoccupation with Kate had made him flub critical tests, might even have suggested he was in a petit mal fade-out.

"I think I can assure Lieutenant Beaupre that you have epilepsy," Dr. Havighurst said as they faced off again across her desk.

The detective's name instantly refocused Daniel's attention. "He doesn't believe I do? What the hell does he think happened to me that Thursday?"

"My impression from talking to him is that he doesn't know quite what to think. He wants medical proof that you had a seizure when you said you did. I can't give him that; I wasn't there. But this EEG and your history clearly support Dr. Loring's diagnosis of classic absence." Her *absence* sounded faintly haughty, as if she thought the concept too complex for Daniel to grasp.

"How about the hoops you just put me through?"

"All normal, just as Dr. Loring found. If you had

any serious neurological dysfunctions, you wouldn't have been able to do several of those exercises.''

"Epilepsy's not serious?''

"Of course it is, Mr. Cooper, when you have a seizure. The rest of the time you're pretty much like everyone else, neurologically. You must know that, given the number of years you were seizure-free.''

Daniel was trying to decide whether this was a reproof when Dr. Havighurst continued. "The lieutenant also wants to know whether, if you did have a seizure, you could have killed that man Rourke without knowing it.'' She introduced the murder so matter-of-factly that the pendulum began oscillating wildly.

"Like Robert Torsney, the cop who shot that kid in Brooklyn ten years ago?''

"Like he's supposed to have. You know the Torsney case?''

"I took an interest in the trial at the time.''

"Then you know no neurologists testified for either side.''

"No, I didn't.''

"If the prosecution had had the sense to call a neurologist, Torsney's epileptic defense probably would have collapsed. But for some reason they didn't, and the jury found him not guilty by reason of mental disease or defect.''

"The jury found him not guilty because the kid was black and Torsney was a white cop.''

"Perhaps, but whatever the reason, the verdict has caused a lot of damage since.''

"How?''

"It's encouraged quite a few lawyers around the country to use the same tactic when defending clients who appear hopelessly guilty. The state epilepsy association knows I keep track of such cases, which is why they steered you to me when Lieutenant Beaupre called them."

Daniel noticed that Dr. Havighurst, strictly business up to now, was manifesting a certain zeal.

"The fact is," she continued, "people with epilepsy simply don't go around committing purposeful violence in ictal states."

Daniel looked perplexed.

"Sorry. That means while having an episode. The research we have gathered in recent years shows quite conclusively that it is impossible to perform direct, motivated criminal acts in the middle of a seizure."

"You mean like deliberately pointing and firing a gun at someone?"

"Precisely."

"So you don't think I could have killed Rourke?"

"Not during an epileptic seizure, no."

This qualification caused the pendulum to agitate again but only for an instant. "Well, *I'm* reasonably sure I didn't do it any other time. Do you plan to tell Beaupre all this?"

"Yes, in my report."

"How long will that take?"

"I'll try to get it to him by Thursday, Friday at the latest."

"I'd appreciate that. I need all the help I can get at the moment." Daniel heard the self-pity in his voice, but another wave of exhaustion left him no will to combat it. He looked hopefully across the desk and asked, "Does your offer to discuss my medication still stand?"

"Certainly. What do you want to know?"

"Isn't there something I could switch to that's less numbing? I can't stand the way I feel."

"If you were my patient, I'd give valproic acid a try. It's proved quite successful in controlling absence seizures, and most people who take it experience little or no sedative side effects."

"None?"

"In many cases."

"Christ, why didn't Dr. Loring mention it?"

"Maybe he did. Did he suggest Depakote? That's the trade name."

"No. All he said right from the start was to take more phenobarb and Mysoline."

"Well, I wouldn't be too hard on him. After all, that combination kept you out of trouble for a long time. It wasn't necessarily wrong to continue them in a higher dose, at least until he determined how well you tolerated the increase."

"I can't tolerate it."

"It's a little early to tell that."

"Not for me. I feel like taking a nap right now. Does this Depa-whatever have different side effects?"

"Depakote. Yes, a few."

"I was afraid of that. Like?"

"We don't know why, but some people experience hand tremors when they—"

"Hand tremors. You mean like palsy?"

"—begin taking the drug. No, not as severe as palsy, and usually they disappear after the first few weeks."

"What else?" Daniel felt himself slipping into a funk.

"A few of my patients still develop GI problems at the outset, but that doesn't happen often anymore because the formulation is enteric-coated. Really, the only serious possible side effect involves the liver."

"What happens?"

"Hepatic failure has occurred."

"Causing death?"

"In a very few cases, yes. I've never had one, and all the literature shows that they are extremely rare."

Daniel prepared himself for the standard lecture on how all anticonvulsant drugs had some side effects and how anyone who took them had to make peace with the trade-off, but it didn't come.

Instead Doctor Havighurst continued. "We don't put patients on Depakote without running liver function blood tests first, and we keep checking at intervals after they start taking the drug. Any trouble signs usually show up in the first six months, and if they do, we stop the therapy, of course."

"Of course."

"Keep in mind, Mr. Cooper, that thousands of people take Depakote with no problems at all. Most of my patients tell me how much more alert they feel once they're off their old medication."

"Well, I'd certainly welcome that," Daniel said sullenly.

"Why don't you discuss it with Dr. Loring?"

Daniel did not want to discuss anything with Dr. Loring but was reluctant to reveal his disaffection, to squeal like a child running to the teacher. Instead he dodged her question and asked, "If my friend Kate had called you that afternoon, would you have let things run their course the way he did?''

"No. I'd probably have had her bring you here in a cab and I'd have given you some Valium intravenously. That almost always brings people out of absence.''

"And I wouldn't have had the convulsion?''

"Not if the Valium worked, which it usually does.''

The possibility that he might have been spared the attack, the chewed-up mouth, the banged hip, the crushing dismay and embarrassment of having lost control in front of Kate enraged Daniel. "Why in God's name didn't Loring do that if it's standard practice?''

Dr. Havighurst stood. "I don't know. I don't know Dr. Loring, but the truth is that quite a few neurologists don't make a point of staying on top of developments. Some, in fact, don't like dealing with epilepsy at all. It's too much trouble. Patients tend to be difficult. They want answers you can't give them, because they aren't there; they want you to hold out hope of a cure, but there is none—at least not in sight. Many patients are also emotionally depressed a lot of the time because of their medication or because society—and sometimes their own families—treat them like lepers.''

Daniel winced at the sound of the word, one he had heard used in this context before but never thought applied to him.

"And there's one other thing,'' Dr. Havighurst continued. "Tonic-clonic convulsions like the one you had make people extremely uneasy; seeing someone thrashing about like that paralyzes people with an almost primitive fear. Including some neurologists.''

"You mean, you think Loring may have stayed away on purpose?''

"No, I think it's possible that a number of things could have contributed to his handling you the way he did, things he may not even be aware of himself.''

Daniel was looking for an indictment now but knew it would not be forthcoming. "Would you take me on as a patient?'' he asked.

"If that's what you want. Why don't you think about it? Then, if you want to make another appointment, give my secretary a call.''

Daniel suddenly wanted to ask her first name, to establish a more binding relationship before he left the room. But her manner did not invite it. He stood, shook her hand, and said, "Thank you, you'll be hearing from me.''

When he arrived back in the waiting room, Sergeant Delvecchio looked impatient.

Chapter XVIII

THE Cathedral of St. John the Divine loomed over Amsterdam Avenue. Even without its two main towers, only now being painstakingly constructed, it dwarfed the residential neighborhood of Morningside Heights like a Gothic non sequitur. Daniel stood on the sidewalk for a moment and examined the facade, its arching portals busy with ornate stone carvings, then mounted the broad steps and entered beneath St. Peter and eight other Christian martyrs. He had never been inside before, and nothing prepared him for the solemn immensity of the great church. He stared up at the vaulted ceiling of the nave and wondered if someone had chosen this vast edifice for Calhoun's service to try to overwhelm the seamy circumstances of his death.

"Twelve stories."

Daniel turned to find Marvin Hinkler standing near the massive bronze doors, a guidebook open. He switched it to his left hand and held out his right. Daniel took it and said, "I thought if I got here an hour early, I'd miss even the *Times*. Friend or foe?"

" 'Without fear or favor,' as we say. Actually, I

came early because I've never seen this place. It's a lot bigger than my *shul* in Forest Hills.''

"Maybe you should start a building fund.''

Hinkler laughed and shoved the guidebook into his jacket pocket. "Any chance I could ask you a few questions?''

"Me? Another reporter? Come on, Marvin, you know how boring journalists are. Anyway, you did a fine job on me Sunday. Page one. Isn't that enough?''

"I just write 'em. They decide how to play 'em.''

"Right.''

"Did I get anything wrong?''

Only by omission, Daniel thought, but then we all do that regularly. Besides, he could hardly raise the point, having refused to return Hinkler's calls Saturday evening.

"The piece was fine, Marvin. I've already had it laminated. But that's it. Talk to the cops some more if you want a story. I'm an empty vessel.'' A sinking one, too, Daniel wanted to add.

"How about after the service?''

"You bet. All the vultures will be assembled by then. I'll get in the pulpit and hold a news conference. You can say, 'Thank you, Mr. President.' ''

"We could go somewhere for a cup of coffee. There's—''

"No, dammit.'' The expletive resounded in the deserted narthex. "Look, I'm sorry. I know about editors, but I have nothing to say. To you or anyone else.'' Daniel began edging away.

"Okay, but if you change your mind, I'll be right here afterward.''

"Noted.''

"If you're going to the chapel already, check out the stained-glass windows along the way. One's devoted to us."

"You and me?"

"Yeah, the media, if you can believe it." Hinkler pointed out the direction and went back to his guidebook.

Looking for some color for his lead, Daniel surmised as he made his escape. He walked past a bank of flickering votive candles and started down the block-long south aisle. Giant piers rose on either side, creating a hushed arbor of towering stone. Its welcome peace was almost instantly broken by a Holocaust memorial, a sculpted Auschwitz figure writhing in agony on a black coffin. In the next bay a huge cross of charred wooden beams commemorated New York firemen killed in the line of duty. Daniel began searching the windows above each bay for relief from these grim shrines and finally spotted Hinkler's discovery.

He had not exaggerated. The morning sun bathed the richly colored glass, illuminating at the bottom of the tall window a reporter bent over his his typewriter and, opposite, a newsy hawking papers from under his arm. Above them, a man with a violin and a woman singer stood before an old-fashioned radio microphone looking like nervous contestants on the Horace Heidt Amateur Hour. Daniel's eyes continued heavenward, revealing a man watching television, a lineman on a pole stringing wire, a linotype operator at his machine, and a telegrapher who looked in his enthusiasm like Samuel Morse asking, "What

hath God wrought?'' Next came Gutenberg with his
Bible, and higher still, in a round window all his
own, a robed host appeared to sit in judgment of all
below. His halo looked like the fat electronic ear-
muffs worn by network sports broadcasters. Daniel
imagined a sonorous announcement issuing from the
kaleidoscopic glass booth: ''But first this message.''

Daniel smiled and wondered what other secular
callings rated such sacred treatment. *Medicine,* came
the answer filtering down from the window over the
next bay, and as he gazed up into the scenes of
healing he began patting his jacket pockets for the
feel of the aspirin tin in which he carried his midday
pills. He thrust his hands inside, then into his pants
pockets. The tin was not there, and he finally admitted he must have forgotten it; then he realized he had
also failed to take his morning dose before leaving.
He looked at his watch. Ten-twenty. Time enough to
dash home and back by cab before the service began
at eleven. But that would mean calling attention to
himself, precisely what he had come early to avoid.
He hadn't recognized any police faces when he arrived, but they were around, or surely would be by
the time he returned, along with the press posse, if it
wasn't unsaddling outside already.

He had forgotten to take his medication many
times in the past, lapses he had come to view with
almost complete equanimity after so many seizure-
free years. Not long after their marriage he and Faith
had tipped over on the first afternoon of a three-day
canoe trip, losing their toilet kits to the river. Despite
a certain anxiety, he had insisted on paddling on; and
they had, to an uneventful conclusion. More than

anything, that test persuaded him that his pills were mostly, perhaps entirely, a psychological prop, a placebo of habit. Hadn't the Army doctor said he could get along without them? Hadn't Dr. Grosbart? If he forgot now and then, it was a misdemeanor at worst.

Now it seemed a major felony, a violation that would put him—*had* put him—in serious jeopardy. He wondered if at least some of the medicine he had taken last night remained in the bloodstream or if he was running on empty, if his brain now thirsted like an alcoholic's for a missed shot and his body was on the verge of retaliating in fury. He cast himself as both doctor and patient, the former reassuring the latter that he was overreacting. "Three or four hours won't make any difference, Mr. Cooper, especially with the extra medication you've been taking. Just go home immediately after the service and take both your morning and afternoon doses." The patient accepted this advice with marked ambivalence, and the curtain came down on the psychodrama, leaving Daniel standing anxiously in the gloom.

Hesitantly he moved on and entered St. James Chapel, one of seven attached to the forward hull of the mother ship like exquisite barnacles. He took a seat in the next to the last row on the far side, hoping to hide his dubious celebrity among the other mourners when they arrived. As much to discourage conversation as to kill time, he withdrew the bible from the rack on the chair before him and opened it at random. Before he could focus on the page, Jennie Mae began telling him, as she had in the Cooper kitchen twenty-five years ago, that Jesus Christ would cure his epilepsy. "It's right in the good book, Dan-Dan, but you got to believe in the Lord. You come to my church Sunday and we'll pray together. I'll ask your momma." Daniel declined and fled to play softball. He loved this devoted black woman, had adored her since she began working for the family when he was six. But at fifteen he found her evangelism embarrassing and her scriptural prescription no antidote for his fear. Still she persisted, bringing in the worn bible the next day and earnestly spoon-feeding him the redeeming passage when he came home from his piano lesson.

It was from the Gospel According to St. Luke, a fact he knew not because of any familiarity with holy writ but because he vividly recalled teasing Jennie Mae, asking if her Luke had watched over the war-time star shortstop of the Chicago White Sox, Luke Appling. Daniel now located the gospel and began skimming the alien terrain, not sure exactly what he was looking for or whether he even wanted to find it. What word or phrase was he seeking? Was the trip wire epilepsy? Or the Falling Sickness? Or the Sacred Disease? Or some euphemism he had never encountered? Then the word *foams* frothed on the page, and Jennie Mae's sermon formed around it.

"And behold, a man from the crowd cried, 'Teacher, I beg you to look upon my son, for he is my only child; and behold, a spirit seizes him, and he suddenly cries out; it convulses him till he foams, and shatters him, and will hardly leave him. And I begged your disciples to cast it out, but they could not.'

"Jesus answered, 'O faithless and perverse generation, how long am I to be with you and bear with you? Bring your son here.' While he was coming, the demon tore him and convulsed him. But Jesus rebuked the unclean spirit and healed the boy, and gave him back to his father. And all were astonished at the majesty of God.''

Jennie May had given this astonishment a hallelujah fervor and endorsed the remedy with an amen that hung in the air with the tantalizing smells of her kitchen.

Daniel lay the Bible in his lap and invested all the majesty he could summon in Dr. Havighurst. He did not believe in the efficacy of prayer but was ready to fall on his knees if it would somehow guarantee her role as his savior. He had left the Neurological Institute yesterday heady with optimism, a hopefulness that even survived Sergeant Delvecchio's renewed grunts of hostility on the ride back to 329. But as soon as he entered the apartment, he began wondering just exactly what Dr. Havighurst would put in her report to Beaupre, and from there it proved easy to conclude that whatever she wrote didn't matter much at all. Her dismissal of the epilepsy defense as nonsense comforted him but went not an inch toward explaining the missing gun or any of the other non-neurological mysteries that enshrouded him. Beaupre had asked him to submit to Dr. Havighurst, but why should he really care what she had to tell him?

When he spun back the Sanyo yesterday, only two calls had registered, both hang-ups. Still no word from Norman Werner or any of his other friends except Henry Spott, in whose doghouse he remained for rejecting both his *pro bono* counsel and his hospitality. Fosdick also had not phoned again, either to commiserate or to criticize. The absence of calls for the rest of the day convinced Daniel that his page-one debut in Sunday's *Times* had turned him into worse than a leper, an epileptic with an unshakable aura of murder and drugs. Kate had more than demonstrated her willingness to stand by him while he grappled with his medical problems, but clearly he had pushed her too far on the other front. She had not called since he left her apartment Sunday night. It seemed as if he had picked up the phone to call her at least once every half hour. Each time he had set the receiver back in its cradle, unable to find the sentences that would bring her back into his camp.

An amplified tapping broke into his brooding, and Daniel looked up to see a minister flicking his finger against the microphone on the polished wooden lectern to the left of the altar. The bible slipped off Daniel's knees and slapped against the floor, causing the clergyman to peer at the perpetrator. If he recognized Daniel, he did not show it but instead turned to the group of women gathering around him. They wore white robes, and their dark faces shone with the promise of gospel singing. The seats were filling up now, and Daniel worked to maintain his anonymity by turning away from the entrance and examining the white marble tomb of Henry Codman Potter: UPHOLDER OF RIGHTEOUSNESS AND TRUTH. SOLDIER AND SERVANT OF JESUS CHRIST. Bishop Potter lay atop the slab, alabaster hands across his chest. "You honkies get even whiter when you die," Calhoun observed, and for an instant Daniel was sitting next to his wry friend at this prelate's funeral.

Daniel imagined a tomb of deep brown marble, Calhoun stretched out on top: UPHOLDER OF THE POOR AND HOMELESS. SOLDIER AGAINST AVARICE AND GREED. He deserved no less, Daniel argued, and then DRUG PUSHER carved itself into the fantasy. He wrested his eyes from the block and permitted himself a quick glance around the chapel. It was only about half full, maybe a hundred people. Most were black: staff members of the West Side Tenants Council, friends and relatives from Bedford-Stuyvesant, a handful of the tenants for whom Calhoun had fought so hard. Daniel recognized the backs of a few heads—the shiny pate of Dick Sanford, Calhoun's "main man" at the council; the fat neck of Victor Kaplan, owner of the Horn— but most of Calhoun's varied white supporters were absent, notably the Brooklyn pols who up to now had missed no opportunity to boast of his achievements and claim him as their protégé. Maybe they would send Mary Bledsoe flowers or at least pat her hand at the cafeteria, once her son's epitaph clarified itself, if it ever did.

Daniel strained to see if Mary and her two daughters were sitting up front, but his view was blocked by two women in animated conversation. He wondered if one of them was Hilda Purvis or if she was elsewhere in the chapel. Perhaps he could get Dick Sanford to point her out after the service and together they would be able to persuade her to trust him, to tell him at last what he needed to know. Yet what made him think that Sanford trusted him? And even if he did, and willingly identified the woman, where could they talk without attracting the attention of

Hinkler and the rest of the press, now seated in the back row like patient buzzards on a fence?

Daniel picked up the bible and stuck it back in the rack as the opening strains of "Swing Low, Sweet Chariot" poured from the organ. The gospel choir joined in, their emotion at once enfolding Calhoun's memory and purging the chapel of its stifling formality.

> *I looked over Jordan and what did I see?*
> *Coming for to carry me home.*
> *A band of angels coming after me,*
> *Coming for to carry me home.*

Many in the pews sang or hummed along, including a tall, erect woman on the aisle in the row ahead of Daniel. Three children sat to her right, a boy and two girls. The woman had managed to stalemate poverty for these few hours, her inherent dignity deepened by her simple print dress. But the children, though well scrubbed for the occasion, wore threadbare castoffs and fidgeted in their hard chairs with a restlessness that seemed to ask where in this mighty fortress they might get something to eat when this ordeal was over.

As the spiritual soared, the smaller girl began inspecting the chapel, fastening first on the recumbent Bishop Potter. Daniel was speculating on her reaction when her gaze shifted to him. He smiled, and she looked quickly away, but not before he recognized the frightened face of the pathetic child who had knocked on Billy Rourke's door three months ago at the Bellemoor. He had lost her name, but her spiritless expression was unmistakable, even without the

black-and-blue welts inflicted by her sodden father.
Was he here too? Daniel scanned the other heads in
the row, then searched the rest of the chapel; he did
not see Jones Williams anywhere. "Mind, Bernice,"
the guardian whispered; she fixed a stern look and
the girl faced front obediently. If Rourke had been
right and Bernice's mother was a hooker, Daniel
thought, than this austere woman was clearly someone else. He rejoiced at the possibility that Bernice
had finally escaped both the Bellemoor and her abu-
sive father and found her way into a decent home.

The minister was at the lectern now, reciting the
Twenty-third Psalm. A big man with a barrel chest,
he reached down and delivered the verse in rousing
cadences that his listeners punctuated with ardent
amens. This passion did not prove contagious, did
not convince Daniel that he should fear no evil in the
mysterious valley of death he found himself passing
through. The reverend, whose name was Sturges and
who had known the Bledsoe family for many years,
said all the right things, charting how Calhoun had
grown from a "dev'lish little rascal" on the streets of
Bedford-Stuyvesant into a scholar, a basketball star,
and a man devoted to helping others. Others stepped
forward and said the right things, too, embalming
"the departed" in a succession of platitudes so inad-
equate that only the speakers' obvious affection rescued their mawkish sentiments. And then the Reverend
Sturges was praying again and the gospel choir was
singing "Sweet By and By."

Daniel felt shut out. He wanted to have spoken
himself, to have at least tried to honor Calhoun with
something more than the somber clichés he had just

heard. Of course, he had not been asked; and now, as the chapel began to empty, he wondered if he could even go say a few words to Mary Bledsoe without causing a scene. He stood for a moment contemplating that course, and also the prospect of talking to Dick Sanford about Hilda Purvis. Then he remembered his pills and opted for a fast exit. Hinkler tried once again to waylay him as he reentered the main church; the rest of the buzzards flapped about with mixed emotions as their redoubtable competitor from the *Times* failed. They followed Daniel nonetheless, as he moved at a near trot back up the south aisle.

He had only gone a short way, however, when the trailing footsteps suddenly faded. Daniel relaxed his stride and glanced back, to see the flock retreating toward the crossing. He stopped for a moment and pondered what could have distracted them, then decided he should be grateful for whatever it was and continued toward the portals that opened on Amsterdam Avenue.

"Leave her alone, you hear!"

Even the echoing vastness could not muffle the angry words of the shout. Daniel turned around again as camera flashes tweaked the cathedral's gloaming. He tried to pierce the distance, but all he could make out was an agitated coagulation of press and mourners. A questioner had probably asked one too many of Mary Bledsoe, Daniel guessed, trying to dismiss his curiosity. It and his desire to get back home collided head-on, strewing the wreckage of indecision across his path. Finally he convinced himself that his medicine could wait a few more minutes. He slipped between two columns, edged across a row of chairs, and joined a tour group coming down the center aisle of the nave. "Isn't this place neat?" said a young woman walking backward so as not to relinquish her view of the great rose window looking down on them. "Aren't those colors incredible?" Daniel nodded.

When they reached the crossing, their guide, a gray-haired woman who relished her instructional role, attempted to resume her discourse. But the nearby commotion distracted her, and she left her charges to put a stop to it. When she returned, the disturbance had not ended and she was furious.

"Can you imagine? A lot of journalists coming into this place of worship and bothering people at a *funeral*."

"Bothering them about what?" The rose window enthusiast asked the question, one clearly shared by the others, who at least temporarily had lost interest in learning who had designed the marble pulpit before them.

"I don't know. Some man is trying to get a little girl to go somewhere with him. That's another thing. He looks like he's been drinking."

That bastard, Daniel thought, he *is* here. He jostled to the front of his group to get a better look, but the band of heathen journalists blocked his view. His every medical instinct told him not to get involved, to go home and take his medication. Besides, this family fight was really none of his business, as had been pointed out in admonitions by such disparate parties as Mac Fosdick and Steven Bromley. But he knew he would not be satisfied, could not leave, until he found out whether the man causing all the trouble was in fact Jones Williams. He left the safety of his neutral camp, walked across the resonant stone, and pushed his way to the core of the dispute.

"Come on, Bernice, I won't hurt you, you knows that. If you comes with me, I'll buy you anything you want. We're gonna have big money soon. Big money." Williams addressed his plea more to the tall woman than to Bernice, who cowered behind her.

"I told you, she ain't going nowhere with you. Ever again. You treat her like dirt."

"Just a few hours, Carrie. That's all. I don't want to keep her. And I'll see you get some of the money too. We's flesh and blood."

"You're no kin of mine. Not no more. Aren't you ashamed coming into a church like you is?" Carrie Williams seared her brother with a glare.

"Look who's back." Joe Balboni, the *Mail*'s photo-dervish, snapped several shots of Daniel. The crowd swung its attention to the newcomer as he tapped Jones Williams on the shoulder.

Daniel had readied a verbal broadside, but when the man faced him, he looked even more pitiable than his daughter. "Don't you think it's time for you to leave now?" Daniel said.

Williams blinked in bleary half recognition.

"You know this guy, Cooper?" asked Rob Samuels of the *Daily News*.

Daniel ignored the question and squatted down. "Don't be afraid, he won't bother you anymore," he told Bernice. The fear in her eyes only dilated.

"Who are you?" asked her aunt.

Daniel explained and quickly described the encounter with Bernice in Rourke's office and his subsequent threatening lecture when he went upstairs to the father and daughter's squalid apartment. Jones Williams suffered this summation in silence, nervously glancing out of the circle like a floundering actor searching the wings for a prompter.

"Why did you come here today of all days?" Daniel said, rising.

Williams again looked anxiously out of the arena.

"I'll tell you why. He came here full of big talk about collecting a reward," said his sister.

"The Rourke reward?"

"That's right. And he says he needs to take this child with him."

"Where?"

Williams stood silent looking down at the floor.

"What's going on here, Cooper?"

Daniel looked over Jones Williams's stooped shoulder to see Sergeant Delvecchio. He had shed his uniform, but his Dacron mufti did little to soften his cop countenance. He stepped toward Daniel and said, "Can't you even go to a funeral without causing trouble?"

"Where's Beaupre?"

"Who wants to know?"

"I do. Is he here?"

"He's at the precinct, which is where you're going."

"Why?"

"I've told you before, you're not a reporter now. We ask the questions. Are you coming, or do I have to get out the cuffs again?"

The possibility of handcuffs put the encircling press corps on full alert.

"How about questioning *this* man? Ask him what he knows about Billy Rourke's murder.

"This guy?" Delvecchio sized up Williams with contempt.

"His name's Jones Williams and—"

"I don't know what he's talking about. I don't know nothin' about that Mr. Rourke getting killed. I jus' wants my little girl."

Bernice pulled closer to her aunt, to whom Daniel now looked desperately for corroboration of her brother's quest for the reward. Carrie Williams stood mute in the threatening presence of the policeman.

"Which little girl?" he asked.

"That one," Williams stammered. "She's my daughter."

"Is that true?" the detective asked the trembling child.

"Yes, it's true," said Daniel, "but it's also true that he beats her and—"

"I asked *her,* Cooper." Delvecchio again turned to Bernice. "Is this your daddy?"

The child nodded and buried her face in Carrie Williams's dress.

"Where are you living now?"

The child looked up at her aunt.

"With me," said Carrie Williams. "And my two children here."

"At the Bellemoor?"

"No, they made us leave that place. We's in another of them welfare places. The Randolph Hotel on Twenty-third Street."

"You can't just let him take her away. This woman's her aunt. She's giving her decent care for—"

"Let's go, Cooper. I haven't got time for family quarrels today. They'll have to settle it themselves."

Delvecchio took him by the arm and began leading him away as the cameras burst about them. The flashes flooded Daniel's eyes, which instantly widened and stared off into the distance, as if no longer registering what was happening to him. They appeared at once dazed and oddly alarmed and remained fixed in that confusion for about twenty seconds when he emitted a sepulchral scream so intense it quavered through the crossing like a chorus of terrified spirits. Daniel pitched backward, striking the stone floor hard. His eyes now bulged up as the onlookers froze in captivity, as petrified as the specter now stretched rigid before them. At the sound of the cry the tour group broke for the scene, arriving as Daniel began convulsing violently. His arms and legs flailed at the surrounding shins and ankles, setting off a counterpoint dance to escape his touch.

Another flash from Balboni's camera finally broke the spectators' spell.

"Joe, you and that paper are really scum," said Hinkler.

"Just doing my job, pal." He took another shot of his writhing subject, and his emboldened compatriots moved in for pictures of their own.

"Lord, someone call a doctor for this poor man." Carrie Williams leaned over toward Daniel, then shrank back as his thrashing intensified.

"What's wrong with him?" said Bernice, recoiling with her aunt and her terrified young cousins.

"He's having a fit, child. Don't be asking questions now."

"Where's the phone in this barn?" Delvecchio barked into the crowd.

"There's one in the gift shop," said the guide, pointing to the opposite side of the crossing. "The St. Luke's emergency room is only a block away."

"Maybe we should just take him there," someone suggested.

"Are you going to do it?" Delvecchio snapped.

The sergeant himself, however, appeared unable to act, seemed glued to the stone, his eyes riveted on the spasming form.

"Tell them it's a grand mal attack. I've seen one before," said Hinkler.

Delvecchio did not respond to the advice but at last slowly began moving toward the gift shop.

"Doesn't 'grand mal' mean epilepsy?" said a woman wearing a backpack. "That's just incredible. He was fine only a few minutes ago. Perfectly normal."

"What if he swallows his tongue? Maybe we should hold it down."

"Yeah."

"With what?"

"I've got an address book."

"No, you're not supposed to do that. It's not physically possible to swallow your tongue."

"How do you know?"

"Because I—"

Daniel rose up into this debate and crashed out of the ring like an escaping maniac. He was already racing up the center aisle before the stunned press corps managed to collect itself.

"Someone go tell that cop," yelled Balboni as he and his jouncing cameras gave chase.

Daniel widened his lead with every stride, disappearing out the portal before his pursuers reached the narthex. When they finally spilled out of the cathedral, they found the steps deep in sightseers just disgorged by three tour buses parked at the curb. Their eyes smarting in the bright sunshine, they squinted frantically among the rubberneckers for some sign of their quarry. Then, almost as one, they saw him, standing near the front of a bus. He seemed to be shouting at it crazily, and when he spotted the journalists now charging down the steps joined by Delvecchio, he clambered into the vehicle and edged out of sight. In the split second it took the press to decide to follow, the detective leapt aboard and yanked the door closed behind him. The sightseers abandoned the cathedral and poured down the steps to find out what was happening to their transportation. But neither they nor the news force could see a thing through the heavily tinted windows, and many in the growing crowd surrounding the bus at first thought the gunshot was a backfire.

Chapter XIX

"STOP beating up on yourself. You're doing the right thing." Maggie Burke looked over her shoulder as Kate followed through the revolving door.

"At least I should have offered to go to the memorial service with him today."

"What I'm hearing is a lot of 'shoulds,' Kate. You didn't know this man Bledsoe from Adam. And you don't know Daniel all that well, either. You're right to keep your distance and you know it."

"Okay, but no more lectures. Where do you want to eat?"

As they stood in the cacophony of midtown reviewing the tired restaurant options, Gretchen Kahn, the twelfth-floor receptionist, spun breathlessly out of the lobby.

"Kate. The *police*. They want to talk to you."

She looked at Gretchen, then at Maggie. "I told them everything I know on Saturday."

"He said it was real important."

"Who?"

"He had, like, a French name."

"Beaupre?"

"I think so. When I told him you had just gone to lunch, he said I should try to catch you. Here's the number." She handed Kate a Glossary message slip. "Are you in trouble?"

"No, of course she's not," Maggie said, too defensively.

Kate reentered the lobby and headed for the pay phones next to the smoke shop. She dialed the Twenty-fourth Precinct as Maggie and Gretchen hovered at a semidiscreet distance.

"Now?" they heard her exclaim, after several seconds; then she hung up quickly.

"He wants me to come up there right away."

"Why?" Maggie asked.

"He wouldn't say."

"Are you going?" Gretchen asked the question as if a visit to the Twenty-fourth Precinct might be rather exciting.

Kate nodded and started back toward the street.

"Do you want me to come with you?"

"No, Mag, I'll be fine."

Beaupre was waiting on the sidewalk when the cab pulled up. He thanked Kate for coming on such short notice and led her into the station house, where the press chase now chattered in the shape-up area. Several reporters moved toward them, but the lieutenant hurried Kate past the booking desk and into the same neon-drab room in which he had interrogated her on Saturday. She wanted to ask about Daniel and why so many reporters were around, but Beaupre's gravity preempted all questions but his own. He had only one.

"I know this can't be much fun for you, Miss

Bernstein, and I apologize for dragging you up here. But I want you to think very hard about what I'm going to ask you. Your answer could be extremely important."

"May I sit down?"

"Yes, of course, I'm sorry." He pulled a chair away from the peeling wall and placed it next to the scratched-up wooden table.

Kate sat down. "I'll try, but I really don't—"

"You said on Saturday that the person who called you at your office told you to tell Mr. Cooper to find a woman, a woman he knew." Beaupre began pacing.

"That's right, I told you that be—"

"Are you absolutely certain the caller said 'woman'?"

"Of course I'm—"

"Could he have said 'girl'?"

The single syllable rose instantly to the surface of her memory and bobbed with a growing embarrassment that in all her reconstruction efforts for Daniel, it had never occurred to her. She looked at Beaupre sheepishly and said, "Yes. It's possible he did."

"Are you certain?"

"No. But when you made the distinction, it definitely rang a bell. I can't be absolutely sure, but I think he did say 'girl.'"

Beaupre continued pacing, as if on a treadmill that would not stop until Kate ruled out "woman" unequivocally. Instead she said, "Even if he did say 'girl,' why does it mean anything? Lots of men refer to women as girls."

Beaupre stopped and frowned. "But you now think he *said* 'girl'?"

Kate nodded. "Have you found her?"

"I'm not sure. But . . . what is it?"

Detective Spofford poked his head in the door. "You wanted the rundown on Garofalo as soon as I got it." He smiled perfunctorily in the direction of the chair.

"I'll be right out." Beaupre turned back to Kate. "I won't be long."

"Do I have to stay here?"

"I'd appreciate it."

"Is Daniel here too?" Kate asked, but the lieutenant was already out the door.

"Tony Garofalo's not his real name," Spofford said when Beaupre joined him in the corridor. "The FBI says it's Vincent Crevani. He's got at least one other alias too: Roy Phillips."

"What's his pedigree?"

"Long enough for all three, starting with auto theft when he was seventeen right up to attempted murder, with you name it in between: drugs, armed robbery, extortion. He gets good lawyers from somewhere, though. He's only done time once: three years in Attica for shaking down a builder in Brooklyn."

"When did he get out?"

"March 'eighty-three."

"Anything else?"

Spofford nodded and took out his notebook. "Ever hear of 'mungo'?"

"Sounds like a new dance."

"It's construction site scrap. A mungo ring steals it, and Garofalo—or whatever his name is—was arrested for running one last year."

"Mob stuff?"

"Together with the builders, who just look the other way."

"The price of doing business."

"Sometimes a high price. They were fixing up the Chrysler building a few years ago, and the foreman told some worker he was being cut out of the mungo profits because he'd been stealing scrap on his own. So this guy hits the foreman on the head with a sledgehammer and sends him out the window on the fifty-sixth floor."

"What happened to our man's case?"

"Out of court for lack of evidence."

"Good lawyers again?"

"Looks that way. Some guy named Canaday."

"Walter Canaday? Of Barron, Grossman and Wilson?"

Spofford flipped through his notebook. "That's the outfit. Why?"

"Just a rather interesting coincidence. I'll explain later. Right now I want you to go get the girl and bring her in. Take Banks with you. Tell her to put on something motherly, and you get out of those blues too. Go real easy. The kid'll be scared enough just having to come in here. Don't use a cruiser, do it by taxi. And bring the aunt."

"The father too?"

"If he's around. But don't waste any time looking for him. It's the daughter we have to talk to. You know where to go?"

"The Randolph Hotel. West Twenty-third Street."

"The aunt's name is Carrie Williams. Don't frighten her, either. Tiptoe, Lewis. Tiptoe all the way."

Spofford nodded and went in search of Officer

Alma Banks as Beaupre sent the desk sergeant in to Kate and then climbed the stairs to the squad room. A half hour later, as Kate unwrapped a tuna salad sandwich, Daniel burst in, took her head in his hands, and kissed it passionately on top.

"Baby, I don't know if you're even speaking to me, and I don't blame you if you're not, but I adore you—especially your brain." He pressed his lips through her hair, as if trying to bless her memory.

"Daniel, I—"

"Beaupre wouldn't believe me. But I think he believes you. He really does. And, baby, you are right. I love you. Calhoun did say 'girl.' I know it. I was all wrong about Hilda Purvis the other night."

Kate looked skeptical. "You were so sure."

"I know. I know. But I was dead wrong. I just wasn't thinking in the right groove, about the child."

"Child? You mean this girl is a *little* girl?" Perplexity erased the doubt in Kate's eyes. "Could you calm down, Daniel, and tell me what's going on?"

He pulled another chair from the wall and sat down facing her, putting his hands on her knees as if to insure that every word flowed into her with the efficiency of an electric current.

"I don't see anything so odd about her being at the funeral," Kate said when Daniel finished explaining how he knew Bernice Williams.

"There wasn't. She came with her aunt, who had lived in the Bellemoor and probably worshiped Calhoun. But, as we were leaving, the father showed up and started hassling the kid to go somewhere with him."

"And, as usual, you jumped into the middle."

"Yes, Kate. I jumped into the middle. You would have, too, after daddy said he needed Bernice to help him claim Bromley's reward for information about Rourke's murder."

"Why did he want the girl?"

"That's what I wanted to know. He was pleading with his sister to let her come with him, but as soon as I got there, he got very nervous. He kept looking off into the cathedral."

"At what?"

"For some quick getaway, I thought. But then I saw our friend Mr. Green Car."

"That's not so strange, either. If he really was a friend of Bledsoe's, he'd be at the service too."

"He wasn't at the service. I'd have seen him. But now he's hanging around the poetry corner, playing tourist."

"The poetry corner?"

"About forty feet from where we were all standing there's an area where prison poetry is tacked up on boards. He was pretending to read it but kept glancing in our direction."

"How could you be sure it was him at that distance?"

"I couldn't at first. It's pretty dim in the cathedral. But when he noticed I'd spotted him, he suddenly started to leave and I got a better look. He was dressed more formally this time—in a brownish suit—but it was the man at the gas station, no question: same build, same crew cut. I was about to go after him when Delvecchio materializes out of nowhere and says Beaupre wants to see me back here, pronto. No explanation, no nothing, except a threat to arrest me on the spot if I don't come with him voluntarily."

"What did you do?"

Daniel leaned back in his chair, withdrawing his hands to break the circuit before the coming surge. He looked at Kate with an embarrassed half smile and said, "I faked an attack."

"An attack? You mean a seizure?"

Daniel nodded, his smile broadening in spite of himself.

"In front of all those people? You just pretended to pass out, I can't beli—"

"More than that. I put on the full show. I screamed. I keeled over. I thrashed about on the floor."

Kate stared at him for what seemed like minutes. Finally she managed, "Why didn't you just tell Delvecchio who you'd seen?"

"I didn't think he'd buy it. Besides, Green Car was out of sight by now. I was frantic. I had to get rid of Delvecchio, and *The Idiot* just popped into my head."

"What idiot?"

"Dostoyevsky's Prince Myshkin. Have you ever read the novel?"

"No, but I know Dostoyevsky had epilepsy."

"So did Myshkin. He has a seizure in the book that saves his life, that so terrifies the man about to stab him that he can't go through with the murder."

Kate shook her head and emitted a small laugh. "I can't believe you got this out of a book."

"I gambled that if I staged a good show, Delvecchio would at least have to go for help. And he did, though for a few minutes there I wasn't sure he would."

"And?"

"As soon as he went into the gift shop to phone St. Luke's, I took off after Green Car." Daniel smiled again as he recalled the stunned assemblage out of which he had bolted.

"So now you're in here again for playing games with the police."

"Not exactly. My little performance is hardly uppermost in their thoughts at the moment." His smile disappeared. "Green Car had such a head start on me, I didn't think I had a chance of catching him, but just as I came out of the church, I saw him duck into one of the empty tour buses in front. So I ran down the steps and started yelling for him to come out. Then Delvecchio and all my pals from the press came charging after me. So I got on the bus."

"By yourself?"

"I wanted to talk to the man alone, if only for a few seconds."

"You are truly crazy. For all you knew he was waiting to kill you."

"Give the lady a cigar. At first it seemed as if he'd completely disappeared, but then I heard his breathing coming from the back, so I started toward it. I got about halfway back when he stood up from behind a seat. I'd forgotten how tough he looked, especially those hands. He was still a little winded but otherwise quite calm. He didn't even raise his voice when he told me that I'd wind up in the foundation of a building—he actually said that—if I didn't get my ass off the bus and keep my mouth shut about him. I started to tell him it was too late, that the Mongol hordes were already at the door, when a flash went off behind me. Correction, I thought, the invaders are already aboard, Balboni in the lead. But then came the explosion, and Green Car sank out of sight. When I turned around, Delvecchio was kneeling on the front seat, his revolver aimed with both hands across the headrest.''

Kate could not speak, but her eyes asked the only question.

"A bull's-eye right through the heart. He was dead before the ambulance could get there from a block away. I took his pulse. I also found the .38 in his belt.''

"He had a gun?'' Kate stood and brushed away sandwich crumbs angrily. "Well, I hope you're through badmouthing Delvecchio. He saved your life.''

"I suppose.''

"You suppose?''

"I guess he did.''

"Who was the man?''

"I don't know his name. Beaupre won't tell me. But I know who he wasn't: a messenger for Calhoun. You were right about that too.''

Kate acknowledged the admission with a nod and asked, "How do you feel?''

"Pretty high, actually. My adrenaline's probably countering the drugs or what's left of them. I forgot to take my pills this morning or bring any with me.''

"Forgot? You really are on a kamikaze run today. Do you want—''

"Okay, Cooper, they're here.'' Beaupre had not knocked.

"The pills can wait,'' Daniel whispered, then asked the lieutenant if Kate could come with them.

He looked dubious but said yes, and they headed for the stairs to the squad room.

*   *   *

Bernice swiveled experimentally in Lewis Spofford's desk chair, chewing on a Baby Ruth Alma Banks had brought for her. Her thin frame seemed lost in the big seat, but neither she nor her aunt, who sat beside her talking to the two calming cops, appeared frightened. Only when the girl saw the three sober white faces coming toward her did she slide out of the chair and clutch at Carrie Williams, smearing chocolate on the sleeve of her funeral dress.

"Child! Look what you done."

Bernice pulled the candy away, fearing she was about to lose it, but her aunt made no attempt to take it away.

"We'll get that off," said Banks, and went to wet her handkerchief.

"That's the sick man, Aunt Carrie. What's he doing here?"

"Hush. He was a friend of Mr. Bledsoe's."

Daniel looked at Beaupre, who nodded permission to proceed and brought over three more chairs.

"You're right, Mrs. Williams, I was Mr. Bledsoe's friend, and I'm your friend too." Daniel turned to Bernice. "I know I scared you in the church this morning, but I was only pretending. I wasn't really sick, I was acting."

Bernice looked at her aunt, then back at Daniel. "You mean like they does on TV?"

"That's right, exactly. Just like on TV. So there's no reason to be afraid of me. You remember, I came to your apartment last July and told your father to stop hurting you."

She nodded, and he wondered what conclusion she had drawn from the fact that he had never returned.

"Why did you pretend such a terrible fit?" Carrie Williams asked.

"Because I saw a man I thought might want to hurt Bernice even more than her father."

Banks returned with the handkerchief.

"Why would anyone want to do that?" the aunt asked as the officer began daubing at the chocolate.

"That's what we've brought you here to try to find out," Beaupre said.

"Bernice, how would you like to help the police?" Daniel squatted down by the chair, holding the arm.

Bernice shifted away. "Is you gonna act again?"

"No, honey, I promise. All you have to do is look at some pictures. Mr. Spofford is going to show them to you one at a time, and you tell him if you recognize any of the faces. Okay?"

Kate leaned over toward Beaupre. "Where's Sergeant Delvecchio?"

"He's downstairs filling out his report." Beaupre looked annoyed and did not explain further.

"Do like the man says, Bernice," Carrie Williams said.

The child looked at Spofford, who pulled the first photograph out of the folder and placed it on the desk in front of her as her aunt leaned over to get a better look.

"He's sure a mean one. Look at that scar."

Spofford put his finger to his lips, silencing the aunt. "Have you ever seen this man?" he asked Bernice.

"Is he the bad man?"

"We don't know. Have you ever seen him?"

She shook her head.

The next two shots were of cops, routinely inserted into these photo arrays. She passed them both, as well as the three felons who followed.

Daniel saw the crew cut the instant Spofford began to extract the next picture. Mr. Green Car stared out of the mug shot looking palpably alive.

"Is that man here?" Bernice asked when Spofford laid the photograph before her. Her small voice quivered, and she looked anxiously around the room.

"No, honey, he's not. He can't hurt you. But you recognize him, don't you?" Daniel glanced at Beaupre, barely containing his triumph.

The girl, her eyes welling with renewed fear, said nothing.

"Answer the man, child, and tell him the truth," admonished her aunt.

Bernice began to cry.

"There's nothing to be afraid of, honey." Daniel was now kneeling by the chair. "Where did you see this man?"

"Is my daddy gonna find out I told you?"

"No, you don't have to be afraid of him anymore, either." Daniel knew this wasn't true, that he could do very little if Jones Williams tried to reclaim his own daughter.

"Where you seen this man, Bernice?" Carrie Williams demanded.

"In the laundry."

"The Laundromat? I never seen—"

Bernice shook her head. "That room where the washers is all broke."

"At the Bellemoor?" Daniel's hands clamped on her chair.

"Uh-huh."

"What was you doing in that place, child?"

Guilt spread across the girl's face. "I went there to hide from Daddy. So he couldn't beat me."

"At night?" Beaupre asked.

Bernice nodded.

"All night, honey?" Daniel asked.

"Most times."

"And it was nighttime when you saw this man?"

"Uh-huh. He came in the room and washed his hands in the big sink."

"How could you see his face if it was night?" Spofford asked.

"There's a light in the hallway that shines through the door."

"Didn't he see you?"

"I was in the dark part, on the floor under the table."

"That's where you slept?" Kate asked, shaking her head.

"Uh-huh."

"Why was the man washing his hands, honey? What was he doing there that night?"

Bernice looked at Daniel as if he were playing some game.

"Don't *you* remember?" she said.

The question ballooned to the bursting point.

"No. No, honey, I don't." Daniel looked at Beaupre, then back at Bernice. "Sometimes grown-ups have terrible memory problems when they get older. So I'm counting on you to tell me."

"You don't look so old."

Bernice was not sure why this remark was funny,

but the laughter it drew diminished her distrust. She looked at Daniel and said, "*You* know, he shot that Mr. Rourke that night."

"Why does Mr. Cooper know?" Beaupre asked.

These important white people were all beginning to seem thickheaded to Bernice.

"Because he come there in the morning, after Mr. Bledsoe did."

"Did you see us?"

Bernice stared at Daniel. "How could I talk to you without seeing you?"

Beaupre stood and motioned Daniel away from the witness, then approached her himself.

"Are you saying that Mr. Cooper and Mr. Bledsoe were both at the Bellemoor the morning of the murder?"

"After this man left," she said, pointing to the picture. "First Mr. Bledsoe came, then him." She swung her finger at Daniel. "He was dressed like one of them runners."

"And you talked to both of them?"

Bernice looked at Daniel for corroboration that didn't come. Finally she said, "Yes, I told them about how the noise of the gun woke me up and how I seen the man come in the laundry to wash his hands, and how I was scared."

"And what did they do?"

Bernice waited again for Daniel to speak, to tell this policeman what had happened, to take charge the way white people were supposed to. But he just stood paralyzed in silence.

"Mr. Bledsoe, he found a gun in his room and got real excited. He said it was the one that killed that Rourke man."

"And then?" Beaupre said.

"Mr. Bledsoe, he said he had to leave there right away and told that man there to take the gun and hide it in his apartment." She looked again at Daniel for some signs of confirmation.

"Did he say why he had to leave and why the gun had to be hidden?"

Her features tensed. "He made me promise not to tell."

"That was then, honey," Daniel said, unable to restrain himself. "You have to tell us now."

The girl's eyes began moving around the squad room, falling apprehensively on the uniformed officers at their desks.

"He said he had to go because he couldn't be there when the police came."

"Did he say why?" Beaupre asked.

"Uh-huh. He said there was a real bad police that helped this man"—she pointed at the picture again—"and that he had a plan to catch him."

"Did he tell you the plan?"

Bernice shook her head and looked at Daniel. "He told him."

"Did he say the name of the policeman?"

She looked at Spofford and Banks, then at her aunt. "It's a bad name they use for black people."

"You can say it." Carrie Williams looked her niece in the eye.

"Sambo," she said.

Chapter XX

SAM Delvecchio's firearms discharge report oozed plausibility. He had, he wrote, "jumped onto the bus to see a Caucasian male, subsequently identified as Vincent Crevani, reaching for a .38-caliber revolver in his belt. I employed deadly force both in self-defense and to protect the life of Daniel Cooper, the suspect I was pursuing." Daniel made it clear to all who would listen that this was bullshit, that he had been only a few feet away from Mr. Green Car, whose rough hands never stopped crumpling the white napkin on the headrest in front of him. The gun remained in his belt as he bled to death hanging into the aisle. Delvecchio had squeezed off his perfectly aimed deadly force with not a word of warning.

The dailies dutifully recorded these conflicting accounts but allotted most of their space to the tantalizing tale of the seven-year-old black kid who fingered the cop nicknamed Sambo. LITTLE BLACK MYSTERY, trumpeted the *Mail* on page one. After reading these headlines, Dennis McGuire, president of the Patrolmen's Benevolent Association, summoned his usual ire and called a news conference on Thursday. With

Sergeant Samuel P. Delvecchio standing humbly beside him in creased blues, he asked the assembled stenographers, "Has it come to the point where some little girl, seven years old, on the basis of no evidence other than what she *thinks* she heard a man say—a man, by the way, now conveniently dead—can destroy the unblemished reputation and career of a dedicated police officer who has been on the force for twelve years? Has it come to the point where a man whose life Sergeant Delvecchio selflessly risked his own to save is so ungrateful that instead of falling on his knees and thanking him, he attacks him with totally unfounded allegations? I don't like to bring up a person's illnesses, but I ask you to keep in mind that Daniel Cooper is an epileptic who, by his own admission, cannot recall hearing Bernice Williams say the name Sambo, even though he claims to have been present. And now he asks us to accept his version of what happened on the bus? I wasn't there, but I know this man standing here, and I know his record. I back up Sergeant Delvecchio's story one hundred percent."

No one besides Daniel even stumbled forward to challenge this view. The late Vincent Crevani, a.k.a. Tony Garofalo, a.k.a. Roy Phillips, a.k.a. Mr. Green Car, lacked a loyal constituency. Had he been black or Hispanic, his friends, neighbors, and the ACLU might be raising hell at the Twenty-fourth about another gunslinging cop. But he was an ex-con with too many names and a record that did not engender much sympathy from either press or public.

They much preferred the next day's happening, one carried off with far more panache than the tacky

PBA affair. In the atrium on the Bromley-Keller Tower, amid finger sandwiches and wine for all, Steven Bromley presented Bernice Williams with a check for twenty-five thousand dollars for identifying Crevani as Billy Rourke's killer. The name Sambo did not come up. "There is a lesson here for all of us," he told the crush, which included momentarily distracted shoppers as they paused in their rounds of the glittering emporia that opened onto the atrium. "This is what good citizenship is all about. The Bromley-Keller family, and I personally, are proud and pleased to give this reward to such a fine young lady." With a flourish he bent down and handed Bernice the check, posed for the photographers and cameramen, and immediately took it back. "We don't want her spending it all in one place, do we?" he told the crowd. He then led Bernice and Carrie Williams into the Citibank branch off the lobby and patiently helped the bewildered aunt open a custodial-money market account, an event that made all the evening news programs.

"Doesn't it make you carsick to read?" Kate asked.

"It makes me sick, period." Daniel dropped the *Times* onto the backseat. "Did you see how much space they gave Bromley's stage show?"

Kate laughed. "Face it. You're upset because Hinkler and the rest of them are slowly chipping away at the story before you can scoop them in *Tabula Rasa* next week."

Daniel looked out the window. They were nearing the end of the Taconic. He had slept for most of the trip, assuaging the exhaustion of a three-day media siege. "The real scoop will take longer than that."

"What did Fosdick say when you talked to him yesterday?"

"He seemed reasonably open to my contention that Bromley is the top banana. All he wants is proof. I'm going in Monday."

"Can you get it?"

"I'm sure as hell going to try. Rourke, Calhoun, and Green Car may be dead, but Delvecchio the Marksman is still with us. I promise you that bastard is going to find it harder to tough it out with every passing day. Not all his brothers are closing ranks like that asshole McGuire."

"Including Beaupre?"

"Especially Beaupre. He's filling out the UF49; that's the report a superior officer submits after any shooting. He assured me it wouldn't be as self-serving as Delvecchio's. There's a Firearms Discharge Review Board, too, and when I get before it, I'm going to hold Sambo's feet to the fire until they turn into charcoal. And he's going to read about himself in *TR* every week until the D.A. impanels a special grand jury to investigate all three deaths. That's the only way we'll ever get at Bromley, by keeping the pressure on Delvecchio until he makes the connection in exchange for reduced charges."

"What are the odds?"

"If Fosdick lets me keep the heat on, I don't think they're so bad. Beaupre told me something else. The firm that does Bromley-Keller's legal dirty work— Barron, Grossman and Wilson—also represented Tony

Garofalo. Pretty high-priced talent for a mug like that, don't you think?''

Kate nodded. ''It certainly looks fishy, but isn't it just circumstantial? And what does it prove about Delvecchio?''

''Come on, Kate. Jones Williams tells Bromley that Bernice may know something about the Rourke murder, and the kid suddenly winds up in a tug-of-war at the cathedral with Garofalo and Delvecchio pulling together on the same end of the rope. And then, when it looks as if I've got Garofalo cornered on the bus, our hero the sergeant plugs him in the heart.''

''Is that enough to get him indicted?''

''Maybe, maybe not; but there's more. Like the rather convenient coincidence of Delvecchio nailing me in Bed-Stuy after Mr. Green Car Garofalo points the way for me. But that's not the best part. Beaupre says Delvecchio's fingerprints are all over the drug cabinet in that basement.''

''Wouldn't he have left them when he looked around after discovering Calhoun's body?''

''Good cops don't smear things up at a crime scene. But that's not the point. He didn't hang around long enough to leave prints that day. He could hardly wait to get me back to the Twenty-fourth. Cops from Brooklyn dusted the cabinet and they found his prints.''

''You mean he'd been there before that day?''

''Many times. He was dealing drugs, together with Rourke and Garofalo. As a sideline he was also getting money from Bromley to blink while Rourke and the other B-K goons terrorized tenants in the conversions. Bromley didn't give a damn about the drugs as long as his buildings got emptied on schedule. Actually, the trafficking helped chase the tenants out. But Rourke got greedy and tried to blackmail Bromley over the Wilder bribe.''

"How do you know *that?*''

"Wilder's finally come to his senses and is spilling everything to Beaupre, whimpering about how he never would have gotten involved if he'd known Calhoun would be killed.''

Kate steered the car onto the exit ramp and made the left toward Chatham.

"Once Rourke got uppity, Bromley enlisted Delvecchio and Garofalo to dispatch Billyboy and hang it on Calhoun. Only, Bernice was in the laundry room, and then Cal shows up before the foreman, who was supposed to discover the setup first.''

"And then you strolled in.''

"God knows why. I suppose that when Cal didn't show up to run, I decided to go look for him, even though I was totally out of it. He was probably so frantic, the poor bastard, that he couldn't see that nothing he said to me about his plan, or Delvecchio or Bernice, was registering. I must have just taken the gun when he handed it to me and waltzed back to 329.''

"Do you think they'll ever find it?''

"The gun?'' Daniel shook his head. "It's probably in the river. I feel like an idiot, just handing over my keys to Delvecchio and letting him pluck the goddamn thing out of my hamper.''

"How could you know?''

Daniel looked out the window. "Yeah.''

They were in the country now, the smooth two-lane macadam road flanked by dairy farms, their silos measuring the serene sky. Daniel watched the Guernseys straggling toward their late-afternoon milking.

"You know how Calhoun was murdered? An overdose of speedball. That's a combination of coke and heroin. The autopsy showed that he died the day before Green Car pointed the way."

"Did he give it to him?"

"No, Delvecchio."

"You think he did or you know it?"

Daniel wrested his gaze from the countryside and smiled at Kate. "You sound like one of those skeptical journalists."

"Well, isn't it going to be hard to prove which one did it?"

"Maybe not. Beaupre says they've found no Green Car prints in the basement—at least so far."

"He could have worn gloves."

"Not just no *finger*prints. No shoe prints in the boiler room dirt, either. If Green Car was in that basement, I doubt he was barefoot."

Kate grimaced.

"Beaupre's also questioning a housewife from across the street who says she saw a man who looked like Delvecchio enter the brownstone—alone—the morning Calhoun was killed. None of this is ironclad, I know, but it's a damn good beginning. It's only been a couple of days."

"I suppose."

"Remember, Kate, we're talking about murder one. Even if it turns out that both were in that basement, Delvecchio still faces a possible life sentence. That's likely to concentrate his mind mightily when the D.A. begins asking questions about Bromley. We'll nail 'em—both.''

Daniel closed his eyes to the sylvan landscape. When he opened them again, the tires were crunching to a stop in the gravel driveway of the barn. The sun was retreating into the Hudson River Valley, but its fading rays still bathed the meadow of tall grass and wildflowers that sloped down to the pond.

''Come look,'' said Kate, leading Daniel onto the deck.

''Spectacular, baby. Just as advertised.''

He pushed his hands hard toward the sky, trying to stretch the fatigue and travel cramps out of his body. A wave of dizziness came over him, dotting the meadow with a profusion of white spots and causing him to grasp the wooden railing for balance. He knew the spell had nothing to do with his epilepsy, but while he waited for it to pass, he reminded himself to make an appointment with Dr. Havighurst as soon as he got back to the city Monday. He liked the promise of Depakote and was ready to gamble on a new trade-off.

''Did you remember to bring your pills?''

''No, I'm winging it the next two days.''

''Daniel, did you?''

''Yes,'' he said, and they went inside.

About the Author

RICHARD POLLAK is the distinguished founding editor of *MORE* magazine and a former literary editor of *The Nation*. He was an associate editor of *Newsweek* and has written for *Harper's*, *The Atlantic*, and many other leading magazines. He is the author of *Up Against Apartheid: The Role and the Plight of the Press in South Africa*, and has taught at Yale and New York University. He is married to the pianist Diane Walsh, and they live in Manhattan with his teenage daughter, Amanda. THE EPISODE is his first novel.